RIVEN

LISSA DEL

First published by Lissa Del, 2017

Cover design by Apple Pie Graphics

Edited by Catherine Eberle of WordWeavers

For those who choose to rise when it would be so easy to fall.

ACKNOWLEDGMENTS

First and foremost, my family deserves a huge round of applause for putting up with me as I wrestled with the beast that is this book. Contemporary fiction does not come as naturally to me as speculative fiction and writing it saps a huge amount of my creative energy, which, in turn, leaves me emotionally exhausted. This kind of storytelling relies on the reader's experience to be truly appreciated and I can only hope that I have done it justice.

To my long-suffering editor, Catherine Eberle of Word-Weavers, who has been with me since the beginning and has become more than just a faceless scrutiniser of words, thank you, for making me better and for encouraging me when you didn't have to.

To my cover designer and very dear friend, Wendy Bow of Apple Pie Graphics; there is nothing like artwork to make a story come alive and you nail it! Every. Single. Time.

A story like this one requires the expertise of professionals and I would like to express my gratitude to Dr Morné

Moolman for his infinite patience and sound advice. I don't think I've ever seen a man so interested in the plot of a romance novel!

To Jane Long, for sharing her architectural expertise and explaining in such detail the process of the qualification to someone who literally had no idea; thank you for giving Sarah's character the credibility it needed!

My beta readers: Fiona McCarthy, neighbour, friend and red-pen professional! Thanks for being honest and for having no poker-face! Wendy Bow, for being blunt and tactless and wonderful – without you I would no doubt embarrass myself! And to Cara Pechey and Candice Fountain for picking up those pesky typos, thank you!

To The Dragon Writers, my online writing support group, who provide a sanctuary and applaud every word from the side-lines. From craft to marketing, there is no better resource for a writer.

And finally, to my readers, especially the Rainfall fans. If it wasn't for you I would never have started, let alone finished this book. You are my inspiration and the reason I continue on this crazy journey.

CHAPTER 1

*E*very beat of my heart brings me closer to the wide mahogany door. My legs are leaden, my mouth dry and bitter, and it takes everything in me to fight the urge to turn and run. My nails dig painfully into the palms of my hands as I place one foot in front of the other. The brass knocker is in the shape of a lion and the symbolism is not lost on me. It is a glimpse into a life I cannot possibly understand, that of a man I do not know and a history I played no part in.

Three tentative raps later I hear a determined voice call, "It's open." I push at the heavy door and it opens slowly, as though the house itself would deny me entry. Standing in the hallway, unsure which way to turn, I feel the unease trickle down my spine. It's too unfamiliar; the sweeping stairway to the right, the gilded-framed paintings adorning the walls. Even the cool air is unwelcoming.

"You must be Sarah." I recognise the same determined voice as before, the same voice on the phone. I turn to face her and my stuttering heart thuds to a halt in my chest. Clare

Russell might not have turned heads if it wasn't for the way she carried herself. As though someone had once told her she was extraordinarily beautiful and she had believed it ever since. Her colouring is pure autumn. With her russet hair and the pale silk scarf around her neck, she reminds me of the red foxes which used to hide in my mother's berry bushes. The milky translucence of her skin is a perfect foil for the faintest smattering of freckles, and her eyes are neither blue nor green, but fall strikingly somewhere in between. She is a few years older than I am, as I knew she would be. I would guess she is not yet thirty, but she seems older, mature, in a way I have yet to experience.

"Thank you for coming," she says, but I detect a trace of staccato in her honeyed tone.

"Of course." I nod, as though this was never in question. As though I haven't changed my mind a million times in the past hour alone. As though my mobile isn't filled with desperate messages from her husband.

"Let's take a seat in the living room." She doesn't wait for a response. Instead, she walks away, moving down the hall to the right. Her soft leather moccasins make almost no sound on the polished hardwood floor.

I follow, wondering if she is used to being obeyed or if it is simply that she cannot bear to look at me a moment longer, but I dismiss this second thought almost immediately. It strikes me that this is just how she is. Decisive, controlled, straight-backed and serious and, no doubt, utterly unthreatened by the silly, simple girl trailing after her. I could never know what Clare really saw when she looked at me. A nervous young woman who couldn't quite hide the wonder she saw in the world. A girl who was the antithesis of herself.

A girl she could all too easily imagine her husband falling in love with.

We sit in the living room - a picture-perfect replica of the cover of every decorating magazine I've ever seen. Despite the opulent setting, I don't like it here in this room which smells of orchids and money.

"Would you like something to drink?" Clare asks, as I sink onto a sofa overflowing with cushions. She seems embarrassed to have forgotten her everyday etiquette and I want to laugh hysterically at the absurdity of it. Instead, I shake my head 'No, thank you' and then I fall silent. It feels as though I'm still sinking, the soft sofa cushions rising up to smother me, and I shift forward, trying to get both feet back on the ground.

Clare straightens the magazines on the coffee table and, for a minute, only the gentle ticking of the clock above the recently swept fireplace fills the space between us. Then I hear her draw in a deep steadying breath and she begins.

I listen to the words, strangely detached, as though I am hearing the story third-hand, as though it doesn't pertain to me or to my life. I think my heart offers that protection from a truth that is so unbelievable that it belongs in the world of fiction. I focus on Clare's lips as she speaks, listening, but not really *hearing* her words. I manage to keep up the barrier my subconscious has put in place far longer than I expect, until I glance up. I watch in mortified horror as her eyes pool suddenly, glittering for only a moment before a solitary tear spills over, gliding quickly down her cheek as if it has somewhere important to be. In the brief time it takes that tear to reach the curve of her chin, my heart breaks. Clare Russell is in pain because of me and because of the extreme circumstances which have brought me here. I finally understand that I am the problem, not the solution.

"I'll help you," I say simply when she is done. There is nothing else to say. It is time to set things right. Doing the right thing is never easy. It takes courage, selflessness and everything you have. It takes far more than I have to give, but I cannot deny her request, not after seeing her like this. I should never have come here. I should never have seen her. But I have, and I did. And the look on her face will haunt me forever.

CHAPTER 2

I met Leo Russell on what would later be recorded as the hottest day that year. It felt as though the devil himself had thrown open the gates and unleashed the furnace of hell's fires upon the earth. Well, upon Manhattan's Arts District, at least. The heat was inescapable and there was certainly no relief to be found in the tightly-packed lecture hall, filled with breath and sweat, to which I was confined for sixty minutes.

"I'm melting," my best friend, Jessica, whispers in my ear. Or at least I assume she is trying to whisper. Jessica is incapable of keeping her voice down. She makes my Aunt Fran, who is partially deaf in one ear and automatically assumes everyone else must be hard of hearing, sound almost dulcet by comparison. Today Jessica's dark hair is tied in two messy bunches on the top of her head, keeping it off her neck and her signature black eyeliner is smudged.

"You're not the only one," I reply, pursing my lips and

blowing a rogue blonde curl which has escaped my bun off my forehead.

Prepared as I was for the unexpected heatwave, courtesy of my brother Dylan, who watches both the weather and Sky News with the alacrity I reserve only for *The Vampire Diaries* and *E! News*, I am still sweating up a storm. My light, summer blouse clings uncomfortably to my body and perspiration beads the fine hairs of my upper lip. The black pants I had donned this morning in an effort to maintain an air of professionalism are doing me no favours either. I lick my lips, tasting the salty tang, and try instead to focus on the droning monotony of the lecturer's monologue, which is difficult, given that I broke up with him two months ago because, quite frankly, he bored me to death. I had hoped that the summer break might have given Noah time to recover and move on to someone new, but, judging by the constant calls and the impromptu arrivals on my doorstep, that hadn't happened.

My first impression of Noah Allen's boyish charm had been that it was very appealing and it ensured that, in a predominantly male-environment he had a small gaggle of women flocking annually to attend his classes. As fifth-years we attend few lectures, spending most of our time working on our theses and doing research, but there are still a few mandatory classes, one of which happens to be Technology, the subject that Noah teaches. He prides himself on having landed a 5th year educator's post, but, in truth, Noah is the prime example of "those who can't do, teach". It's no wonder that his course covers only the driest aspects of architecture – after all, there's no changing the chemical composition of concrete. It is a subject to be learned, rather than one to be experienced or evolved.

Glancing around, I notice that the few other women in the room are making a conscious effort to pay attention and hanging onto Noah's every word. Beside me, Jessica shows no such compunction. She is texting frantically, in between her incessant checking of the clock hanging on the auditorium wall. Noah is about as enthralling as the subject he teaches. The problem is that he loves the sound of his own voice far more than the art of architecture. I know this, having dated him for six months. Suffice it to say I barely got a word in edgeways.

Despite the cloying heat, it settles on me slowly that I am being watched. First, the prickling of the hairs on the back of my neck, and then the unnerving sensation of simply knowing - knowing that a set of eyes is boring into you. I shift uncomfortably in my chair, discreetly scanning the room, but I cannot find the source of my discomfort.

"Sit still!" a female voice hisses from behind me and I resign myself to facing forward for the remaining period, not daring to distract Noah's female fans.

"Why don't you go and eat something," Jessica snaps back at the girl, coming to my defence.

"You eat enough for the both of us, Atkins!"

I roll my eyes, recognising Samantha Simpson's voice, but I am hyper-aware of Jess's hackles rising beside me. My best friend is highly emotional and she yo-yos between startling euphoria and manic depression. She's as likely to break into song as she is to burst into tears at any given moment. Sensing her steeling herself for a comeback, I place a restraining hand on her arm. "She's not worth it, Jess."

Samantha has been Jessica's nemesis since the first day of second year. A five-foot-nine student transfer, with a three-inch waist and a curtain of naturally-bottled honey-blonde hair that falls beguiling over one periwinkle-blue eye, Samantha is the yin to Jessica's yang. When she celebrated her twenty-fifth birthday last month, Jessica finally abandoned all and any hope she might have harboured of losing her puppy fat. Jessica is not only buxom and curvy, but she errs on the side of being just too short to be taken seriously. Her redeeming features - huge, caramel-coloured eyes that domi-nate most of her face and a perfectly sculpted mouth, complete with cupid bow and fleshy bottom lip, are enhanced by an ironic sense of helplessness that men cannot resist responding to. Jessica epitomises the damsel in distress. Ironic, because she is neither ladylike nor helpless. In fact, her father is the chief-executive officer in a multi-national development company worth millions of dollars.

Jessica is two years older than I am because she spent her first two years out of high school trying her hand at everything from fashion-design to flight-programming, determined to make her own way. As it happened, she made her way down to the bar on Fourth Street every night with a slew of unsuitable suitors until Mr Atkins put his foot down and recalled her Visa Card. Jessica is just as obstinate as her father so, when he failed to pay the rent on her loft apartment, she promptly called his bluff and landed herself a job at Hooters, waiting tables. Not to be outdone, Mr Atkins booked a table for two and proceeded to watch Jessica's courage fail her as she served her seventy-four-year-old grandfather a plate of *Hooterstizers*.

When Mr Atkins Senior clutched at his chest in the middle of dessert, both sides finally admitted defeat and Jessica and her father came to a compromise. Jessica would gain a degree in Architecture which would serve her well if she ever decided to join the Atkins Development Co. and, once she had attained it, her father would fund whatever lifestyle she preferred. Secretly, I think that Mr Atkins was hoping that Jessica would grow up in the five years it took for her to complete her degree. With less than a year left, he was fast losing faith. Jessica's grandfather, to everyone's astonishment, had lived to tell the tale. As it turned out he was not having a heart attack due to the spectacle of his granddaughter's ample bosom in a tighty-whitey that afternoon at Hooters, but had simply developed a bad case of indigestion from the chilli. Either way, the deal had been struck and neither Jessica nor her father would concede defeat.

I am still watching Jessica when she picks up a piece of paper, conspicuous by its lack of even a single note taken, and fans her face. "He's definitely practicing for hell," she whispers loudly, casting a snide look over her shoulder toward Samantha. Samantha's envy of my relationship with Noah is common knowledge. She spent the better part of the last year trying to lure him away from me, without success. Neither Noah nor I had publicised our break-up, but by the snide remarks Samantha's been throwing my way since the semester started, I know she's been well-informed. Samantha eyes Noah with the same lascivious expression with which Jessica eyes a cheeseburger, but it doesn't bother me. Further proof yet that I no longer feel anything for him. Truthfully, I doubt I ever really did.

I grin at Jess, offering moral encouragement, but I'm distracted. I can still feel eyes on me, the feeling of being watched growing stronger by the second. I cast another furtive look around but it's hopeless. There are too many people in the room to single out anyone in particular without it being obvious.

To my surprise it is Noah himself who tips me off to my watcher's identity. Despite the interruption of Samantha and Jessica's mini-confrontation, Noah hasn't so much as paused for breath, but suddenly, mid-speech, I notice his eyes narrow at someone in the far corner of the lecture hall, someone who is sitting behind me, just out of my field of vision. Jessica doesn't even notice the pause in Noah's lecture, bored into a state of slack-jawed stupor as she is, but I do. And, drawn to the person who could prompt such an expression of ill-concealed irritation on Noah's face, I swivel right around in my chair, my eyes scanning the room.

I find him immediately; a tawny giant of a man with an enviably dishevelled head of hair that is neither brown nor blond, but a perfect coppery blend of the two. The moment my eyes meet his, he gives me a lazy, insolent smile which creases the corners of his arresting eyes. That particular shade of blue shouldn't be an eye-colour. It should be reserved for paintings of crystal clear lakes and cloudless summer skies. He doesn't even try to hide the fact that he is staring, and I am so flustered by his brazenness that I flush, the heat rising from my neck and up to my cheeks. I should look away, but I don't. Instead, I glare at him, silently calling him out and daring him to look away first, which of course, he doesn't. Instead, he holds up a piece of paper on which is written in an untidy scrawl: *Only six more minutes.*

The gesture is so unexpected that I press my lips together to keep from laughing, my eyes flicking to the clock above his head. His timing is exact, down to the minute, and I wonder how many drafts he wrote before he got my attention.

Amused, I shake my head and turn back to face Noah, who is now apoplectic with indignation and outrage. Of course he saw the note, how could he have missed it? My amusement diminishes rapidly as I gaze down at Noah's sullen face.

Thankfully, Noah is the only exception in a course teeming with colour, texture and beauty. I hadn't always wanted to be an architect, in fact I'd spent most of my high school career entertaining the notion that I would become a chef. Then, in my senior year, my parents took my brother and I to London on a family vacation. The beauty and diversity of the buildings had taken my breath away. I had always loved old buildings, finding the form, space and ambience fascinating, but my senses had been assaulted by the flamboyant face-off of the old and the new world. Something about that trip had sparked a flame of yearning inside my eighteen-year-old self and I returned home with a new dream of becoming an architect.

The Holmes Institute, situated in Los Angeles' famous Arts District offers Advanced Placement Opportunities for their top students in final year and I've applied for a position at Burke & Duke, a prestigious architectural firm renowned for its innovative concepts and forward thinking. Hard work and natural flair have ensured that I've placed top of our class since the very first year of my B. Arch studies, but now, entering our fifth and final year, I am even more determined to prove myself, particularly after the disastrous six-month courtship with Noah, who is still rabbiting on below us. I had dearly hoped that my schedule this year wouldn't include him, but alas, here I am, listening to the rambling of an ex-boyfriend, who, every now and then, throws me a wounded, doe-eyed look for good measure.

I barely notice. In the few seconds that I'd held the

stranger's gaze something had shifted within me - something that could never shift back. I was drawn to him from the moment I laid eyes on him and our story would play out with, or without, my consent.

CHAPTER 3

"*I* saw that," Jessica smirks beside me, blatantly blowing a kiss over my shoulder to the stranger. I can still feel the heat of his gaze on my neck and I shift awkwardly in my seat, still half-heartedly trying to focus on Noah, who seizes the opportunity to give me a lingering look that would probably make Samantha Simpson self-combust.

"Saw what?" I reply, feigning nonchalance.

"Oh please," Jess snaps. "Don't act like you didn't see Mr Sex-on-legs over there undressing you with his inhuman eyes. You need a good cleaning out," she adds, chewing on her thumbnail. "It's been what, over two months since old Noah hosed your pipes?"

"Hosed my pipes?" I exclaim, finally turning to face her. "Who actually says things like that?"

Jessica ignores me, a thoughtful expression coming over her pale face.

"The question is though, how will Needy Noah handle seeing you with another man?"

"Stop it," I laugh, shoving at her shoulder with my own.

"Is there something you would like to share with the class, Miss Holt?" Noah's eyes bore into mine and I can imagine the perverse pleasure he's taking in calling me out.

"No, nothing, Mr Allen," I call out clearly across the room.

"You won't mind, then, informing the class of the benefits of double-glazing that we've been discussing?" Noah traps his bottom lip in his teeth as he crosses his arms over his chest. It's his smug look and I know it well. Heaving a sigh, I sit forward. Noah should know better, I think resignedly. I may not have been paying attention the past few minutes but, up until two months ago, I had helped him prepare his lesson plans for this semester. Lessons that I'd hoped I wouldn't be subjected to.

"Double, or insulated glazing is separated by a vacuum or gas-filled space and reduces heat transfer across a part of the building envelope," I recite easily. "The key advantages are energy cost savings, limited condensation, sound insulation, safety, and reduced damage to furnishings." Jess gives a low chuckle beside me as Noah visibly twitches with annoyance before unravelling his arms and resuming his wounded expression.

The small female contingent of the class cast me dark, dirty looks. Noah, despite the tedium of the subject matter that he teaches, is good-looking and charming. He is also young enough, at twenty-nine, not to be considered pervy for dating his students. I know for a fact that I'm not the first student Noah has become romantically involved with, but I am the only one who ended it before he could. I think it is the brutal blow to his ego that has him so worked up, rather than the actual loss of me as his girlfriend, although I'm still fairly certain he felt more for me than I ever felt for him. I already knew he wasn't for me by our second month of dating but I hadn't known how to end things, and the fact that my parents adored him made it hard for me to break it off. After six months, however, I was done trying to please everybody.

"Well, that certainly puts it into perspective," a deep voice utters, dead-pan, and I glance across the lecture hall to find the golden-haired man chuckling. He has made a paper airplane out of his note, which he unabashedly sends soaring in my direction.

"Excuse me, but who are you, exactly?" Noah demands, consulting the roster at the edge of his desk.

"Leo Russell," the man replies smoothly. The paper airplane has landed in Samantha's hair and she rips it out, tearing it in half and shooting daggers at Leo.

"You're not on my list," Noah announces pointedly.

"That's probably because I'm not supposed to be in this class," Leo grins. "I'm actually registered for Art History 101, but I stumbled into the wrong lecture hall and I thought I'd look a right ass if I got up and left." He gives me the ghost of a wink and I turn back to the front of the class, bemused.

"Two words," Jessica hisses in my ear. "Pipes. Cleaned."

"That is enough," Noah orders, narrowing his eyes at the newcomer, but, as he opens his mouth, no doubt to evict Leo, the bell sounds and forty or so students get to their feet, scrambling for the exit. All save for Samantha, who makes a show of leaning forward to retrieve her brightly-coloured notes, her pink push-up bra creating a veritable Silicon Valley right here in the Arts District. Sadly, her practiced movement is wasted on Noah who only has eyes for me. I step aside, offering him a better view of Samantha's cleavage, hoping he might be distracted, but he barely notices.

"Miss Holt, a word, please!" Noah strains to be heard over the mass exodus of students filing from the room in their haste to get to our next period. In an act of pure sadism, according to Jess, the university had scheduled most of our compulsory lectures on a Thursday rather than spacing them out.

"I'm going to be late for class," I reply, as Jessica scuttles past, leaving me to deal with Noah on my own.

"You can tell Luke I kept you back." Luke, or Professor Hanson as he is more commonly known to his students, is one of Noah's lecturer friends and we had double-dated a few times while Noah and I were together. It irks me that Noah would use that fact to hold me up, as though our personal lives are a perfectly reasonable excuse for being late to class.

"Don't you think that's a little nepotistic?" I ask, only to be rewarded with yet another petulant look. "What is it, Noah?" I watch longingly as the last straggler disappears through the double doors. They swing shut behind him, rocking to and fro before closing properly with a depressing thud.

"Sarah," Noah murmurs, in his most charming voice. "We need to talk."

"No, we don't. We *really* don't," I argue, trying to keep the irritation out of my tone. Noah has spent the better part of the past two months trying to get hold of me, leaving numerous text messages and voice mails which I refuse to answer. When that hadn't worked, he had come to my apartment bearing flowers and wine – which is usually a guaranteed entry, but which, in Noah's hands comes at too high a price - and eventually, out of sheer exhaustion, I had banned him from the building.

"You can't just forget the time we spent together," Noah whines.

"I didn't, Noah," I reply kindly. "What you and I shared... it was special." The bald-faced lie tastes sour on my tongue but I continue, determined to keep things between us amicable. For all his idiocy, Noah could make my college life difficult if he really set his mind to it and I just want to get through my final year without incident.

"If it was so special, why aren't we together?" Noah's tone is harder than before. *Not as stupid as he looks then, folks.*

"I told you at the end of last semester, I have too much on my plate to be in a relationship right now." This of course, is only partially true. My plate may be full, but that had nothing to do with my breaking it off with Noah. The sad truth was that I'd come to realise that Noah cared for me far more than I had ever cared for him and I didn't want to lead him on. He was a nice enough guy, if a little self-absorbed, but he wasn't the man for me. Even so, I had expected him to bounce back quickly and transfer his attention to another, far more willing, student. Instead, my rejection had spurred him to unbecoming heights of desperation.

"Sarah..."

"I have to go," I insist, cutting him off and throwing my bag over my shoulder. "I'm going to be late." Without waiting for a response, I hurriedly make my way from the room.

"So, did he fling you over his three-by-two and have his wicked way with you?" Jessica grins as I emerge into the corridor. She is leaning against the duck-egg blue wall, one black-booted foot placed flat on the clean paint.

"Don't be ridiculous," I mutter.

"It wouldn't be the first time," she points out wryly and I can't help but laugh.

"Thanks for waiting."

"No problem. It seems I wasn't the only one." She inclines her head and I follow the direction of her gaze. The tawny giant from inside is leaning casually against the wall a few yards away speaking into a mobile phone.

"He isn't waiting for me, Jess, he's on the phone." I take a moment of undetected scrutiny to admire the breadth of his shoulders and how his torso tapers, criminally narrow, shape into his hips. He looks a lot older than the average first-year student and I wonder why he is only starting his studies now. As I watch, he lifts a dinner-plate-sized hand and runs it through his hair, leaving it standing up at all angles. All the relaxed teasing is gone from his face. Instead, his forehead is furrowed and his broad shoulders are bunched up under the cotton of his shirt.

"He looks furious," I whisper, as he hisses something inaudible into the handset.

"He looks like coffee and hot buttered toast," Jess sighs, adding a suggestive growl for effect, then, sashaying towards him, she hollers in a voice loud enough to be heard across the state, "Hey, new guy!"

I flush as he whips around to locate the source of Jess's voice. His eyes move over her and back toward me and the same lazy grin settles crookedly on his lips.

"I'll talk to you later," he announces abruptly, ending the call. "Hi," he says, looking directly at me.

"Hi," I say.

"I'm Leo."

"I know," I tease, reminding him of the incident in class.

"So, you got lost huh? From what I recall Art History 101 is on the other side of campus."

"I have a terrible sense of direction," he says, his eyes directing their way up and down my body with the precision of sat-nav. "I didn't catch your name?" He leaves the question hanging in the air, his head cocked slightly to one side.

"Sarah," I offer.

"Sarah," he says, as though tasting the name to see if it's palatable. I wait, expectantly, but Leo doesn't offer anything else. He seems to enjoy making me feel uncomfortable, his eyes boring into my own as though he is waiting for something.

Jessica, who is easily bored, thrusts her hand between us, engaging Leo in an arm-pumping hand shake. "Jessica," she introduces herself. "So, now that we're all acquainted, how about we get our asses to room 27 before Hanson locks us out?"

"He won't lock you out," I correct, "you're his favourite." Luke Hanson is not only one of our fifth year lecturers, he's also Jess's mentor. In this final year we are each assigned a professor to mentor us through our final projects. Jess is certainly not Luke's most talented student, but she's probably the most fun to work with.

"Says she of Marchant stock," Jess teases, referring to my own mentor, the Dean of the Holmes Institute and a legend in Architectural circles. "Anyway, let's hustle!"

"I'm free this period," Leo says, pointing to his chest, "first year, remember?"

"You were being serious?" Jess's jaw drops, revealing a row of perfect white teeth, courtesy of a lifetime of private health.

"Yes," Leo's amusement is plain to see, but Jess looks horrified.

"You're too old to be a first year." She narrows her eyes at him. "How old are you, exactly?"

"Thirty-two," he replies easily. To Jess's credit, even I'm stunned by this revelation. He looks younger, not by much, but I certainly didn't expect a thirty-two-year-old man to be beginning his studies now. My disappointment must show, because he scrutinises my face, a thoughtful look coming over him.

"Bit of a late bloomer, then?" Jess sighs, giving me an apologetic look. I know exactly what she's thinking. All her high hopes of hooking me up with the sexy new student have shattered. So much for her pipe-cleaning project! After all, it doesn't matter how good-looking Leo is, nobody wants to set their best friend up with a loser.

"You could say that," Leo says. "Or," he adds, as Jess turns away, pulling on my arm, "you might say that I've had a change of heart."

"Sounds fascinating," Jess grumbles, still leading me away. Sometimes her lack of tact is mortifying.

"A change of heart?" I ask politely, throwing the words over my shoulder. Leo is leaning back against the wall, watching me go, his lips pressed together to keep from laughing.

"I'll see you around, Sarah," he winks, and then we turn a corner and I can't see him anymore.

CHAPTER 4

"False representation, that's what it is," Jess says. "He deliberately presented himself as one thing and it turns out he's another."

"He didn't present himself as anything and he clearly said he was a first year. How is that false representation?" I ask, trying to talk out of the very corner of my mouth. Luke had given us a hard look when we scuttled in at least five minutes after everyone else. I hadn't mentioned Noah keeping me back, but, at the very least, I wanted to look as if I was paying attention to make up for it.

Jess looks alarmed. "Is there something wrong with your lip? Are you having an allergic reaction? I swear they put dishwasher in the coffee here."

"Miss Atkins," Luke Hanson growls a warning.

"Sorry, Professor!" Jess mock whispers, her voice carrying across the lecture hall and no doubt to the pedestrians on the street three storeys below. Luke cringes, but when I catch his eye he smiles. Luke is a nice enough guy, and, to be honest, I

21

don't think he's quite as fond of Noah as Noah likes to think. Unlike Noah, Luke is actually a professor, and a visionary. He is also mercifully pro-cooling and, for the first time today, I'm not genuinely concerned that I might vaporise.

Out of respect for Luke, Jess waits a full seven seconds before resuming our conversation.

"I mean, why would you go and sit through an entire lecture of a class you're not even supposed to be in? Especially one of Noah's lectures," she adds meaningfully. Like a dog with a bone, Jess refuses to let the subject of Leo go, as though he has insulted her personally, his mistake a deliberate affront to her matchmaking skills.

I nod sagely. "I'm sure he only does it to seduce innocent fifth years."

Jess looks pensive, considering this, until she figures out that I'm pulling her leg. "Oh ha-bloody-ha!" she snaps.

It's only when we reach the cafeteria that she finally lets the matter rest and then only because she's distracted.

"I heard Tom Cruise is filming Mission Impossible 37 or something down on Alameda Street," she takes a monumental bite of her burger before continuing almost intelligibly, "we should totally blow off the rest of the day and go check it out."

"First up, Tom Cruise is a little long in the tooth for us to be stalking him," I say.

"Tom Hardy's in this one, apparently," she interrupts, through a mouthful of food.

"Second," I say, "what part of Advanced Placement at Burke & Duke do you not understand?"

"Oh please!" Jess washes down a mouthful of food with water. "The AP's in the bag. You know it, I know it. *Everybody* knows it. You're leagues ahead of everyone else in this place, myself included and you have *the* Dianna Marchant as a mentor. Now stop setting such an impeccable example and let's get the hell out of here!"

"Bunking again, Atkins?" a deep voice interrupts. Thomas Brooks has been the only other constant in my four years at Holmes. Devastatingly handsome, incorrigibly lazy and undeniably gay, Jess, Tom and I had met during our very first week at Holmes. It had taken only one wild Wednesday night and five bottles of wine to bring us together and we'd been inseparable ever since. Tom's barely been in class this week as he's been scouting for a location for his final project. Tom shares Jess's distaste for the institution of learning, but, despite his frequent truancy, he's in the top ten percent of our class.

"Hey Thomas!" Jess insists on using the French pronunciation, even though Tom was born and raised in Manhattan. He once ventured out of the city on a dirty weekend away with one of his many boy toys and now refers to himself as being internationally-travelled.

"Pull up a seat," Jess says, sliding back the plastic chair beside her with an almighty screech. Tom drapes himself over it, looking more like a Calvin Klein model than an aspiring architect. "I was just telling Sarah we should blow off the rest of the day and go and watch Tom Cruise doing all his own stunts."

"Actually the set's closed for the day. I just came from there."

"You two are as bad as each other!" I scold. Tom meets my shocked disapproval with defiant nonchalance.

"All work and no play makes Sarah a dull girl," he teases, breaking off a piece of the demolished remains of Jess's burger and throwing it at me.

"Fine," Jess concedes dramatically. "We'll go to the library," she gives a little shudder at the word, "but we better be on for tomorrow night." There's a pause and they both turn to look at me, the eternal party-pooper.

"Oh come on! When have I ever cancelled Game Night?" Friday nights are a ritual for the three of us. Copious amounts of junk food are ingested and, depending on how much wine is consumed, we sometimes head out on the town after.

The terrible twosome are already ticking instances off on their fingers.

"The time you had to help Noah, the needy, plan his lessons..."

"The time your mom came to stay..."

"The time we had a philosophy final..."

"Now hold on a minute," I raise my hands to stall the onslaught. Once they build up steam there's no stopping them. "I think you'll find we *all* had a philosophy final, and, if it wasn't for me, you two would've failed dismally!"

They pause, heads inclining toward one another, Jess's messy buns contrasting spectacularly with Tom's perfect blond bed-head.

"We have to give her that one," Tom concedes.

"Regrettably," Jess agrees, giving me the benefit of her dazzling smile, which is not in the least bit diminished by the piece of lettuce caught between her teeth.

After a gruelling couple of hours working on my digital 3D model, my back is aching from being hunched over the screen for so long. Most of my work is done on my personal computer but I do use the online library resource allocated by the Institute. My designated work station is in the far section of the library building and, while it's perfectly functional, it's hardly comfortable.

I arrive home and drop my purse and keys on the table in the hall, rolling my shoulders to try and relieve some of the tension that has built up in my neck. My apartment is modest, but comfortable, courtesy of my parents who understood my need for independence and even better, the sensibility of being closer to college. They had bought the apartment outright with most of what remained of their savings – my dad's rationale being that it was still his money, but that it was now far better invested. My parents hate the bustle of the big city. They still stay in the same house I grew up in, in Arcadia. It's only about fifteen miles away and, at least once a fortnight, my brother Dylan and I drive out to see them. A couple of times a year mom comes down to spend the weekend, most of which she spends preparing and freezing ready-made meals for us, much to Dylan's delight. My brother is the most undomesticated twenty-first century man I know.

I'm halfway to the kitchen when there is a knock at the door. As if my thoughts had drawn him, Dylan stands outside my door.

"I told you it was going to be a scorcher," he grins, smug in the knowledge that both he, and the weatherman, by association, were right.

"You need a haircut," I say, stepping aside to let him in. Like me, Dylan inherited my mother's curls and green eyes, but the rest of him is all dad, right down to the dimple in his left cheek and his love of Sky News. Dylan is an attorney, a good one if you ask him himself, and a full seven years older than me, although sometimes it feels more like twenty and at other times I want to feed him a jar of Gerber.

"Don't even go there," Dylan yawns, clapping a hand leisurely over his mouth, "I've had a week from hell."

"I don't want to hear about your cases, please," I moan, not in the mood for the usual play-by-play of his prowess in the courtroom.

Dylan glances around the spotless kitchen, unfazed. "What's for supper?" he asks.

"I just got in, as you obviously know, seeing as you got here about three seconds after me," I reply pointedly. The downside to my parents' generosity, coupled with their fear of sending their only daughter out alone into the city, is that the apartment they bought me came with one sole condition - it had to be in the same block as Dylan's. The Gods were working against me the day that an apartment just a few doors down from his became available just when we were looking. Seven floors and I had to end up on his.

"Just following the parentals' orders," Dylan grins unapologetically. "You know they told me to keep an eye on you."

"Yes, but I'm pretty sure that was more for my safety than for your convenience. You're going to be thirty next month Dyl, you should at least know how to boil an egg by now." Despite my teasing I open the fridge and stick my head inside.

"That's what wives are for."

"So why haven't you found one, yet?" I ask sweetly, backing out of the fridge with a block of Gouda and a pack of pre-sliced ham. "Pass me the bread, will you?"

"Grilled sandwiches?" Dylan pouts his disapproval.

"Yes, Dyl, grilled sandwiches. I haven't had time to go shopping, so you can either like it or lump it."

He doesn't leave. Of course he doesn't leave. Most nights Dylan eats out with any of the dozen or so single men from his office, but, whenever he stays in, he expects me to feed him, without warning I might add.

"Mike was asking after you today," he announces casually while I'm washing up. "We have a corporate dinner coming up and he doesn't have anyone to go with. I said you might be available." Dylan is always offering me up to his single friends in need of a date, my present relationship status notwithstanding. I vaguely remember Mike as a rather over-weight introvert with ketchup down the front of his shirt.

"I won't be," I reply, "I have plans."

Dylan gives me a dark look. "You don't even know when it is, yet."

"When is it?"

"December fourth." It's over two months away.

"Then I definitely can't make it."

"You are so full of shit!"

"I'm not. For your information, I have every intention of having stomach flu that day."

"You've been single for over two months. It's not healthy."

I arch my brows. "And this coming from a man who has been single for the better part of a decade?"

"I haven't been single for a decade! I've dated plenty of women."

"Oh yes, how could I forget the memorable Sandy, Mandy and Candy line-up?"

Dylan laughs out loud at that. It's a long-standing joke

between us that the only women he ever dates are young, gorgeous and absolutely lacking in ambition or brains.

"You know if you actually tried dating a girl for something other than her cup size, you might find someone you could bear to spend more than three months with," I point out.

"I'm taking it, then, that you dated Noah for his electrifying personality?" he asks innocently. Dylan spent enough time with Noah to know that he bored the life out of me and, unlike my parents, he wasn't as taken with Noah as he made believe.

"Touché," I grin.

Dylan leaves around nine o'clock. I take a much needed shower, washing away the sweaty stickiness of the day and then I fetch a bottle of water from the fridge and make my way to my room. The night air is still stiflingly warm and I switch on the air-conditioning, determined to sleep comfortably, utility bill be damned. As well as the apartment, mom and dad had set up a small trust that I could live off so I wouldn't have to work through college. I usually err on the side of being conservative, but it's just too hot to go without it. Embarrassingly, in the quiet stillness of my bedroom, my thoughts turn to Leo. In my defence, the unusual blue of his eyes and the wicked curve of his mouth are hardly easy to forget.

It is only when I switch off my nightlight that I notice the annoying blink of the red light on my answering machine. There are two messages from Noah, both asking me to call him as soon as I get home. I delete them and curl up in my bed, pulling the beautiful patchwork quilt mom made for my sixteenth birthday around me. It has adorned my bed ever since, despite the fact that the pale pink and lavender squares don't really match the rest of my bedroom. There is a still a faint smell of enamel in the air, as a result of the gorgeous side-table that I got for a steal online and which I only painted last night. I'd been going for a shabby-chic washed effect, but, in truth, the best I could manage was a smeared, globular mess. I make a mental note to sand it down over the weekend and then close my eyes, scrunching my pillow beneath my head.

I am almost asleep when the phone rings.

"Hello," I croak, and for a fleeting moment in the place between sleep and wakefulness, I forget that the only person who would be calling me at this hour is the one person I really don't want to speak to.

"Don't you check your messages?" Noah's voice is playful, but I can hear the underlying irritation.

"Noah," I moan, rubbing my eyes. "It's late."

"Not that late," he teases. "We used to stay up a lot later, if my memory serves."

"I'm really not in the mood for your sexual innuendos right now. I'm tired." A long pause follows this, and, realising I may have been a bit abrupt, I quickly add in a far gentler tone, "Can we talk tomorrow?"

Noah is silent for a long moment and I can practically hear the cogs of his brain turning. Since our break-up he's fluctuated between being charming and light, and downright angry that I refuse to get back together with him. Thankfully, tonight, he takes the high road.

"Yeah, okay, sure. Sleep tight."

"You too, Noah."

CHAPTER 5

*T*he next day I barely make it home with enough wine to sink a small country before Tom and Jess descend on me like a pair of F5 tornadoes.

"Stop that!" I slap Jess's hand aside as she tries to grab a packet of crisps. "I'll put everything out in a second." She completely ignores me, ripping open the bag and spilling a liberal pile of Jalapeno Poppers all over the kitchen counter. "Why are you two so early, anyway?" I grumble, scooping the crisps into my palm and tossing them back into the bag.

"We ditched last period," Tom mumbles through a mouthful. "Mr Hardy is back on set." He fake-swoons and I shake my head.

"You're both incorrigible. You can't get near those sets, anyway. I don't know why you even bother."

"We bother, dear Sarah, because you never know when old Tom might feel the heat of my yearning and stalk off set into my open arms. The press would dub us Tom-Tom and we'd adopt a whole basketball team of adorable orphans from Africa."

"If he's going to be embracing anyone, it would be me," Jess corrects, her brows narrowed in earnest, "I'm pretty sure he doesn't bat for your team."

"That's only because he hasn't met me yet."

By 9.15 we have consumed at least five bottles of wine and Jess and Tom have joined forces to coerce me to go out. It's futile arguing, so I allow myself to be led downstairs and bundled into a cab. By 9.30 I am wedged between them at the bar counter, yelling for the barman's attention and waving a twenty in the air as though my life depends on it. Less than five minutes later, thanks to Jess's criminally low-cut top, we are on the dance floor, each with a beer in hand.

I dance half-heartedly for a few songs, laughing at Jess and Tom's shamelessly sexual display, until I hear the first bars of Ellie Goulding's 'Something in the way you move'.

"I love this song!" I shriek, doing a few energetic dance jumps and spilling at least a third of my beer over my arm.

Let me just say that dancing has never been my strong suit. On a good day, Jess says I look like a baby giraffe trying to find her feet; on a bad day she insists I resemble a Parkinson's patient being attacked by a swarm of bees. Nevertheless, with the amount of alcohol sloshing around in my system, I feel suddenly inspired. I wiggle my hips like they don't lie and I wave my hands in the air like I just don't care. I'm pretty sure I look like the girl in *Flashdance* – all long limbs and feline grace. By the time the song ends Tom and Jess are doubled over in fits of hysteria and Jess is laughing so hard that her mascara has run down her cheeks.

"It's not funny!" I yell above the thumping of the next number, but, in truth, it is. It's hilarious. I start to giggle while Tom mimics my antics. "Okay, drinks!" I shout, pointing in the direction of the bar.

Jess's mascara-streaked face seems to have hindered her capacity to attract the attention of the barman and we stand in the queue much longer than before. While we wait I cast a lazy look around, closing one eye when the crowd starts to spin around me. A familiar face comes into view and I give a start of recognition, ducking my head before Leo can spot me.

"What?" Jess asks.

"It's him!" I hiss, jerking my head in Leo's direction.

"Who?" she scans the sea of faces.

"If it's Tom Hardy I have dibs," Tom interjects, looking around intently as though he might spot the superstar any minute in this seedy, downtown bar.

"Not him," I slur, "Leo!"

"Who's Leo?" Tom yells, his timing coinciding spectacularly with a lull in the music. I cringe, ducking below Jess's shoulder.

Jess ignores Tom, her eyes sweeping the room with single-minded purpose. "Oh, there!" She swings me around so that she can spy over my shoulder and watches for a minute. "Hmmm," she murmurs after a time.

"Hmmm what?" I'm itching to turn around.

"Oh, give me that!" Tom snatches the twenty-dollar bill clutched in Jess's hand and turns back to the bar. "You two better fill me in as soon as I have our drinks," he announces.

"What's hmmm?" I demand of Jess.

"Well, for someone with no prospects, he certainly seems

to hang with the 'it' crowd." She gets up on her toes to get a better look.

"What?" My curiosity gets the better of me and I turn around, immediately finding Leo, still standing in the same position, talking to a man who is dressed a lot like Mike from Dylan's office, only without the ketchup. They are in the centre of a small group of men, most of whom are drinking water. I spot the beer in Leo's hand and heave a sigh of relief before returning my attention to the people surrounding him. They're older than us, probably in their early-to-mid-thirties, and Jess is right. Their clothing, haircuts and even the way they hold themselves suggests money. Money and ego. I narrow my eyes, partly to try to see better through the throng of bodies, and partly because it's the only way to focus through my alcohol-induced haze.

"Right!" Tom hollers, returning with three tepid beers, "who is Leo?"

"A first-year who has Sarah's panties in a twist!" Jess yells back. "Well," she adds, giving me a look, "what are you doing? Go say hello!" She gives me a small shove in Leo's direction. It seems like a perfectly reasonable idea for the space of five tottering steps before I have a change of heart. I swivel, intending to beeline straight back to my friends, but I find myself hemmed in by the masses desperate to get to the bar. Right, then, only one way to go. I let the crowd push me forward and find myself at the counter.

A burly youngster with a ring through his lower lip slaps the counter in front of me.

"What can I get you?"

"Um… a beer, please." He casts a curious look at the full

bottle in my hand. "I'm double-parking!" I yell, grinning like the village idiot. "You know; in case I can't get back for a while. This place is pumping!"

Lip-ring rolls his eyes and slams a beer on the counter. With one practiced move he flips the top off and I hand over the money. "Keep the change!" I say, but he doesn't respond. Too late, I feel a presence behind me and from the way the hairs on my neck rise, I'm pretty sure it can only be one person.

"Hello Sarah," Leo's voice is low and friendly.

"Hey!" I say brightly, turning to face him. Seeing as how we don't really know one another, I'm unsure how best to greet him. I offer him my right hand, realise it's holding a beer and instead extend the left. *Dammit!* Also holding a beer. Leo grins, going in for a hug instead. God, he smells good. *Don't think about it, don't think about it.*

"You must be thirsty," he says, completely at ease. I try to do the same, giving a casual shrug as if to say, 'haven't you ever seen anyone order themselves two drinks before?"

"I saw you dancing earlier," Leo admits, and the words send my dignity darting out of the bar and straight up 7th Street. It's hit the state line before I can even think of a response. "So," Leo continues, saving me the mortification of talking about it, "are you intentionally trying to avoid me?"

"Avoid you?" I splutter, making a noise that sounds oddly like I just farted with my mouth. "Of course I'm not avoiding you."

"Oh," he takes a small step back, the sheer size of him parting the crowd around us and giving me some much-needed breathing room, "it's just, I thought you were coming over to say hi but then you seemed to change your mind?" He words it as a question, rather than a statement of fact.

"Nope," I shake my head, "I didn't see you."

Leo's lips press together as though he is trying to keep from laughing.

"Okay then. Well, it was lovely running into you, Sarah."

He's leaving. He's leaving and there's not a damn thing I can do about it. Fortunately, Tom decides he cannot contain himself a moment longer and charges toward us to scout out this shiny new toy. As Leo turns to go, Tom barrels into him. Leo is knocked backward by the force of the impact and six feet of solid muscle is too much for my jelly arms. Both bottles of beer hit the ground, sending fragments of glass sliding in all directions. Leo gives me an apologetic look, his eyes roaming up and down my body as if to reassure himself that I'm okay, before he rounds on Tom.

"Hi there," Tom grins, his hand extended, "you must be Leo."

"Kill me now," I groan, holding my head in my hands.

"It really wasn't that bad," Jess says. The two of us have come outside for air, leaving a practically salivating Tom alone with Leo and have taken shelter in the small outdoor section of the bar. It's quieter out here, a few forlorn-looking wooden tables surrounded by plastic chairs that must once have been black but which have been faded by the sun to an insipid shade of grey.

"He's such an ass!" I say for the twentieth time, and then, in my best Tom-impersonation; "Ooh, you must be Leo. Not that Sarah mentioned your name or that you were here!"

"He's an ass," Jess agrees sagely, "but, look on the bright side – Leo's getting you a new drink." Her low opinion of him seems to have lifted, although whether it's due to the booze, or his posse of successful friends, I'm not sure.

"That's the last thing I need, Jess." The fresh air is doing little to sober me up, and I have a sinking suspicion that my eyelids are flying at half-mast. I make a conscious effort to open them as wide as I can as Leo approaches.

"Are you okay?" he asks, looking at me in mild alarm. Tom, who is standing beside him, shakes his head urgently, opening his own eyes so wide that he looks freakish. Fair warning. I blink quickly a few times, trying to regain some semblance of normal.

"Thanks." I take Leo's proffered beer and give up trying to look sober as he clangs his own bottle against mine. He looks far too composed, far too cheerful and, as I have a feeling he is laughing at me anyway, I may as well just be myself.

"How're your classes going?" I ask.

"Good. I'm struggling a bit with the history theory – I'm more of a practical kind of guy - but I've made a few friends who seem to know what they're doing, so I'll rack their brains closer to exam time."

"If you need a tutor, Sarah's been top of our class for four years now," Jess offers on my behalf. It seems her opinion of Leo has risen enough in the past twenty minutes that she is once again ready to offer me up on a silver platter.

"Sure," I smile up at him, "I'd be happy to help."

Leo is silent a long moment and I feel my bravado fail me. He has an unnerving way of holding my gaze without an inkling of discomfort. Eventually, he gives me a small, sympathetic smile.

"Thanks for the offer, but I think I'll be okay."

"He could've at least pretended to be interested!" Jess's indignation on my behalf is touching, but my cheeks are still flushed with humiliation. The offer to tutor Leo was so clichéd it couldn't have been a more obvious excuse to spend time with him, but he rejected it. He rejected me! Not that I think I'm above rejection, but all the signs were there. I was so sure he was into me.

"Maybe I was imagining his signals?" I muse out loud. We are wandering aimlessly in the general direction of my building, but have yet to find a cab.

"No way!" Jess raises a hand to emphasise her point as I hop over a huge crack in the sidewalk. "He was putting out major vibes. And let's not forget, he was the one who practically eye-fucked you in class. And he held up that note. No," she shakes her head so vehemently that her braids whip across her face. "The signs were there. That man wanted you."

"Maybe he changed his mind after seeing me in all my drunken glory?"

"Probably," Tom hiccups, oblivious to my feelings. Jess punches his arm.

"Sarah's adorable when she's drunk," she says, although her tone implies that this is less of a compliment and more an indication that there is something seriously wrong with me. "It can't be that – something else spooked him." She considers this for a second and then snaps her fingers. "Maybe you're too smart! I did say you were top of our year. If he's a bit useless, he might've been intimidated. Maybe he doesn't want you to find out that he's all penis and no brains."

"I think the correct term is all brawn, no brains," I point out, but she ignores me.

"What we need is a plan. Maybe we should invite him to Game Night next Friday?"

I turn to gape at her. Jess has spent the past four years advocating the sanctity of Game Night. *No-one* is allowed inside our inner circle. Once, when my brother Dylan rolled up halfway through a particularly gripping game of Monopoly she actually threw an empty champagne bottle at him.

"Game Night Jess, really?" I ask incredulously. I look at Tom to gauge his reaction, but he is standing in the middle of the road, shirt hitched up, admiring his abs. "You're going to get run over," I point out before turning back to Jess.

"Yes, Game Night. Nobody gets away with snubbing you." The only thing that Jess loves more than Game Night is a challenge. Her eyes are narrowed and she has adopted the same fierce look she usually reserves for her mortal enemies - the likes of Samantha Simpson and her gaggle of silicon slappers. That look never bodes well.

"I think we should just let it go," I mumble.

"Agreed," Tom announces, appearing at my side. "He already turned her down once. Sarah's not exactly a sucker for punishment."

Jess's eyes narrow even further, although I honestly didn't think it was possible.

"Besides," Tom continues, "Sarah Russell really doesn't have a nice ring to it."

"Russell?" I ask, confused.

"Yeah, that's his name. Leo Russell. I asked him at the bar."

"We'll ask him on Monday," Jess announces, and it takes

my fuzzy brain a moment to realise she's still talking about Game Night. The look on her face is so fierce that neither Tom nor I dare argue. When Jess makes up her mind she is a force to be reckoned with. I should be more upset that I'm about to commit social suicide, but, in truth, the enigma that is Leo Russell is a challenge I can't back down from either.

CHAPTER 6

*B*y Thursday I haven't seen Leo once, which is not really surprising given the size of the Holmes Institute's campus, and the fact that he hasn't snuck into any of my lectures again. Jess, who is behaving like a woman possessed, has assured me she will handle what she dubs the 'Pipe-Cleaner' project, so I try to focus on my classes instead. Rumours are flying around campus that two representatives from Burke & Duke have asked to meet with the Institute's nominated candidates for the Advanced Placement Program, but, being one of the only two candidates, along with the dreadful Samantha Simpson, who is not as stupid as she looks, I know this to be false. The interviews won't take place until after our thesis submission, toward the end of the academic year. This placement is something I have been working toward for the past four years, and any mention of it gets my nerves firing. I want this placement. I want it more than anything else in the world. I've worked for it and secretly, I know I'm the better candidate.

Surprisingly, today's Technology lecture has been cancelled. I saw Noah coming out of the lecturers' lounge on my way to class this morning so I know he must be here. It's not like Noah to miss a lecture - not because he takes any pride in the grades of his students, but the opportunity to be fawned over is not something he avoids. Presented with a free hour, I find an empty table in the cafeteria and make notes on my final project.

"I hope that's your thesis you're working on," a gravelly voice interrupts and I can't help the smile that pastes itself on my face as I look up. Dianna Marchant is well into her fifties and terrifies most of the students here at Holmes. She is tall – over six feet – and slim, with broad shoulders that carry most of the weight of the college upon them. Students can only guess at the length of her nothing-natural-about-it black hair because her trademark tight bun gives nothing away. Dianna is stern and intimidating, but the mischievous twinkle in her blue eyes gives her an air of youthfulness. I think so, anyway. Most students don't let her get close enough to notice.

"Dianna!" Yes, I am on a first-name basis with the Dean. I make no apologies. She has her favourites, all of whom work harder than most. She is also my allocated mentor for this final year and the person to whom I report my thesis and ideas. It's no coincidence that in a class of almost a hundred students, only Samantha and I were allocated Dianna's tutelage – she works exclusively with those nominated for the Burke & Duke Advanced Placement program. Technically, we began our mentorship with Dianna at the end of last semester, in our fourth year, making preparation for the mighty workload that we would be set this year, and it hadn't taken long for me to grow comfortable with her. I set down my pencil and get to my feet, my eyes reaching the uncomfortable level of her insignificant bosom. "How lovely to see you!"

"You too, Sarah," a pause and then, "how's it coming along?" She gestures at the stack of papers on the table.

"It's a work in progress," I stammer. Dianna had approved my thesis topic only last week but she expects almost immediate results.

"Did you find a location yet?"

"I think so, I'm going to check it out next week." My thesis involves tearing down an abandoned warehouse and building an art gallery in its place, right in the heart of the district. After weeks of walking the streets I ironically found the location online, but next week I will conduct a site visit to see if it will work for my proposal.

"I'd like to see your progress by next Friday."

"I'm sure I'll have the location finalised by then." I nod convincingly.

"I'm counting on you," Dianna reminds me, "I'm sick to death of losing out to ATC and Monet." At the mention of the rival colleges her lip curls. The Burke & Duke placement hasn't been won by a Holmes graduate since... well, since Dianna herself was a Holmes graduate and won it. She is possibly the person I admire most here at Holmes. She still lectures occasionally and, when she deigns to do so, the lecture hall is full to bursting. Unlike Noah, who is as sub-standard an educator as he is in terms of professional practical skills, Dianna's skills are legendary. After winning the Burke & Duke placement over thirty years ago, she went on to become one of their most successful architects, earning herself a full partnership in just four years. Dianna is what Noah is simply not: enormously talented. She spent fifteen years with the company before, in what many refer to as a moment of insanity, resigning from the firm and returning to Holmes to pass her knowledge on.

"You can't possibly put in a good word for me, can you?" I tease, knowing full well what her answer will be.

"No," she replies firmly and expectedly, "and even if I could, I wouldn't. You shouldn't need me to." Her voice drops even lower and a satisfied smile tugs at the corners of her lips. "You *don't* need me to," she corrects, and her meaning is clear. "Why aren't you in class?" she adds, as if she is aware of being too kind and is looking for something to take me to task about.

"Noah... Mr Allen's class was cancelled."

"Of course it is," she snaps impatiently, "he's probably schmoozing the B & D reps."

"They're here?" I gasp, a surge of panic coursing through me. I hadn't given the rumours that the Burke & Duke representatives were here a moment's thought, but it appeared that they were true after all.

Dianna waves her hand breezily through the air between us. "No need to panic, dear. They're not making any decisions about the internship. They just need to review some of your previous work. Not that Mr Allen," she emphasises the title, "would be required to assist."

"Then, why would he cancel his lecture?"

Her eagle eyes fix me in their stare. "That is something you should think about," she says, and I detect a warning in her tone. "I don't like to get involved in the private lives of my students, but between you and me, Sarah, I am relieved that that particular affair is over."

I can feel my jaw tightening as the blush spreads unbidden

across my cheeks. I tried to be discreet about my relationship with Noah but it was common knowledge on campus. Never, though, had I expected Dianna Marchant to know about it or to have an opinion about it, one way or another. But know she must and I am mortified. Strictly speaking, there is no law against student-lecturer relations, but that doesn't stop it creating a scandal.

"I... I..." I mutter, trying to form a coherent response. Fortunately, Dianna isn't expecting one.

"Noah Allen is charming," she continues, "and certainly very easy on the eye, but he is also narcissistic and petty, and not above taking the low road. You have a bright future ahead of you, Sarah. Don't let someone like him be your downfall."

"He won't be," I insist, "it's over. I called it off months ago. We've both moved on."

"Are you sure about that?"

"I am."

"Good. Keep your eye on the prize and don't do anything to antagonise him, not when you're so close to getting what you want. Noah may be a lot of things, but he's not stupid. And I wouldn't put it past him to hit you where it hurts most if he feels inclined."

"But he couldn't interfere with the internship? You wouldn't allow that, surely?"

"I think you give me too much credit," she smiles again, and the atmosphere lightens perceptibly. "Just keep your head down, keep your nose clean and stay away from trouble until the internship is awarded."

As she walks away, students parting like the Red Sea in her path, I mull over her words: stay away from trouble, and, at that precise moment, Leo Russell looms large in my field of vision.

"He said he'd think about it!" Jess hisses triumphantly in my ear, the sound carrying across the cafeteria to where Leo is standing. Dianna had barely taken five steps away from me before Jess dashed forward. Leo tries to hide a smile, fails miserably, and then, as if to save me from any further embarrassment, he turns away and strides out of the cafeteria, the doors swinging innocently behind him. "Oh," Jess follows his departure and then gives a little shrug, "oops. I thought he'd left already."

"You are so bad," I say, gathering my paperwork and stuffing it unceremoniously into my book bag. "And what do you mean he said he'd think about it? It hardly sounds promising."

"Beats me." She shrugs again, the padded shoulders of her military-style jacket making the gesture far more effective than it would usually be. "I asked him while you were chatting to Dianna and he said he'd think about it. Of course he's coming, though. I mean, who turns down an invitation to Game night?" This is said with all the confidence of a woman who always gets her own way.

"Jess," I groan, slinging my bag across my shoulder and meeting her eyes.

"He took the address," she says, as though that decides it.

"Just stop," I say, "enough with the Leo project."

"It's actually the Pipe-Cleaner..."

"I know!" I cut her off before she can finish her sentence in that high-pitched voice of hers. The cafeteria is filling up as the lunch crowd descends upon us. Lowering my voice to a whisper I continue. "Enough with the Pipe-Cleaner Project. In fact, you're never allowed to mention my pipes again. Period."

"But…"

"No buts, Jess," I laugh at the look of desolation on her face. "Let's try and retain just a little dignity for me okay?" Her answering grumble is barely audible but I catch the words "fine" and "ruin all the fun" and with that I'm content to be satisfied.

I'm waiting for Jess and Tom on the steps outside at the end of the day when the topic of my earlier conversation makes his appearance. A shadow falls across the page of the textbook I'm browsing through, blocking out a large portion of the sun.

I look up, shielding my eyes automatically, but Leo is so broad-shouldered that I am completely shaded. Dropping my hand, I close the book, carefully marking the page with a Post-it.

"Hey," I smile up at him.

"Hey," he replies, "do you mind if I sit?"

"Sure!" I gesture at the spot beside me and he curls his body into it. His name suits him; I find myself thinking. He's all tanned, toned skin and lithe grace, despite his size. The sunlight catches the copper in his hair, which flops into his insanely blue eyes and I fight the urge to brush it aside. His eyebrows slightly darker and perfectly shaped, in contrast to his wild hair, arch enviously over his dark lashes. *Don't look at his lips, Sarah*, I chide myself, an instant before I do exactly that. No man should have a lower lip that full. Too late, he catches me mid-stare.

"So, what's up?" I ask, clasping my hands together between

my knees and praying that Tom and Jess are delayed. There's no telling what inappropriate comments they might send my way if they catch me talking to Leo.

"Not much." His voice is ocean deep, soothing and intense at the same time. "It's been a quiet week. I think I'm finally getting ahead in history theory," he adds, his mouth twitching as if there is some private joke in his words. I don't respond, feeling the embarrassment of my offer to tutor him rising again. Leo seems to realise this and he quickly changes the subject. "So… your friend Jess invited me to a Game Night tomorrow." He has an unnerving way of holding my gaze when he speaks, maintaining the direct eye contact that is only truly comfortable when you know someone intimately. His knees are spread, his hands hanging casually between them. The position is relaxed and graceful, with no air of insecurity. Leo is as confident as he is forthright.

"She may have mentioned that," I say, feigning nonchalance. "Are you coming?" This close up I notice a jagged scar just above his left eye which zigzags back into his hairline. *Not perfect, then*, I tell myself unconvincingly. Seeing where my gaze wanders, he shifts imperceptibly, turning his face and I wonder if he has a complex about the scar. He certainly doesn't need to; it does nothing to detract from his appeal.

"That depends," he replies enigmatically, and then, out of the blue; "do *you* want me there?"

I open my mouth to answer yes – yes, yes and absolutely yes – when, over his shoulder I catch sight of Noah. His eyes are narrowed, fixed on the two of us, and a dark scowl mars his usually handsome face. Dianna's warning not to antagonise Noah comes back to haunt me as I become aware of the two people standing beside him - the older man and an attractive woman who appears to be in her mid-thirties. Both are immaculately dressed and I don't need to be able to read the fine print on their white visitor cards to know that these are the Burke & Duke Representatives. Seeing that he has my attention, Noah deliberately turns his back on me and places a hand on the woman's sleeve. The gesture seems innocent enough, but I know Noah and there is nothing innocent about it.

To his credit, Leo doesn't turn around to see what has captured my attention. He must notice the change in my expression though, and he shifts slightly, a small frown creasing the skin between his eyes.

"I'm going to take that as a no, then," he says. Is it my imagination or does he actually look disappointed?

"No… I mean, that's not what I… you're more than welcome to join us. It's not exactly a private function, you can come if you like. I mean, it's not only up to me…" I trail off, perplexed at my sudden inability to articulate.

Leo stares at me in that unnerving way for a long moment before speaking.

"You know, Sarah, I'm hearing a lot of 'I mean's' but I don't think you've meant any of it." His blue eyes dominate my vision as he leans in close to me, unashamedly invading my personal space. "Do you want me there or not?" His words are almost lost in the intensity of those incredible eyes, but they echo in my subconscious and I stifle the urge to close the distance between us. Our mouths are only inches apart. I lean back, intentionally, trying to put some much-needed distance between us. I can see Noah in my peripheral vision, still hovering, watching my every move.

"Like I said," I shrug, "it's up to you."

This time I'm not imagining it. Leo's disappointment is palpable. He wanted this invitation to come from me. Shouldering his bag, he gets lithely to his feet, his shirt pulling up to reveal a flat stomach, a line of dark hair burrowing below his waistband.

"Well, maybe I'll see you there." His parting line is as unpromising as the emptiness he leaves behind when he's gone.

CHAPTER 7

"*Y*ou said what?" Jess is a formidable sight, hands on her hips, shoulders pushed back as she faces me in the kitchen like a matador challenging the bull. Tom backs away slowly, conveniently needing the bathroom. "Why? Why wouldn't you say, yes Leo, please come over and tickle anything that tickles your fancy?"

"Jess!" I laugh. "That's disgusting."

"No," she corrects, "you're disgusting. I bet Leo's amazing in the sack – he's so controlled and dominant. And do you know how hard it was to track him down? To get him to even consider coming tonight? And then you go and give it a 'oh, if you wanna… do what you want to do'! What the hell, Sarah? It's like you're trying to destroy me!"

"You may be being just a little bit dramatic right now, I don't know, it could just be me."

"That's totally not funny."

"It's a really busy year," I try to justify, "I don't need any distractions. Besides, he's single. You don't get to be single at his age unless you play the field. I don't want to be another…"

"If you say feather in his cap, I'm going to punch you in the face."

I keep my lips firmly closed.

"Sarah!"

I sigh. "You know what I mean, Jess."

"No," she announces confidently, "I don't. I'm calling bull-shit right now. You like him, he's hot, and, as you so clearly pointed out, he's single. I don't understand what the problem is."

She's not going to let it go, I can tell. When Jess sets her mind to something, there is no force on earth powerful enough to stop her. Relenting, I exhale deeply, mentally preparing myself for the shit-storm I'm about to unleash.

"It's Noah," I admit, and then, before she can interrupt, "he's buttering up the Burke & Duke reps. And, before you say it, I know I'm probably being paranoid, but I'm worried he could try to destroy my chances at the internship."

The singular pause that follows this admission is far more terrifying than the outraged outburst I had been expecting. Jess is silent for at least a minute, her mouth opened in a perfect 'O' and then she shuts it abruptly. When she opens it again, what bursts from her lips is a screeching summons. "Tom!" Oh God, it's worse than I thought. She's calling for back-up.

Tom practically falls over his feet as he rushes back into the room.

"Who died?" he yells, his eyes darting between us.

"You, sit!" Jess hands me a wine glass, the meniscus teetering dangerously over the rim. I take a huge gulp, partly to ensure I don't spill all over my new vinyl flooring and partly to ease my nerves, while Jess fills Tom in. Obviously the story is embellished and convoluted to the point where Noah is the sole thing standing between me and my one true love. I'm starting to get the distinct impression that Jess is basing my life deep within the latest episode of *The Vampire Diaries* when I finally interject.

"Guys! Enough! Let's just move on, please. We have a whole night of games planned."

"Games?" Jess's eyebrow disappears into her hairline. "Do you think I wasted half my allowance buying all of this," she gestures at the expensive cheese platter and snacks she brought with her, "for us?"

I have no idea what answer she is looking for, or whether I am supposed to take that as a compliment or an insult, so I simply shut my mouth.

Tom shows no such compunction. "That's not even a tenth of your allowance," he drawls.

"This was for Leo!" Jess continues, ignoring him. "I invested good money in your sex life, Sarah, and I expect a return on my investment!"

Later, no one could recall exactly who had left the front door unlocked, but it hardly mattered. The point was, that at this particularly crass proclamation, Leo Russell stepped into the kitchen, his crooked smile so broad that his white teeth flashed under the low-hanging bulbs. With Jess's decibel levels reaching new heights, no one had heard him knocking.

"I'm sorry I'm late," Leo announces, holding out an expensive bottle of red and a crumpled packet of crisps. "And the door was open." No one speaks. It's one of those awkward, I-would-rather-be-anywhere-but-here silences that nobody wants to be the one to break. Leo, far from looking uncomfortable, turns to lock his blue eyes on my magenta face. "Where would I find a glass?" he asks politely.

Ten minutes later, I emerge from the bathroom where I fled after the mortifying start to my evening, to find Leo ensconced on my two-seater sofa with Jess. Tom is hovering above them, holding a tray of cheese and hummus and looking for all the world like a *maître d'*. Jess and Leo fall silent as I enter the room – a bad sign in itself. Knowing Jess, I can only pray that she hasn't offered Leo hard cash for his sexual services.

"Are we ready to play?" I ask innocently.

"Yes!" Jess leaps from the couch and perches herself daintily on the arm of my one-seater. "And for once, we have even numbers, so we can play teams! You and Leo can pair up, I'll take Tom." She pats the chair beside her, managing to sound as though she is doing Tom the hugest favour. There is no point arguing, so I settle into the spot she has just vacated. Leo is so big he takes up most of the sofa, only a few inches spared between the two of us.

"What are we playing?" Leo asks.

"Charades?" Jess asks the room at large.

"What about truth or dare?" Everyone swivels to face Leo, not sure of how to respond. "What?" he shrugs. "Haven't you ever played that?"

"Not since I was thirteen," Tom announces, "and Patrick Jones's mother has never been the same after what she witnessed. I hear he's married with a kid now, so I guess all that therapy worked out well... for mama Jones at any rate. Poor Patrick's spending his life in denial." He pauses thoughtfully, and then with a memorable sigh, "He had such potential, too."

"Oh-kay then," Leo grins, completely unfazed by Tom's over-share. "So, who's going first?"

"We are not seriously playing truth or dare?" I ask.

"Why not?" Leo teases. "Are you scared, Sarah?"

"Oh, hell no!" Jess announces, moving from Tom's side to the other single-seater in the room. "Let's do it!"

The game starts out innocently enough. Jess dares Tom to kiss me, which he does with great flair, complete with lip-smacking noises and a great deal of moaning, while keeping his lips firmly closed against mine. When it's done, I fake giddiness and take a huge swig of wine, emptying my glass which Jess immediately refills. I dare Jess to take off her shoes, knowing full well she hasn't cut her toenails in weeks, but the dare backfires on me as, with no shame whatsoever, she kicks off her sneakers and the stench of smelly feet fills the room. Within minutes we're all begging her to put the shoes back on, but she refuses until Tom is forced to waste a dare in getting her to do so.

"Your turn," Jess announces happily, turning to Leo. Tom scowls darkly at her, annoyed at having to relinquish his turn, but Jess is oblivious.

"Truth or dare?" I know he's talking to me because he's staring intently, his eyes locked on mine.

"Truth," I reply immediately, too intimidated to go with a dare. My stomach is flip-flopping like a wet fish on dry sand.

Leo grins in Machiavellian style, his teeth catching the light of the lamp beside him. *Uh-oh*, I think, knowing that I'm about to be embarrassed. Jess and Tom seem to have come to the same conclusion and both have leaned forward in their chairs, looking positively euphoric at the thought.

"Sarah," Leo says, almost purring, "do you, or do you not..." he tapers off, his blue eyes twinkling, and then he shakes his head, laughing at some private joke. When he speaks again, his voice is perfectly neutral. "Do you or do you not usually have fancy cheese platters every Friday, or is Jess just trying to impress me?" Jess and Tom both slump back in their chairs with annoyed sighs of disappointment as I release the breath I had been holding. Surprisingly, I'm disappointed that he so obviously changed his mind about the question he wanted to ask, but I do think it's kind of cool that he chose to embarrass Jess instead of me.

"We do not," I reply gravely, taking a sip of wine. "In fact, none of us can actually stand the stuff. It's your turn, Jess," I add, grinning at her.

"What an anti-climax," Jess huffs, shooting daggers at Leo, who shrugs his broad shoulders. He doesn't drink much, but I'm the only one who notices, probably because I'm hyper-aware of every move he makes.

We continue to play, Jess and Tom doing their utmost to embarrass each other, while Leo and I simply fire meaningless, superficial questions at one another until Jess eventually calls the game to a close for 'fear of being put to sleep'.

"Let's go out," Tom suggests and I immediately set my glass down, shaking my head.

"I'm actually going to call it a night, you guys, I have an early start." Jess and Tom look as though I've just announced my intention to enter a convent. "Dylan and I are off to see the folks tomorrow," I explain, sounding lame even to my own ears.

"I should get home, too." Leo gets to his feet. While he's dusting the crumbs from his pants, Jess takes the opportunity of his distraction to cast me a look of disgust. She is still jerking her head in his direction by the time he straightens up and he watches her antics for a few seconds before she realises.

"Tom, let's you and I go and paint the town red," she grins, hauling Tom off the sofa.

"Red is so hetero," Tom pouts, "but I'm all for streaking it scarlet."

"Deal," Jess pushes him toward the front door, winking at me as they pass. "See ya!" she sings. The door slams shut a moment later and I am left alone with Leo, who is staring at the spot they have just exited from with a bemused, but startled look on his face.

"Well," I dust my hands together, "thank you for coming." He doesn't reply and I start ferrying dishes to the kitchen for want of something to do. "You don't have to do that," I insist a moment later as he joins me at the sink.

"I know," he replies evenly, going back to retrieve the virtually untouched cheese platter.

I breathe slowly in through my nose and exhale through my mouth, fighting the hysterical urge to giggle. By the time Leo saunters back into the kitchen the hilarity of the situation has me in its clutches and I turn to face him, a huge grin on my face.

"I'm so sorry about all of that," I wave my hand airily in the direction of the front door, where Jess and Tom departed only moments ago. "Sometimes they get a little wild."

"I think they're great," he says, his own crooked smile making an appearance. "I think you're all great, actually."

"Great being a new kind of crazy?" I ask, raising my brows.

"No," he chuckles, "great being great." He pauses, glancing over his shoulder at the door and then those blue eyes find mine again. "Do you have any idea how awesome this whole dynamic is? You have pretty amazing friends, Sarah." As he says it, I realise how true the words are. Jessica and Tom are unique and quirky, but they're my unique and quirky and I wouldn't change them for the world.

"There's never a dull moment," I agree, "but why should there be? We only have one life, after all, we may as well make every second count."

I'm not sure why but my words seem to unsettle Leo. His usually open face shuts down, his lips tightening into a flat line and he raises a hand to his left temple. It's a subconscious action, one I doubt he's even aware of, but the movement draws my eyes again to the half-hidden scar there.

"How did it happen?" I ask, stepping forward automatically, but Leo drops his hand and turns to the fridge, giving me the benefit of his broad back. He sets the cheese platter carefully on the second shelf, not answering the question.

"I should get going," he announces suddenly, and I nod, too stunned to argue.

"I'll walk you out."

We reach the front door and I pull it open. Leo's arm brushes against mine as he moves past me in the narrow hall, the fine hairs tickling my skin. I've had just enough wine that I'm feeling reckless, sentimental, and more than a little horny. All thoughts of Noah and the Burke & Duke representatives have been tempered by the pinotage. Normally, I'd take the proverbial bull by the horns and lean in for a goodnight kiss, but Leo's abrupt mood swing has me filled with uncertainty.

"I'm glad you could make it," I say, far too brightly,

directing the words at his back as he steps out of the doorway. He turns to face me and I'm relieved to see that the crooked smile is back in place.

"Thank you for not inviting me," he replies teasingly, "I'm glad I came." There's an infinitesimal pause where I'm so certain he's going to kiss me that I actually incline my body toward him, and then he's gone, walking towards the elevator with his hands in his pockets and not looking back.

CHAPTER 8

"What do you mean he didn't kiss you?" Jess mumbles, only half-listening. I glance at the clock in the kitchen and cringe at how early it is. Jess is probably nursing a hangover, but I wanted to ask her opinion about the non-kiss before Dylan picks me up to drive down to see our parents.

"I mean, nothing. Not even a cheeker, or that weird, kiss-the-air-next-to-your-cheek thing that some people do."

"And you made it clear that you wanted to kiss him, right? I mean, sometimes you can be a bit hard to read."

"He knew, Jess." I fob off the implication that this could be my fault. "And the funny thing is, I had already decided that this whole thing would be too complicated and that it would be best if I just avoid him. But then he shows up here, with that hair and those eyes and..."

"That crotch," Jess intervenes.

"How is it that even when you're half-asleep you have sex on the brain?"

"It's a gift... Oh my God!"

"What?"

"What the actual fuck!"

"Jess, what?" I yell into the phone.

"Oh please, please tell me we didn't do anything last night?" Jess roars, still ignoring me.

"Have you actually lost your mind?" Tom's deep voice is muffled, and a mental image of him buried deep under Jess's duvet springs to my mind. "I don't care how tight your ass is, Jess, I am G-A-Y girlfriend. Like, that's just gross!"

"Oh thank God!" Jess's relief is tangible, even over the phone.

"Um... hellooooo?" I snap. "Do you guys mind? This is kind of important!"

"What is?" Tom sounds slightly more alert, "the fact that Jess's first waking thought is of my penis, or the fact that she acts like we've never slept in the same bed before?"

"Actually, this is all about me."

"Leo didn't make a move last night," Jess's voice. "Hang on, I'm putting you on speaker," she adds.

"So what happened?" Tom asks.

"Nothing, literally. He left just after you guys did. Not even a goodnight kiss." My cheeks flame as I remember how I'd leaned toward him, expecting one.

"He seemed pretty into you when we made our discreet exit," Tom points out and I wonder if he's taking the piss, or if he's actually delusional enough to believe they weren't obvious. "Maybe Jess's direct approach scared him off?"

"No," I muse, actually giving this some thought.

"Maybe the cheese disagreed with him and he had to high-tail it to the visitor's bathroom?"

"He didn't actually eat any of that cheese. None of us did."

"Such a waste," Jess grumbles.

"Maybe the lingering stench of Jess's feet made him physically ill and he had to leave before he blew chunks all over your pretty vinyl floor?" This last suggestion is followed by a thud and the sounds of a struggle. "Get them away from me!" Tom yells.

"You slept in the same bed as these feet all night and I didn't hear you complaining!" Jess's retort is loud and clear.

"The smell probably induced a mild coma!"

"Take it back!"

"No!"

"Then sniff away my boy!"

"Guys!" I yell into the handset.

After a brief pause, Jess is back. "It's nothing I did, Sarah. When we left, Leo was still hot to trot, I could see it in his eyes."

"In his eyes?" I ask dubiously.

"She means he was staring at your ass the whole time we were heading for the door," Tom quips helpfully. "I saw it too. I hate to say it, sweetheart, but Jess is right. It must have been something you did after we left."

"Hmmm..." I pause, thinking about our brief encounter in the kitchen. "I did ask him about the scar above his eye..."

"Ooh, I noticed that!" Jess loves a good mystery. "What did he say caused it?"

"He didn't."

"Oh, flashback!" Jess yells suddenly. She must have turned to face Tom because her next words aren't as clear. "Do you remember the hottie from the bar last night? The one with the goatee and the tattoos? He was so into me!"

"Oh please," Tom's derision is clear, "he was not into you Jess. He was into me."

"No way!" Jess insists, and I bite the tip of my thumbnail waiting for them to remember I'm on the line.

"How can you be best friends with me and still have the worst gaydar in New York?" Tom says.

"He was not gay!" Jess draws every word out.

"Girl, the man was staring at my zipper with his teeth!"

Knowing I'll get no joy out of either of them before Dylan arrives, I interrupt.

"I've gotta go, you two, Dyl will be here any minute. I'll call you later when I get back." They barely miss a beat and I'm still chuckling as I hang up.

"You look pale, sweetheart. Are you eating properly?" These are my mother's first words as I step over the threshold.

"She's hung-over," Dylan corrects, coming in after me. He dips his head to kiss her cheek, ever the perfect son.

"That's my girl, taking after her old man!" Dad's voice booms as he makes his way down the stairs and pulls me into a bone-crushing hug. My mother giggles in the way she always does when my father makes any sort of joke, and he lets go of me to sweep her into a hug of her own. Dylan and I wait patiently as he dips her toward the ground, her pale curls trailing along the mahogany floor before he lifts her back up again and plants a kiss on her nose.

Long gone are the days when my parents' constant displays of affection made us feel uncomfortable. We're used to it, although when they really get going in a busy restaurant Dylan usually puts his foot down. Mom and Dad have always been this way. I cannot remember a time that they didn't feel the need to touch one another, a simple passing of the peas across the dinner table leads to a quick squeeze of the hand, and Dad has a habit of giving Mom an ass-grab every time they pass in the hall. I have spent the past ten years trying to convince myself that this doesn't mean they have an active sex-life, but sadly, they keep trying to prove otherwise.

"Something smells good," I say, as Mom stares adoringly into Dad's eyes.

"Oh! My potatoes!" Mom shrieks, bustling off to the kitchen. Dad grabs a handful as she rushes away, but thankfully, it's mostly skirt.

I follow Mom into the kitchen, which opens onto the patio outside. The table, as always, is beautifully laid out with Grandma Holt's best china which Dad inherited after she died and a tall glass beaker of iced water in the centre in which bob a few slices of lemon and a sprig of mint from the herb garden. My mother is one of those people who takes the time to cut sprigs of lavender to adorn the plates and who folds the napkins into swans. Sometimes I wish some of her attention to detail had rubbed off on me, but then I remember that Jess and Tom would hardly appreciate it. The only thing they want handy when they come for dinner is the bottle-opener and an unending supply of ice.

Dylan and Dad take a seat on the antique wicker chairs on the opposite side of the patio and immediately start discussing current affairs.

"Sarah," Mom throws over her shoulder as she turns the roast potatoes in the pan, "fetch the boys a beer, will you?"

"Dylan's driving," I point out happily.

"It's only one beer," my mother gives a little giggle, "and besides, you can always drive him."

I roll my eyes behind her back, but I do as she's asked, fighting the urge to remind her that she was born in the era of Women's Liberation and should start acting like it. This is exactly why Dylan is like he is, why he has such archaic expectations of women, but my mom has always doted on the men in our family and she's not about to change her ways now. Dad, at least, is grateful and he gives me a fond look as I set down his Bud Light. Dylan, on the other hand, loves to rub it in.

"You're going to make someone a very good wife one day, little sis," he teases. I hurl one of mom's many scatter cushions at him, but he catches it easily, much to my chagrin.

"You shouldn't speak of wives as if you know anything about them," I say, flipping him the bird as I walk back inside.

"Your sister makes a good point, son," I hear Dad say and I grin, knowing that for the next few minutes Dylan will have to deal with yet another talk about how he should find a wife and settle down.

Revenge, however, is a dish best served cold. We are not five minutes into Mom's homemade lasagne when Dylan pipes up, "So, Sarah, who was that man who left your place so late last night?" His voice is casual, but the devilry in his eyes gives him away. Dylan has been trying to get me into trouble with Mom since we were kids and he usually succeeds. Our mother has high moral standards about unmarried women being alone with a man, unless that man is her son, of course, because he's the epitome of moral responsibility.

"Sarah?" Mom rounds on me, her green eyes wide.

"It was Game Night, Mom," I reassure her. "Jess and Tom

were there too. And what are you doing spying on my place anyway?" I ask, lobbing a bread roll at Dylan's head. It lands innocently on his plate next to a mountain of chicken. "Don't you have anything better to do with your life? Like finding a wife?" I arch my brow at him suggestively.

"I thought Game Night was a limited invite event," Dylan says. "Only you, Jess and Tom allowed. So when I heard a new voice, I was concerned for your safety."

Oh he didn't! He drew the safety card, ensuring that Mom would now go into a thirty-minute long sermon lamenting how I was living all on my own in the dangerous cesspit of the city.

"Dad!" I say brightly, turning to my father before Mom can begin. "What do you think of Trump running for office?"

Distracted by the light of her life's precious opinion, Mom turns to listen and I'm spared, but I spend the rest of lunch shooting dagger eyes at Dylan for good measure.

CHAPTER 9

*C*onscious of Mom's high opinion of him, Dylan only has two beers and then moves on to coffee for the rest of the afternoon. By the time he pulls his Mustang into the underground lot, two spaces down from my little Fiat, I'm feeling the effects of last night's wine and the restless lack of sleep.

"I'm going straight to bed," I announce as Dylan locks the car and follows me to the elevators. We part ways on the fourth floor and I let myself into my apartment with a yawn. A lightning shower later and I'm tucked up in bed, checking my Facebook notifications, when I hear a rapping in my front door. The sound is amplified by the complete silence in the apartment and I hasten to answer, the vinyl flooring warm beneath my bare feet.

Assuming its Dylan, no doubt needing to borrow milk or a roll of toilet-paper, I yank the door open and Noah practically falls into the apartment, his arm raised heroically over his head. He was obviously lounging against the door in what he thought would be a sexy pose, as I eyed him through the peep-hole. Recovering quickly, he drops his arm and rights himself, smoothing down the pale yellow, woollen sweater I bought him for his birthday. It fits his lithe frame beautifully and I know from experience that it feels like cotton candy on my cheek when we watch TV and I lay my head on his shoulder. Looking at it now I can't help but think how much better it would look on Leo.

"Noah, what are you doing here?" I ask pointedly. I had banned him from the building after a series of late-night, unannounced visits and he hadn't been back in a while.

"I was in the area," he replies easily, "and I thought I'd pop in to see you."

"That's really sweet of you but I was actually just about to go to bed." I gesture at my Snoopy pyjamas as if I need to prove it.

"To bed? It's a Saturday night and the sun's barely down?"

"I know, but I had a late night last night and Dylan and I drove down to Arcadia today."

The tightness that settled on his lips when I mentioned my late night softens ever so slightly at the mention of my parents' home town.

"How are Robert and Eleanor doing?" The names drip familiarly from his lips, smug in the knowledge that my parents adore him.

"They're fine…"

He doesn't even wait for me to finish. "I hope you sent them my regards?"

My anger spikes. His assumption that he would even be worth a mention is so typically Noah.

"Funnily enough, you weren't mentioned," I say.

He barely hears me. He is already moving into the living room, his blue eyes sweeping the apartment. I always thought Noah had the nicest eyes, but they pale in comparison to Leo's. *Stop it!* I mentally chide myself. *You have Leo on the brain.* I turn my attention back to Noah. I'm sure he's looking for evidence of another man; a coat draped over the sofa, a pair of shoes on the floor or a secret lover stashed in the hall closet. Not that he's going to find anything remotely inter-esting – I haven't been with anyone since our split.

"You look tired." Noah is staring at me and for the first time in forever, he actually looks like he used to back when we were together. His eyes are soft and the concern in his voice is genuine. The sweet effect is slightly dampened by the fact that I just told him I was about to go to bed and yet he refuses to leave and let me sleep, but I force that thought from my mind. I try to remember why I fell for him in the first place. Noah is not all bad. He can be funny and caring, but, in hindsight, I believe that the real reason I stayed with him as long as I did is because of the way he made me feel about myself when we were together: Like I was important, like I mattered. I didn't realise at the time that the only reason he made me feel this way was because I was an extension of him. I was only impor-tant because I was dating him, I only mattered because of my status as his girlfriend. It was never really about me and only ever about him. Still, we had good times and it was never my intention to make an enemy of him, so I resign myself to being polite and making small talk.

"How about I make us a cup of tea?" I offer.

"Sounds good." He shrugs out of his coat and lays it across the back of the sofa. "Maybe we could catch a film?"

"Sure." I gesture at the set and leave him to flip through

the channels while I put the water on. I glance down at my cotton pyjama top. Snoopy stares balefully up at me between the curve of my breasts, the thin fabric doing nothing to conceal them. Oh well, it's not as if there's anything here that Noah hasn't seen before.

The kettle takes forever to boil and I stifle a yawn as I carry the steaming mugs back to the living room. I sit on the other side of the sofa, curling my feet beneath me to ward off the chill.

"So, how was Game Night?" Noah, of course, knows all about our Friday ritual, having taken part more times than Jess or Tom could bear – which was once. Noah had whined so badly at being excluded when we were dating that I had finally coerced Jess and Tom to make an exception for him. Unfortunately, even though logistically, Game Night works better with four people, after having to endure a couple of hours of Noah's participation, both Jess and Tom had decided we would make do. Until last night, that is. Leo is the first person who has been invited to join us since Noah's exit. Thinking of Leo brings a smile to my lips.

"That fun, huh?" Noah probes, noticing my expression. He doesn't look pleased. I don't answer and he turns his attention back to the television. "It doesn't look like there's anything good on." He switches the set off and swivels to face me, his left arm draped casually along the head-rest. His lean fingers are close enough to brush my hair and I shift uncomfortably.

"What are you really doing here, Noah?"

"What, now I can't even come and visit?" he replies.

"It's just a little unorthodox. We broke up. Normally when people break up they don't get together much."

"I don't see why we can't still be friends."

I can't think of a valid argument so I settle for taking a sip of my tea.

"We always got along so well," Noah reminisces, "that's why I still don't understand exactly why we broke up."

Not this again. "You know why. It just wasn't working. I didn't feel the same way you did."

"The way I do, you mean." The emphasis on the 'do' is yet another way for Noah to remind me that he didn't want the split. Not that I need reminding. I'm fully aware of the fact that, with the slightest click of my fingers, I could have him back. Unfortunately for Noah, my fingers have absolutely no inclination to do any clicking.

"I know this has been hard for you," I say, "but it's only going to make it more difficult if you keep popping around and staying in contact."

"So I should just accept that what we had is over?" There is a challenge in his voice now, and I sense we're moving into dangerous territory.

"I don't want to fight with you, Noah."

It's like he doesn't even hear me. "How can you just forget everything we had?"

Quite easily, I think. Our relationship wasn't exactly the stuff you read about. It was pretty sub-standard, but, conscious of his feelings, I set my cup down on the table and give him the benefit of a nostalgic smile.

"I didn't forget. Of course I didn't forget - we were together for six months. And we had a lot of fun. I just didn't see the point of continuing when I didn't see a future for us."

"So now you're single? You'd rather be single than give us the benefit of the doubt?"

"No," I answer honestly. "I'd rather be open to new opportunities. I don't plan on staying single indefinitely."

Noah's face is pure outrage. He stiffens, his hand clenching involuntarily on the head-rest beside me.

"Are you seeing anyone?" he asks, his mask of composure slipping on a fraction too late.

"No. But you need to accept that I might meet someone, possibly in the near future."

"You've got to know how hard that is for me to hear." His voice is a low reproach, and I find myself feeling guilty even though I shouldn't.

"I know and I'm sorry."

Noah drains his mug and sets it down beside mine on the table. I sigh inwardly, expecting him to leave, but instead, he fixes me with his blue eyes, which have turned as cold as the arctic winter.

"How's your thesis coming along?"

The abrupt change of topic catches me unaware.

"Good," I say, neglecting to add that it's going a lot better now that he isn't trying to interfere with it. When we were together Noah was constantly trying to influence my thesis and tell me how it should be done. Given his own mediocrity at college, I hadn't been too eager to follow his advice, a fact that he soon discovered. It had caused a fair bit of friction and added strain to our already volatile relationship.

"I still think your approach is too dangerous," he says. "An art gallery? I mean, I know you're influenced by Wright but you can't compete with the Guggenheim."

"I'm not trying to compete with the Guggenheim. It's a thesis, designed to showcase my vision. It's not actually going to be built."

"I still think it's a huge risk."

"Which is why I'm not asking for your help."

That brings him up short. "I only want what's best for you, Sarah. I know you don't value my opinion very highly but I'm always here if you'd like me to read it over." And just like that, he is once again the victim.

"I'm not doing this now," I insist. I'm not prepared to get into this vicious old cycle with him especially since I no longer have to. "And seriously, I'm tired."

"Okay, I'll go." He gets to his feet and holds up his hands in mock surrender. Then, as if considering whether or not he should tell me, he adds lightly, "I just thought you might be interested to know that I spent last night entertaining the Burke & Duke selection panel."

He lets the words hover in the space between us, a calculated, ugly implication that is so very beneath him and yet not altogether surprising. This is why he's really here, I realise. Not to see how I'm doing, not to offer support, but to remind me that he holds a position of professional power over me.

"Really?" I ask, crossing my arms across my chest. "And why would I be interested to know what you do in your private time?" Of course his comment wasn't about him, but I refuse to snatch at the bait he is laying out.

"Oh Sarah, you know what I mean." Noah smiles down at me, the pretty boy charm almost disguising the cunning look in his eyes. Almost, but not quite. For a second I am actually shocked to my core. Noah has always been needy, but I've generally thought of him as harmless. Even Dianna's warning seemed too removed to be plausible. A huge part of me had wanted to laugh it off - after all, Noah wasn't like that. He wasn't that smart, that conniving. Now, looking up at him, I'm not so sure. As quickly as I feel the weight of Noah's infatuation, I shrug it off. I will not be bullied by this man.

"Actually, I don't," I say, holding his gaze levelly. "What exactly are you implying?"

"I'm not implying anything."

"Get out."

"Sarah…"

"Out!"

He hesitates, and for an awful moment I think he's going to refuse. Then he stalks across the threshold and I heave a sigh of relief.

I lie awake in bed long after he is gone, tossing and turning. As tired as I am, sleep evades me. It's still early but I feel exhausted and yet my mind will not shut off and, deep within me, a fire grows, an ugly black heat that beats its chest at the injustice of it all. I want to kick something, to release the emotion that is clawing through my chest. I should've slammed the damn door in his face.

When I hear the knock at my door it occurs to me that I might get the chance to do just that. I grit my teeth, determined to tell him off and let him know exactly what I think of his dirty tactics. I swing the door wide, my mouth already forming the words, but it is not Noah lounging casually against the door frame.

"Leo!" I gasp, clamping my arms to my chest as the night's chill reminds me poignantly that Snoopy is a sorry excuse for modesty. "What are you doing here?"

Leo pointedly raises his eyes as the crooked grin tugs at his lower lip. He stares at me for a long moment, his head cocked slightly to the side. "Leo?" I ask again, the hairs on my arms standing on end, whether from the cold or his presence I can't be certain.

"I like you, Sarah," he announces, as coolly as if he were telling me the time. "And I think you like me." My only reaction is an involuntary widening of my eyes. "You find me attractive, yes?" he prompts and, despite myself, I smile, then nod my head.

"I thought so." Oddly, he doesn't sound altogether pleased with this revelation. Lifting his hand from the door frame he plunges it into his coppery hair. "I really shouldn't be doing this," he groans, without any further explanation.

"Why?" I ask. Such a small insignificant word, but so monumentally unfitting when my mind is screaming 'why not?'

"It's complicated." A cryptic answer, but all I'm aware of is that his gaze has found my mouth and is lingering there.

"It occurred to me that I didn't kiss you goodbye last night." At this casual observation, my stomach flip-flops, and there is no blaming the weather for the way my skin prickles in anticipation.

"You didn't," I agree, "which was really rather rude of you after I plied you with all that expensive cheese." The tension building between us is delicious and so very inviting.

"Jessica supplied the cheese, if I'm not mistaken," he says, taking a step forward and towering above me, "perhaps I should be knocking on her door?"

"No, you have the right door."

"Hmm," he murmurs. He stands still, assessing me for a long moment.

"I should go." He says it as though he's willing me to contradict him.

"Why?" I challenge, my arms still crossed over my chest.

"Because I want you." It's a bold statement.

Locking my eyes on his, I lift my chin.

"Then going is the last thing you should be doing."

The words are barely out of my mouth when he lowers his burnished head and the involuntary gasp of breath I take is sucked from my mouth as his lips crash down on mine. Of their own accord, my arms unravel, my hands running up his hard chest and over his shoulders to bury themselves in his unruly hair, which is just as thick and as soft as I imagined.

Leo's kiss is gentle at first, his tongue exploring my mouth as though it might dissolve under his touch, but my own reaction is anything but gentle. I feel faint with desire and my patience wears thin quickly. I snatch a handful of his hair, pulling him down toward me and his shoulders jerk with the pain. His hands trap my waist, yanking me toward him and crushing my body up against his. I rise up on my toes, trying to make contact with every glorious inch of him, and, sensing my need, his arms encircle my waist, lifting me clear off the floor so that the evidence of his own desire is clear.

When I wrap my legs around his waist, Leo kicks the door closed and, for a heart-stopping moment I think he is going to carry me to the bedroom, or at the very least, to the sofa. I want nothing more than to get horizontal with this man, but instead, he leans back against the door, his mouth searing a blazing trail down my neck. There is an infinitesimal pause and I hear a low chuckle, his breath blowing hot on my throat. He lifts his right hand, holding my weight easily with only his left, and runs his index finger deliberately from the hollow of my throat down between my breasts and rests it on the faded black of Snoopy's nose.

"That's adorable."

I glance down, and, of course, my nipples are practically piercing the thin fabric of my nightshirt in their desperate attempt to get attention.

I'm not quite ready for the kissing to be done so Leo actually has to physically remove me. His hands are warm on my waist as he gently pushes me away from him, his eyes twinkling.

"I'd like to take you out," he announces suddenly.

"Out?" I sound breathless and groggy, the way I imagine the female lead would sound in all those bodice-ripper books my mom devours.

"Yes, out. To dinner. Tomorrow."

"Is that an invitation or an instruction?"

"Whichever has the higher chance of success."

"Okay," I nod, "Dinner."

"Tomorrow?"

"Tomorrow."

"I'll pick you up at eight."

Leo looks gratified as he opens the door. *He's leaving?* I'm too stunned to argue, but as he steps out into the hall he turns to me, the crooked smile fading slightly. It's as if the last few minutes never happened as we stand facing each other once more on my threshold.

"I really shouldn't be doing this," he murmurs, almost to himself.

"So you keep saying." I give him an arch look but he doesn't respond. Instead, he kisses me chastely on the cheek.

"Goodnight, Sarah," he whispers.

CHAPTER 10

"*A* date?" Jess frowns, as though the very concept is alien to her. It's lunch time and the cafeteria around us is teeming with students trying to grab a quick bite to eat before classes resume.

"Yes, Jess, a date. I really can't fathom why this is so hard for you to understand."

"It's not the date," Tom says, through a mouth crammed with pie. Oblivious of the flecks of pastry projectiling onto Jess's salad, he continues. "It's the fact that he came to your apartment and stuck his tongue down your throat but he didn't stick anything else anywhere else." He grabs the bagel off my plate to emphasise his point with a wildly inappropriate gesture and I snatch it back.

"You are so disgusting," I grumble. "And I wanted that!" I toss the bagel aside.

"Tom makes a good point," Jess nods sagely. "He was in your apartment and you were enjoying this orgasm-inducing snog, then he just ups and leaves? It's not right." She says this in a tone that implies Leo might actually need therapy.

"He did seem to be holding back. He said he shouldn't be doing this before he kissed me and again when he left."

"Why?" Tom asks.

"It's probably because he's a first year and Sarah's the Institute's golden child."

"I'm not the golden child, Jess."

She ignores me.

"Well, look on the bright side, his superhuman restraint kept you chaste."

"What makes you two think I would've slept with him anyway? Give me some credit – I mean I don't even know the guy."

There's a moment of silence in which their eyes lock, a caramel-chocolate stare-down and then they burst into simultaneous hysterics.

"Right," Jess manages to choke out between guffaws, "I'm sure you wouldn't have done anything I wouldn't have done."

"And seeing as there's absolutely nothing she wouldn't do…" Tom waggles his perfectly arched brows.

"Hey!" Jess throws my discarded bagel at him.

"Truth hurts, Jess baby," Tom replies wickedly. "In fact, I consider myself lucky I escaped your bed unscathed."

"We said we weren't going to talk about that. I still have nightmares about it. And anyway, this isn't about me, or what I would and wouldn't do. It's about Sarah."

"I'm perfectly okay with the way this conversation is going," I point out.

Jess fixes me in a beady stare. "Face it, Sarah, you want him. You want him to do unspeakable things to you."

"For what it's worth, it's nothing to be ashamed about," Tom adds. "Hell, I want him and he's as straight as those God-awful jeans Jess insists on wearing."

"There's nothing wrong with my jeans!"

"Yeah, except they went out of fashion with tie-dye and the banana clip. Nobody wears straight jeans anymore." He gestures at his own skinny Levis to prove his point.

I drain my water bottle and toss it into a nearby trash-can.

"I've got to hit the library; I've got a mountain of drawing to do. Any last minute tips for my date tonight?"

"Try to make it to second base, at least," Jess grins.

"And wear skinny jeans!" Tom yells at my departing back.

Six hours later it looks as though Hurricane Sandy had come and gone within the vortex of my bedroom. Although, technically it's called Hurricane Jess, because it is my pint-sized friend who is streaking around my room, hauling item after item from my closet and discarding them in a frenzied fashion across every available surface.

"Easy there, Flash," I say as she hurtles past me and yanks open my underwear drawer. A flurry of red satin, white cotton and black lace flies over her shoulder until, with a triumphant 'aha' she turns to face me holding a hot pink twin-set.

"You think?" I eye the pants dubiously. They're practically non-existent, just a scrap of silk with high hopes and big plans.

"Definitely! And they're brand new – look they even have the tag on!" It's not hard to miss, given that the tag is bigger than the actual pants.

"That's because I've never worn them." I lower my voice automatically as I admit, "They're a bit too small."

"Not tonight, they're not!" Jess bites through the plastic tag with great gusto, tossing aside the price label.

I should know by now never to underestimate Jess. She always pulls through for me. She and Tom might like to tease, but, at the end of the day, she's my best friend for a reason. She was waiting at my door when I got home, rapping her nails impatiently on the smooth wood. Tom had bowed out, nobly, claiming he had a date, but he refused to tell us who with. Which of course we interpret as code for him not wanting to be exposed to nude female flesh.

"Okay," I announce, determined, and I haul on the bra and panties. The bra pushes my boobs up near my chin and the panties provide about as much cover as a button on a beach ball, but I grit my teeth and bear it, or, as it happens, bare it. "Now what am I wearing over this, or are you expecting me to go to dinner in my underwear?"

"Hang on, I'm still looking." Jess's muffled voice sounds from the bowels of my closet.

I glance at my watch. It's almost half-past seven. Leo will be here in thirty minutes and I'm nowhere near ready.

"What about this?" Jess asks, holding up a fire-engine red top with a cowl neckline, scooped low in the front. It's a bit outrageous but very flattering.

"My bra might show."

"So?"

"The bra's pink." I point unnecessarily at my chest.

"So?" Jess asks again. "That looks amazing, by the way," she adds, running an expert eye over my underwear. Jess should know – she earned more tips than most of the other waitresses combined during her Hooters stint.

"Let's try it." I nod.

Twenty minutes later I usher her out of the apartment. She beams at me in pride, admiring her handiwork. I'm wearing the red top with a black pencil skirt which falls to just below my knees. Considering the low scoop of the cowl neck, I figure anything shorter and I may as well hang a For Sale sign around my neck. My stiletto-heeled boots earn me at least an extra two inches, and, considering Leo's colossal height, this will definitely work in my favour. My eyes are ringed dark and smoky, but not too overdone and Jess very carefully painted my lips the same fire-engine red as my top. It's a daring look, one I would never attempt myself because I'd end up looking like a two-dollar whore. Thanks to Jess's prowess with her make-up brushes, however, the combination is vibrant and feminine. For someone who usually wears only mascara and lip gloss, I feel wildly desirable.

I tell myself that I won't be having sex with Leo tonight, but I still perform an emergency clean-up of my room. I sling most of the discarded wardrobe items over the back of a chair and leave the cosmetic paraphernalia strewn across my dresser, but I do stuff all of my underwear back into the drawer. Hearing a knock at the door, I spritz on a liberal spray of *Dolce & Gabbana Light Blue*, and, snatching up my purse, I hasten down the hall.

"Wow! You look amazing." Leo brushes a kiss across my cheek and the faint tang of his aftershave assaults my senses. "These are for you." He hands me a tight cluster of tulips.

"You didn't have to do that."

"It's our first date, remember? It's customary to bring flow-ers, or so my sisters always told me." I take them from him and quickly set them in a vase of water in the kitchen. Leo waits patiently in the hall and I try not to dwell on the 'first date' comment, which would imply there will be a second. Best not to get my hopes up too early.

When we emerge onto the street I hesitate a moment. The only car parked outside my building is a sleek, shiny SUV with a panoramic sunroof that glints under the light of the street lamp. Leo, a few steps below me, notices my reticence and offers me his hand.

"Shall we?" he asks lightly.

"This is your car?" I ask as he moves deliberately towards the charcoal SUV. As we get closer I notice the small crest on the hood, the rearing stallion impossible to mistake. "You drive a *Porsche*?"

"It's a bit flashy, I know." He opens the passenger door for me and helps me in. I sink into the leather seat which is warm despite the cool interior of the car. Leo curls himself into the driver's seat and, with an almighty growl, the engine comes to life.

"You drive a Porsche?" I repeat. "What are you, a trust-fund baby?"

"In a manner of speaking," he replies. "Why, you don't like the brand?"

"I wouldn't actually know," I admit, "I've never been in one. I just wouldn't have pegged you as a Porsche kind of guy."

"Oh, really? What kind of guy would you have pegged me for, then?"

"Oh, I don't know…" I pause, considering the question. "Maybe a truck?"

Leo laughs at that. "I'm assuming, by your tone, that you're thinking of a used model, probably with a few chips in the paintwork and a missing tail-light?"

I blush, grateful for the dark interior so he can't see it. "I didn't mean it like that. It's just… well, this is a very expensive car and you're a student."

"Yes, it is, and I am," he replies enigmatically.

The restaurant is gorgeous, an out-of-the-way bistro with rickety tables spread haphazardly across an outdoor patio. Dinner will be served *al fresco* and I can't help but wonder what they do when it rains. The patio overlooks a picturesque garden. A fountain gurgles just below us and fairy lights cast a magical glow over the nude statues strategically placed around it. It's the type of place that feigns modesty while charging a small fortune for delectable food that I can barely pronounce. Leo beats the waiter to pull out my chair and I shoot him an apologetic smile.

"Can I get you something to drink?" he asks quickly, regaining his composure.

"Sarah?" Leo asks.

"I'll have whatever you're having," I say, gazing up at the limitless sky. "The view is stunning," I tell Leo when the waiter leaves to fetch us a bottle of wine.

"I would have to agree," he says, but his eyes never leave my face.

I give him an arch look and he chuckles.

"I'm sorry, that was a pathetic attempt to charm you."

"It was," I agree.

"I can do better, I promise. You just make me a little nervous."

I'm delighted by his admission which makes me feel a bit better about the butterfly farm carousing around in my stomach.

"Can I ask you a question?"

"Sure."

"Last night, before we kissed… you said you shouldn't be doing this."

"I did," he replies lightly, but I can tell by the set of his jaw that he's a little uncomfortable.

"Why?"

His lean fingers drum the table as he regards me thoughtfully. Then he leans forward, perfectly at ease once more.

"I don't know. I've just started at Holmes and I guess I was worried about having such a beautiful distraction." The smile he gives me is one of dazzling charm.

"You were right, you definitely can do better," I admit.

"How are you enjoying your Holmes experience so far?" I ask, guiding the conversation into neutral territory.

"It's good. A lot more work than I expected."

"You thought it would be easy?"

He shrugs. "Easier than it is."

"Why architecture?" It's something I genuinely want to know. Being so passionate about it myself, I'm always curious as to why others are drawn to the field.

"Honestly?"

"Yeah," I laugh, "honestly."

"I like the idea of making something strong. Something that can't be broken." He stops as the waiter returns.

"May I pour for you, Sir?" he asks Leo.

"That's okay, I can do it." Leo waves him away. He catches me watching him, still waiting for him to explain and his lip twitches upward. "It sounds stupid, I know."

"No," I interrupt, "it doesn't, actually." I notice that he only pours for me. "You're not drinking?"

"I'm driving."

"My mother would approve." I raise my glass at him and he clinks his own water-filled beaker against it.

"So, do you have any particular influences yet? Any buildings that stand out, that inspire you?"

"Honestly, I can't even get my head around most of them. I had no idea how complex a simple structure could be. I do prefer simple, elegant lines, though. I'm a modern man. Our lecturer showed us a slide-show the other day of a couple of the most amazing buildings in the world. I had to pick my jaw up off the floor when he was done."

"Mind if I test your general knowledge?" I ask, recalling the slide show I'd seen four years ago.

"Be my guest."

"The Basket Building?"

"Perfect place for a picnic."

"Gagster House?"

"Too many stairs."

"The Dancing Building?"

"Lonely."

"The Crooked House?" I am trying desperately not to laugh. Leo considers this last one for a minute and then nods sagely.

"Crooked."

"Not bad," I conceded, taking a sip of wine. "I think you have a real knack for this."

"I'm glad someone thinks so. My family are convinced I've taken leave of my senses."

"Your parents?"

"No," he shakes his head, "they passed away when I was fifteen. Car accident."

"I'm sorry." It's an automatic response, but Leo brushes it off, completely at ease.

"It was a long time ago."

The waiter arrives again to take our order and I realise I haven't even looked at the menu. I open it, take one look at the foreign terminology and snap it shut again. I was right about the pronunciation and there's no way I'm going to attempt any of those foreign words.

"Anything you'd recommend?" I ask.

"Yes," Leo grins, "steak."

"So, who took care of you after your parents passed away?" I ask, once the waiter has taken our order and defiantly refilled my glass.

"My older sister, Ellen. Technically, we lived with our aunt, my mother's sister, but Ellen was the one who made sure I brushed my teeth and did my homework. My aunt wasn't exactly the maternal type."

"So it's just you and Ellen?"

"And my kid sister Trisha. She's a teacher now, ironically."

"Ironically?"

"Ellen was always the bossy one when we were growing up. Trish couldn't wipe her own ass until she was about nine."

We dine on rare steaks dripping in butter and the most delectable French beans I've ever eaten. I clean my plate, finishing long before Leo, who takes his time. Every movement is precise, his deft fingers slicing and shifting the food on his plate to create the perfect bite.

"You're in your final year, right?" he asks, when he eventually lays his knife and fork together and lifts the napkin to his lips.

"Yes."

"So you're conducting your thesis?"

"Hmm mmm," I reply, having just taken a sip of my wine.

"Who's your mentor?"

"Dianna Marchant."

"Wow," Leo looks impressed. "You're that good?"

"I'm that good," I grin.

"Doesn't she only take on two students a year?"

"Yes," I nod. "This year it's me and Samantha Simpson."

"Ah," he leans back in his chair, clasping his hands behind his neck. He is so confident, so assured, that again I fail to reconcile this man with the late blooming student I thought he was. "She's the blonde with the cleavage?"

"Nice to know you pay attention," I tease.

"I'm human," he shrugs, "but she's not really my type. Besides, she didn't like my paper airplane."

"She didn't. In fact, if I recall correctly she tore it up."

"After all my hard work."

"Why did you hold up that note?" I ask, the wine giving me courage. "Not that I'm complaining, but why me?"

"Actually, it wasn't meant for you," Leo replies, deadpan. "I was trying to get the attention of the cutest little brunette two seats in front of you."

I stare at him, unsure if he's teasing or not, until he gives an amused shake of his head. "I don't know; do I have to have a reason? I saw you as you came in and you looked kind of sad. I thought it might cheer you up."

I cast my mind back to that day. I had been disappointed to find myself back in Noah's class, but the fact that he noticed is unbelievably perceptive. I take another sip of my wine to fill the silence.

"What's your thesis proposal?" Leo asks eventually.

"Um…" I falter, not sure how to explain it to him. "Rejuvenation. I'm proposing to tear down a warehouse in mid-downtown and build an art gallery."

"You're creating art to house art?" he asks, but to my surprise he doesn't sound patronising, as Noah did when I first pitched the idea to him.

"Basically," I confirm.

"Like the Guggenheim?"

"That is one of my influences but I have my own vision."

"And the audacity to challenge, apparently." He lifts his glass of water in a toast, "I like that."

CHAPTER 11

*B*y the time we leave the restaurant the roads are quiet, not surprisingly, as it's after ten on a Sunday night.

"Thank you for a lovely evening," I tell Leo as we pull up to the curb outside my block. He gives me an easy grin, his blue eyes almost black in the darkened interior of the car. He seems completely at ease, whereas my stomach has been wrapping itself into a tightly-wound knot of anticipation the whole drive home. I'm still internally debating whether I should ask him up, when he saves me the trouble.

"I'll walk you up," he says, easing himself out of the car and coming around to open my door for me. I don't expect it – this isn't the fifties, after all – and so, of course, I open the door from the inside just as he leans in to grab the handle. The cold metal connects spectacularly with his temple.

"Ow!" Leo howls, clapping a hand to his head. It practically covers his entire face.

"Oh God!" I stumble onto the sidewalk, reaching for him

before I realise that the only places I can reach are his chest, his torso and his crotch. I drive away the wicked thoughts that this conjures and step closer to him. "Are you okay?" I ask hesitantly.

"Hm' fine," he mumbles from behind his hand, "just give me a second."

I shift my weight from foot to foot, waiting. Leo has fallen silent and I start to wonder if he's bleeding, or worse, if he might be a little concussed. I dart a glance up and down the street but all is absolutely still. If he needs to go to the emergency room I don't think I can drive this beast of a car. I cast a dark look at it for good measure. My trusty little Fiat is parked in the underground lot, and worse, the key is hanging on a hook next to my front door. Leo is still just standing there, but at least he's on his feet. He would've collapsed if he'd fainted, right? You can't be unconscious on your feet... or can you? I automatically open my purse to retrieve my cell phone, the urge to consult Doctor Google coming over me, but then I realise how inappropriate that would be. I pick at the hem of my shirt for a minute, feeing utterly helpless and ridiculously uncomfortable when, out of the corner of my eye, I spot Leo's shoulders shaking. Narrowing my eyes, I bend down, peering up at his face. Half-hidden by his palm, Leo's mouth is curved up in that wicked, crooked grin.

"Oh, you asshole!" I yell, slapping his shoulder with my purse. The hand drops to reveal blue eyes glistening with mirth. "I nearly had a heart attack!" I add, hoping he feels guilty. To his credit, there is a definite purple-tinged lump above his left eye. It draws my attention to the scar above it and I almost miss his question when he asks.

"What were you looking for?"

"What?"

"You reached for your purse. Do you have a first-aid kit in there?"

"No, I was reaching for my phone."

"You were going to call for help?" he asks, practically in hysterics. If he thinks that's funny, there's no way I'm admitting to Doctor Google.

"Yes," I nod firmly. Leo takes a bold step toward me, the humour in his eyes morphing into something else, something more intense. The shift in tension crackles between us and I draw in an involuntary breath of air.

As he advances I feel like a deer being stalked by a large cat, wild and beautiful. If the deer was attracted to the lion, of course. If it wanted to grab hold of the lion and do unmentionable things to him which would make even death worth it. Staring up into those electric eyes I find it hard to steady my hands and I clutch my purse to my chest like a shield protecting my heart. The gesture is futile, because every inch of my body is screaming for the distance between us to be obliterated. Leo moves until our bodies are touching in only the most insignificant of places, his knees brushing mine, chest pressing against my purse. I try to smile, but my lips won't cooperate and I just stare mutely up at him as he lifts a blonde curl off my shoulder and winds it around his finger.

"Should I still walk you up?" he asks, throwing down the challenge.

I nod, placing one hand on his chest and feeling the taut muscle beneath my palm. Leo places his one hand over mine and weaves his fingers through it so that when we turn toward my apartment block we are holding hands. His palms are dry and he swings his arm slightly as we walk, his thumb weaving tiny circles on my palm, sending shivers of anticipation through me. He doesn't let go of my hand until we reach my door and I have to fumble for my keys.

"Can I get you anything to drink?" I ask over my shoulder as I dump my purse on the table in the hall. The response is an abrupt 'no' and then his hands are on my hips, encircling my waist and drawing me back against him. The action is so sudden I give a small cry of surprise, but the feel of his hard body against my back is heavenly. My stomach dances in tune to his fingers which are gently stroking my belly and skimming just a hairsbreadth below my breasts. I try to turn around, but his arms tighten like a vice-grip, pinning me in place. Jess was right, he does like to be in control. He hasn't spoken since we left the car and the silence seems to exacerbate my other senses. I can smell him, the faint trace of aftershave which lingers on his jaw, the lemony scent of fabric softener, and something else; something more primal – the scent of hot-blooded man. I don't think I've ever wanted anyone as badly as I do right now.

Keeping one hand around me, Leo slides the other up my arm and over my shoulder, lifting my hair off my neck. Even though I'm anticipating it, I can't suppress the shiver that runs through my body when his lips drop onto the topmost point of my spine. I can feel his small, satisfied smile at my reaction, and he kisses me again, brushing feather-light kisses across the nape of my neck and across onto my shoulder. I squirm against him, but the consequence of that rebellion is that he drops my hair back into place and draws himself up to his full height, withdrawing his attention. Looking up I catch sight of us in the mirror above the hall table. My cheeks are flushed and my eyeliner has smudged under my eyes, making me look wanton and desirable. Or it could just be the light – there's a bulb missing directly overhead. The lack of fluorescence, however, does nothing to dull the unnatural blue of Leo's eyes as they lock on my own in the reflection of the mirror. He gives an imperceptible shake of his head, warning me to be still and, coyly, I let my head fall to the side, exposing the arch of my neck for his undivided attention.

Of course, knowing what I want, he deliberately ignores me. Instead, he slips his hand shamelessly up inside the waist-line of my blouse, grabs hold of one side of my bra and yanks it southward. My breast falls out of the bra like an overripe plum and, to my horror, I can see my nipple practically conga-ing its way through the fabric. Leo is still watching me and it's both unnerving and erotic. My body feels weightless and liquid, and when his fingers close over my nipple it is almost my undoing. My knees groan in protest at having to hold me up. Leo pushes aside the cowl neckline of my blouse so we can both watch as he expertly caresses me, his fingers moulding and kneading me into delirium. Just when I think I cannot take another minute of this relentless torture, his left hand plunges fingers first into the waistband of my skirt. I experi-ence a nano-second of burning, core-rocketing pleasure, in real danger of simply collapsing in a heap, when there is a musical rat-a-tat-tat drumming on the door beside us.

CHAPTER 12

I am going to kill my brother. I'm going to murder him in his sleep when he finally decides to leave and take his interrupting ass back to his own apartment where he will climb into bed alone, much like I'll be doing, thanks to his impromptu, unannounced visit.

"You seem upset," he asks, a snide grin plastered in place. "I'm assuming your visitor wasn't actually 'just leaving' when I arrived, as he so politely claimed?"

Leo has just left, making his exit shortly after Dylan's arrival and subsequent introductions. He had kissed me chastely on the cheek as I let him out. It had taken me only a second to yank my bra and shirt back in place after hearing the knock, but now, ten minutes later, I still hadn't brought my heart rate under control.

"Why are you here, anyway?" I demand, rounding on my brother. "It's almost midnight!"

"I couldn't sleep," he shrugs, "and my cable's on the blink. I thought I could watch over here."

"I hate you."

"You hate that you didn't get your obviously anticipated leg over," he corrects, utterly unapologetic.

"Dylan, I'm being serious. This is my house. You have to respect my privacy!"

"Okay, okay," he relents. "I didn't know you had someone here. Honestly, Sarah, I wouldn't have knocked if I'd known." He looks sincere and my irritation subsides slightly. Until he opens his mouth again. "Hey, you should get one of those signs – you know, the ones you find at those fancy hotels that say 'occupied'? That way I'll know when to steer clear."

"Get out!"

"That's a no to the cable, then?"

"Out!" I point furiously at the door. "Now! And don't you dare come back here without phoning me first. And if it's after nine, I don't care if your house is on fire, don't call, don't visit!"

"You must really like this guy," is all he says as he lopes out of the apartment.

I stomp into the kitchen, snatch a bottle of water from the fridge and take a huge swig before pressing the cold plastic against my cheek. What a shitty way to end my evening. I flip off the kitchen light, plunging the apartment into darkness save for the low glow in the hall. I really must get that bulb replaced. Drawn to the window, I heave a sigh and glance down at the street. My heart stutters in my chest at the sight of Leo's SUV still parked outside. What... where? As I spin around I only just clap my hand over my mouth in time to smother the scream that bursts from my lips.

"That's not how I say goodbye, Sarah." Leo is standing in the hall, his coppery hair even more tousled than when he left, as though he has spent the last fifteen minutes running his hands through it. As frustrated as I am, I can totally empathise.

"I should hope not." I say, feeling the excitement that I have only just managed to clamp down burst back into being. Leo grins, turning to lock the deadbolt. He crosses the room in a few strides and I close my eyes, praying he doesn't trip over any furniture in the dark.

"Just so you know, that door doesn't open again until morning," he growls, towering over me.

"I have no problem with that," I breathe.

His eyes dip to my cleavage, but he hesitates. We're both unsure how to continue, exactly how to pick up where we left off. Summoning my courage, I reach for the zipper of my skirt myself, undoing it and letting it slither down my legs. Leo watches me intently, his eyes following my every movement as I step out of the skirt and kick it aside. I'm no exhibitionist, but his hungry gaze gives me courage. I want to be sexy for him. I lift my shirt slowly, inch by inch, exposing the pale flesh of my torso for his benefit alone. When I drop the red satin to the floor, leaving me naked save for the hot pink scraps of lace and my stiletto-heeled boots, Leo lets out a breathless sigh. Thrilled with his response, I do a quick mental calculation. My boots aren't as easy to take off and I really don't want to bend in front of him and expose my inadequately-covered ass. Still, they have to come off. Gritting my teeth, I start to move, but Leo grabs my arms.

"Leave those on."

I am twenty-four years old and I've had my share of lovers but never have I felt so horny as I do now, hearing those words. If I had to tell Jess or Tom about this they would laugh, because saying it back sounds like a line right out of a cheesy movie, but in this moment – right now – it's the sexiest thing I've ever heard. The lower half of my body contracts.

Through eyes heavy-lidded with desire, I watch as Leo lowers his head. My mouth meets his and the same fire as before ignites as though it never went out. As his head moves lower I suck in a shaky breath, feeling his warm lips and flickers of the wet heat of his tongue against my neck, my collar bone, the dark valley between my breasts. His expert hands slip beneath my bra, igniting duel fires as he squeezes my nipples. It's hard enough to hurt, but it doesn't. Instead, it only leaves me wanting more. His movement is limited by the bra and, desperate for his mouth to join his hands, I lift my arms, unclipping the offending garment and hurling it away from my body. Leo moans, a deep, satisfied sound that merges with my own cry of contentment as his mouth covers first one breast and then the other. By the time he lifts his head I am squirming with desire and his blue eyes are heavy with lust.

"Don't stop," I plead, grabbing a fistful of his hair and trying to pull him back to my breast. He issues a low throaty chuckle and resists me, my desperate hauling no match for his quiet strength.

"Come here," he pulls me toward him and lifts me in the air, turning a full 180 degrees before depositing me on the arm of the sofa. He lifts first my left leg and then my right, slowly unzipping my boots. Once duly divested, Leo grins, the crooked smile that I already adore. Placing his hands beneath me, he grabs two fistfuls of ass and hoists me up. My legs come up around his waist of their own accord and, despite the gloomy interior of my apartment, he kisses me all the way to my bedroom, without tripping.

CHAPTER 13

*J*ess's jaw drops when she spots me getting out of Leo's Porsche in the morning. Conveniently, Leo had an overnight bag in his car – "A bit presumptuous, don't you think?" I had asked teasingly after the most exciting dual shower I've ever experienced – and it seemed only logical that I travel with him to the Institute on Monday morning.

"What are the chances," I grumble under my breath as she bears down on me, looking like an anime character on a mission. Jess is never here before me and she never waits outside. I blame her freakish intuition. She knew about the date last night and the fact that I hadn't called her after to dissect every minute was probably all the proof she needed that I'd finally gotten laid.

"Well, hello, Sarah," Jess calls brightly the second she is within earshot – which, by Jessica's standards, means she is still only halfway across the busy lot. A few curious glances swing my way and I hear Leo laughing from the other side of the car.

I had threatened him with his life if he dared open my door for me on campus, although he was welcome to do it anywhere else. "You're looking awfully perky this morning!" Jess muses. I cringe, but hold my head up high, and finally, to my relief, she reaches us. "Nice to see you, Leo." Jess grins up at him, her eyebrows waggling, before turning back to me. "I'm taking it your evening went well?"

"Okay, enough," I grin, shooting Leo an apologetic look as I lead her away. "I'll see you later," I mouth at him and he winks in return.

"Spill."

"Not now, Jess, there's like a million people here!"

"Right," Jess says, as if this has only now occurred to her. "Coffee."

We head for the cafeteria. There aren't any classes today but we're both up to our necks in work and I'm determined to finish researching the local building codes before my site visit tomorrow. The abandoned warehouse I've earmarked is currently being used by teens as an unauthorised party venue, which, according to my research, includes underage drinking, and it has been frequented by several known drug peddlers, making it easy to justify on a moral basis, but there is also town planning to consider. Dianna, while being the most coveted mentor on campus, is also the toughest, and she doesn't allow us to leave anything to chance.

The cafeteria is quiet this time of the day but, to Jess's disgust, her old rival, Samantha Simpson is seated alone at a table by the window.

"What the hell is she reading? The bloody dictionary?" Jess mock-whispers, catching sight of the enormous textbook open on the table before Samantha. "Why's she trying to act smart?"

"She is smart, Jess."

Jess gives me an arch look before continuing. "She's also dumb. God, I don't know how you deal with having to work with her."

"Technically I don't have to work with her." Samantha and I share Dianna as a mentor, but we seldom get asked to present in each other's company. I know it's only a matter of time, though, before Dianna starts requesting group discussions and getting us to critique one another's work. I shudder at the thought. As if drawn by my dislike, Samantha glances up, giving us a dirty look.

"Let's sit over here," Jess indicates a table as far from Samantha's as one can humanly get. I've barely pulled my chair out and she is looking up at me expectantly.

"Okay, so he picked me up at eight," I begin, but she waves her hands at me in annoyance.

"I don't want to hear about that. Forget dinner, the drive, the way he opened your door..."

"How do you know he opened my door?"

"He looks the type," she snaps, impatiently. "Now, did you or did you not have sex last night?"

"I did," I nod solemnly. Jess fist-pumps the air as if this is a personal triumph and then poses her next question.

"And was it or was it not mind-blowing?"

"It was mind-blowing."

"Best you've had, right?"

"Definitely."

"I knew it!" she grins. I await the next question but she's distracted, pulling out her mobile and typing frantically.

"What are you doing?"

"I'm texting Tom. He wanted me to keep him informed."

"You're texting Tom about my sex life?" She glances up at the indignant tone of my voice.

"What?" she asks, "I'd do the same for you."

I open my mouth to protest that I wouldn't ask her to, but then realise that I would and shut it again. "As you were," I gesture for her to continue.

Jess hits send with gusto and then slips the phone back into her bag.

"That's all he gets for now," she says, and then clasps her hands together on the table. "Tell me everything."

"I still can't believe he actually said 'leave those on'," Jess says an hour later. We are ensconced in the library, working for the most part, but every now and again she brings up my evening for dissection.

"I knew I shouldn't tell you that part."

"Why? It's so freaking Fifty Shades. Did he pull out a riding crop?"

"No, thank God."

"I don't know, Sarah. I think there's something to be said for all that kinky fuckery."

"Well why don't you give it a go and let me know?"

"I might just do that. Did I tell you I got the number of that guy that Tom claims is gay? He's so not gay, by the way."

"Did you ask him?"

"No," she sounds affronted. "You don't ask a man who looks like that if he's gay! Anyway, he's *not*, trust me."

"He's totally gay, I took him home on Saturday night," a voice interrupts. We turn to find Tom stifling a yawn, his phone in his hand. "And if you think that a two-line text is all the information I'm getting about Sarah's enviable sex life, you need more coffee."

"You're lying," Jess hisses, "you didn't take Jackson home last night!"

"Scouts honour," Tom holds three fingers up to his forehead, "but, in your defence, Jess, he's definitely been straight before. The things that man can do with his tongue are definitely new."

Catching sight of Jess's face, my laughter dies on my lips. She actually looks hurt. Is it possible she's really interested in this guy?

Tom notices too and he's taken aback. "Jess?" he asks gently, "are you okay?"

"Did you really take him home?"

"No," Tom shakes his head, "but honey, the man is gay. You need to trust me on this one. Don't go getting your hopes up."

"Too late," I murmur, seeing the relief wash Jess's features back into their normal upturned position.

"We'll see," she smiles, and I sense trouble.

Wanting a change of scenery, Jess, Tom and I bypass the library and head to one of the fifth-year lounges where we work in semi-companionable silence. Jess is acting decidedly chilly toward Tom, no doubt punishing him for his earlier comment, but Tom is so deep in his own project he doesn't seem to notice. Eventually he snaps his laptop shut and clicks his neck from side to side.

"I'm done," he announces, cramming his laptop and a stack of books into his bag. "I'll catch up with you guys later. Let me know if we're doing anything exciting."

Jess spends another hour working half-heartedly between

frequent checks of her phone, and then she also gives up. "Good luck," she calls as she leaves.

The sky outside darkens but I haven't so much as glanced at the window. My shoulders are aching and my vision starts to blur as I sit hunched over my laptop, but I don't pause to rest. Once I get into a rhythm I find it hard to break away.

"Hey!" Leo's voice sounds behind me, "I've been looking everywhere for you." He drops a kiss on my head as easily as if he's been doing it for years and then flops into the chair beside me, the one Jess vacated earlier. He kisses me again, full on the mouth this time, and I blush, smiling shyly as I rest my head on my hand to look at him.

"How's your day been?" I ask.

"Good, for the most part. I saw your ex in one of my classes."

"What?"

"The lecturer – Allen, right? You used to date?"

"How do you know that?"

"It's a small campus."

"I guess student-teacher relations are kind of big news."

"If I didn't know before, I certainly would have after today."

"How so?"

"He popped in to speak to Professor Hanson in second period. He shot me daggers the whole time. I don't think he likes me very much," Leo pauses to coil one of my curls around his finger, "and I think I know why."

"He needs to get over it," I say. "It's been two months since I broke it off."

"Maybe you're not that easy to forget," his finger traces my jawbone and the room seems to shrink to just this desk, these chairs and the two of us. I clear my throat.

"Why were you looking for me?"

The crooked smile. "Really? Aren't I supposed to be giving you a ride home?"

"Oh my God!" I glance at my watch. Classes ended hours ago. "I'm so sorry!" I slam my laptop shut and get to my feet.

"Hey," Leo gets leisurely to his feet. "It's no sweat. I didn't have anywhere important to be."

"But still, it's so late. I completely forgot I didn't bring my car today."

"You mean my super fancy Porsche didn't leave a lasting impression?" He is poking fun at himself as much as he is at me. I like that about him. He's about as unpretentious as they come.

"You sure you're ready to go? I'm happy to hang around, or I can come back and fetch you later if you need to stay?"

"No, I'm done. I'm starting to see spots."

"Shall we then?"

I check that I haven't left anything behind before I nod. "Let's go."

In the car, Leo glances sideways at me.

"What?" I laugh.

"I just don't know where I should be going," he admits. "I mean, I know technically I should be dropping you off and then heading home, but that's not what I want to do."

"Oh really? And what do you *want* to do?" I emphasise the word with a husky inflection straight out of an X-rated movie.

"Nice," Leo approves, grinning. "What I want to do is grab another change of clothes and spend the night with you."

"You didn't get enough the first time?"

"I didn't get enough the first three times."

I blush, recalling our antics the night before. "Well I'd hate to leave you unsatisfied, so I guess we're taking a detour."

"Really?" I announce twenty minutes later. The building towering above me is a luxury studio apartment block, the kind with a roof terrace and a state of the art fitness centre. Oh, and there's a doorman. I know this because when we walk into the opulent foyer, I see him sitting behind his big shiny desk.

"You have a doorman!" I hiss under my breath, as if this is a crime against humanity. Leo doesn't reply but he greets the man cheerfully. Despite his crooked smile I can see the uncertainty etched on his brow. Only once the elevator doors close with an expensive chime does he respond.

"Yes, I have a doorman. And a resort-style swimming pool and a theatre room. No, I don't want to hear your opinion," he adds as I open my mouth.

"But... how can you be so... so..." I can't say rich, I just can't. Wealthy either. "You *know*," I improvise, "and be a student?"

The elevator opens onto a wide corridor that smells like genuine leather and sandalwood. There are only two doors on this floor.

"We may as well get this over with," Leo says, moving toward the door on the left. "I have money. And I'm a student. I make no apologies," he adds jokingly.

"How wealthy are you?" I can't help but ask, and the question sounds disapproving even to my own ears.

"Not as wealthy as you seem to think." He opens the door and we step into a very comfortable, but rather sparse apartment. "I'm comfortable," Leo admits, "but I have to be careful, particularly if I want to spend the next four and half years at Holmes."

I can only assume that Leo's parents must have left him a tidy inheritance, but he doesn't elaborate.

"Can I get you something to drink while you wait?" he asks. "I have beer, water and soda. Or," he turns to a stainless steel wine-rack, on which sits one lonely bottle of red, "I have wine."

"A beer will be perfect," I say, still taking in my surroundings.

He hands me an opened bottle. "Make yourself comfortable. I won't be long."

Initially, I meander around the living area, examining the surround-sound system and the enormous TV that takes up most of the far wall. The sofa is surprisingly comfortable and oddly feminine, in an off-white fabric that wouldn't last a day in my apartment – not with Jess's propensity to slosh red wine around. Even the floor is white, a painted concrete screed which contrasts beautifully with the bare brick walls. There aren't any photographs on display, but the room is adorned with a few gorgeous pieces of abstract art, painted in vibrant primary colours.

The door that leads onto the terrace is a full glass-plate concertina, and when I push on it, it slides aside easily. A slight breeze lifts my hair as I step outside. It's so peaceful up here, removed from the hustle and bustle of the street below. The terrace is bigger than one would expect, with only two wooden loungers and a table between them to take up space. There is an empty glass on the table and a stack of magazines. I flip idly through them – Men's Health, a travel publication and a medical journal. It's like the waiting room at my local GP's office.

"All set." Leo's voice comes from the living room. A moment later he pokes his head out through the door. "There you are."

"It's beautiful out here," I say.

"I like it." The crooked grin. He has a Nike gym bag hanging from his shoulder and he's changed into a pair of dark denims and a branded white T-shirt. The tan flip-flops on his feet complete the casual look. "You ready to go?" he asks.

I down my beer. "Ready."

CHAPTER 14

*S*ex with Leo only gets better, I discover, over the course of the next few weeks. We have officially started "dating" as he calls it, and, insulated in my Leo-love capsule I can overlook the fury in Noah's eyes every time he sees us together on campus. To be fair, Leo and I rarely see one another during the day and, when we do, there are no obvious public displays of affection but Noah must suspect something is up. He has taken to calling me every few days but I don't answer, and thankfully he hasn't popped by my apartment, given that Leo spends almost every night at my place.

My workload has increased dramatically over the past month. With less than a month until we break for Christmas, Jess's nightmare has finally come true and Dianna is having Samantha and I present to each other every other week.

Samantha's project is a high-end commercial studio complex.

"Solid and safe," Dianna remarks in one of our meetings. I

don't know that I would necessarily call that a compliment, but Samantha simpers with gratitude and casts a smug look my way as Dianna pauses, frowning at my own work in progress.

"There are still a few holes in your practical," Dianna tells me. "As I've told you from the start, this is a challenging approach you've taken. Your design is very good and you certainly have the artistic flair to pull it off, but this could be risky."

Samantha is practically orgasming in her seat, but Dianna continues, oblivious.

"You quote Gehry and Wright as your inspiration?"

"Yes," I nod. "The Bilbao and the Guggenheim specifically. I want the building itself to become a piece of art."

"Art housing art..." Dianna trails off, thoughtful. "Your approach is very *avant-garde*, which I personally adore. The problem is that it's experimental. More to the point, it's experiential. They are either going to love it or hate it." By 'they' she means the Burke & Duke Selection committee. This is the crux of the matter. Samantha is also applying for the internship and she's played it safe. I've taken a gamble. If the committee experience my project as it is intended to be experienced, I'll have the internship in the bag. If they don't like it, Samantha will win simply because I will lose, not because of her project's merit.

"I guess I just have to hope they love it," I say, swallowing down the lump in my throat.

Dianna doesn't reply. I know she's rooting for me, but she would never say so in front of Samantha, who is looking thrilled with the way the conversation is going.

"Okay," Dianna claps her hands to her knees. "That's quite

enough for today. Go and enjoy your weekend and I'll see you both next week."

Samantha gathers up her things and sashays to the door, glossy and sleek and dressed to kill, no doubt off to celebrate her weekend. Judging by the lack of dark shadows beneath her eyes, I doubt she's losing much sleep. The simplicity of her design makes it easier and she is far further ahead than I am.

I hang back, mulling over the title on the front page of my draft. "Experiential gallery space in a revitalised environment". The closer I get to completion, the more the self-doubt creeps in. I had been so confident, so cocky, at the beginning of the year. Now, however, I'm starting to wonder if I shouldn't have played it safe, like Samantha.

"Everything all right, Sarah?" Dianna has stopped at the door.

"Oh, yeah," I nod, forcing a smile. "I'm just thinking."

"Thinking you might have made a mistake?" she probes.

"I don't know," I shake my head, uncertain.

"Sarah," Dianna insists that I look at her, "do you want to be an architect or a revolutionary?"

"Ideally I'd like to be both."

"And you will be. Whether you land the internship or not. You are one of the most talented people I have ever taught. It's possible that the selection committee may not understand your vision, but do you really think that Gehry or Wright didn't take any knocks? Your theory is sound, it's well-developed and well thought out. You'll get the practical perfect, too, if I know you as well as I think I do. Just make sure that your justification is sound. You need to make sure they interpret your design as you intended – don't give them any option."

"You're saying I should force them to experience it, on my terms?" I say, half in jest.

"Exactly," Dianna replies and she's deadly serious.

Leo is waiting at the car when I emerge from the campus building.

"Hey, Scarface!" I tease, standing on my toes to kiss him. I run my hand through his hair, tracing the ridged scar. Just beyond his hairline it is smoother, but raised, forming an egg-shaped lump of scar tissue. So much for my theory that he was sensitive about it - it turns out that it's from a bog-standard car accident.

"Someone has to be the beast to your beauty," he retorts. As I step away to move around to the passenger side, he grabs my hand and pulls me back. "I have a surprise for you."

"Please tell me it involves getting out of Game Night," I tease, "I've had a hell of a week."

He cups my face in his hands and kisses me again.

"Actually," he murmurs, resting his forehead on mine so that his breath is a whisper on my lips, "it does."

"Really?" I can't contain my elation. "And does Jess know about this mutiny?"

"She helped me plan it."

"Why am I not surprised? Is there no one you can't charm?"

"I'm sure there's a woman out there who's immune," he concedes, "but if she exists, I haven't met her yet." He kisses me on the nose and releases me. "We're going home to pack."

"Pack?" I'm intrigued.

"Yes. You need a break. You've been working far too hard

and you deserve it," he adds as I open my mouth to protest. "I'm taking you away for the weekend."

The thought of breaking the monotony of my days is too good to refuse.

"Where are we going?"

"You'll see." He gives me a little shove and then swats my backside as I walk around the car.

Leo refuses to give me any information about our weekend destination on the drive home. I'm still trying to get it out of him on the elevator ride up to my apartment but the best I can elicit is a lopsided grin. My happy mood dissipates as soon as the elevator doors open.

Noah is standing at my door. He smiles at me but, when he catches sight of Leo, his expression tightens, his lips pressing into a grim line. The look on his face tells me everything I need to know. Noah may have suspected Leo and I were together but he wasn't sure until this moment.

"Hi Noah," I say, trying to smooth over the awkward situation.

Noah doesn't respond, his gaze fixed on Leo. He draws himself up to his full height and pushes his shoulders back, which would be impressive, if Leo wasn't almost a whole head taller than him with shoulders twice as broad.

"I'll meet you inside," Leo offers, relieving me of my keys. I think he's going to leave it at that but the opportunity to piss Noah off proves too much for him. "I'll get started on the packing," he declares, winking at me over his shoulder. As he moves past Noah, Noah glares at him like a schoolboy in a locker-room fight. Leo grins in return.

The second the door closes, Noah rounds on me.

"So," I feign brightness, "what's up?"

"Packing?" His clipped, curt tone is a sure-fire sign that trouble is brewing.

"Yes, we're going away for the weekend."

He stares at me in disbelief. "So it's true. You're actually dating that idiot?"

"I am," I answer without any hesitation. "I'm sorry, Noah I thought you knew."

"How would I know, Sarah? It's not like you tell me anything these days. You don't even have the decency to return my calls."

"I didn't think it would be appropriate for me to keep talking to you now that I'm in a relationship."

"A relationship?" he sneers. "With him? Tell me you're joking!" His derogatory implication stings because, until I knew better, I had wondered about Leo's lack of ambition myself.

"That's really none of your business. And now that you know about it I think you'll appreciate that its best if we only communicate professionally. During college hours," I add meaningfully.

"Professionally!" Noah snorts. "Well, perhaps if you had bothered to answer any of my calls you would know that what I wanted to discuss is actually relevant to your career."

"Oh yeah? How so?"

"I've become quite friendly with one of the advanced placement panellists. From Burke & Duke," he adds when I don't respond. "I thought perhaps I could put in a good word for you."

"I'm assuming this panellist is female?" I ask dryly,

recalling the attractive woman I saw a few weeks ago. I keep my face neutral, not wanting him to know how affected I am by the thought that he could interfere in my application.

"Yes, actually. Her name is Amanda and she's become a friend."

I can't help myself. "I'm sure she has," I say, rolling my eyes. Noah reads my reaction completely wrong and I see a small smile play about the corners of his mouth.

"Are you jealous, Sarah?" *Oh God, can he really be that stupid?*

"No, Noah," I insist, "I'm not jealous. What I am, is wondering what on earth this has to do with me?"

"Like I said," Noah leans casually against the wall behind him, "I thought about putting in a good word for you."

"You thought about it… so you haven't actually done so yet?" He blinks, trying to establish where I'm going with this. "Let me ask you something," I continue, before he can answer, "who do *you* think is more worthy of the Burke & Duke internship – me or Samantha?"

Noah narrows his eyes, finally realising he's walking into a trap.

"Because if you believe I deserve it, then you should tell this Amanda woman," I say. "And if you don't, then don't. Like *I* said, Noah – I'm still not sure what this has to do with me or why you needed to speak to me about it or why you're here at all," I add pointedly. Despite my determination to stay calm my cheeks are flaming and my voice has risen.

"It has everything to do with you." The words drip incitingly off his tongue. "I'm giving you the opportunity to get ahead in your career. I'm offering to do you a favour. Amanda has become a good friend, yes, but she wants more. She wants us to move forward, but I've held back because I still believe that there's a chance for *us*, Sarah. What are you doing with that first year loser in there? He can't do anything for you – he can't challenge you. You're wasting time. There's so much I can do for you. Why won't you let me help you?"

"You still don't get it." I shake my head in disgust, deliberately ignoring the slights to Leo. "I don't want any favours. I want to earn this internship. I have *earned* it. I don't need you to manipulate the system." I fix my eyes on his, holding his gaze steadily. "If you have feelings for this woman, you should act on them, because you and I, we're over!"

I start to move around him to the door, but he blocks my path, his face losing all trace of softness.

"You should think about this, Sarah." A low warning. "You don't want to make an enemy out of me."

It takes a moment for the meaning of his words to sink in. "Are you threatening me?"

"I'm telling you not to throw your life away on some jock who hasn't got even an ounce of the potential you do."

"How is this about Leo?" I yell, finally losing my temper. "If you want to help me then do it, and if you don't, then don't, but stay the hell out of my personal life!"

"You heard her," a low voice interrupts. I didn't even realise Leo had emerged from the apartment but his face is a terrifying sight. His blue eyes are icy and boring into Noah and the muscles in his shoulders are bunched beneath his collared shirt. I can see him trying to get a grip on his temper but he's not doing a very good job of it.

"Go, Noah," I say, moving to stand beside Leo.

Noah issues a nasty little laugh. "You've just thrown your career down the drain," he sneers. "And you," he adds, disparagingly to Leo, "good luck with her. You're going to need it."

We leave him jabbing at the elevator buttons and close the door behind us.

"Do I even want to know what that was about?" Leo asks.

"No," I knead my temples, feeling a headache coming on.

"What did he mean by throwing your career away?"

"It's just an empty threat. He's trying to intimidate me," I reassure him, wishing I could believe my own words.

"Sarah…"

"No," I say brightly, "we're not talking about Noah. He's not worth it. And besides, don't we have packing to do?"

CHAPTER 15

*A*s we leave the City limits the knot in my stomach slowly unravels and all thought of Noah and his disastrous visit blow away in the breeze that rustles my hair through the open window. Leo's hand rests on my thigh, a mini-inferno of heat that seems to spread as the miles go by.

"On a scale of one to ten, how excited are you?" Leo asks.

I pretend to seriously ponder this.

"A solid two-and-a-half." I grin.

Leo moves his hand further up my leg. "And now?"

"At least a three."

The trip takes only forty-five minutes but, as we pull into a sweeping drive, I feel as though I'm in an entirely different country. Everything is so green; nothing but endless fields in either direction and behind us, haughtily defying the breeze, a forest of regimented trees.

"A spa?" I exclaim, spotting the granite plaque beside two imposing wrought-iron gates. "We're spending an entire weekend at a spa?" My excitement is evident in the squeakiness of my voice.

"Indeed," Leo says, opening his own window to address the guard who approaches. He checks Leo's licence against a list and then signs us in before waving us through the boom. The gates open and we pull up the gravel drive, to the crunch of stone beneath the enormous tyres.

We follow the clearly marked signboards to reception and enter the main building which must once have been the manor house. Immediately, a caramel-skinned man dressed in a grey suit steps forward and offers us a tray laden with glasses of champagne. Completely unselfconscious, Leo takes two and hands one to me. The bitter crisp tang is a welcome sensation on my tongue.

"Cheers." Leo raises his glass to me and I clink my own against it before following him to the reception counter, behind which sits what I can only describe as a Scandinavian supermodel. Her arctic white hair is pulled into a bun and her cheekbones are so sculpted that we could safely rest our champagne flutes on them without spilling a drop. The elegant name badge fixed to her collar tells us that her name is Susan.

"Welcome to Serenity," Susan purrs, her voice a honeyed bell. "Will you be checking in, Sir?" she asks, looking at Leo like she'd prefer to be checking into his pants. I clear my throat and she dazzles me with a smile of perfect porcelain veneers.

"We have a reservation under Russell," Leo replies politely, giving her the benefit of his own crooked smile.

Susan leans forward and presses a button on her switchboard telephone. A second later a feminine voice sounds through the speaker.

"Yes?"

"Mr and Mrs Russell have arrived," Susan informs the faceless voice before cutting the link. I open my mouth to correct her and then think better of it. Being mistaken for Leo's wife is not an altogether unpleasant experience, and besides, with the way she's looking at Leo, it gives me a sense of satisfaction.

"Mr and Mrs Russell!" I recognise the voice from the speaker phone. A middle-aged woman with a trim waist and eyes the colour of crushed coffee beans has emerged from a hallway behind Susan. Her grasp is cool and professional as she shakes my hand and then Leo's.

"Welcome to Serenity. My name is Ingrid and I'll be coordinating your stay with us."

"It's very nice to meet you," I say.

"Your treatments have been scheduled for tomorrow, as requested," Ingrid continues warmly. "There's not much to do this evening except relax. Our listed menu will be served in the main restaurant which is just through there," she points down the hallway to our left," or, if you prefer, we can have something sent to your room."

"Perfect, thank you," Leo says.

"You're welcome. Your car is right outside; I presume?"

"Yes."

"Wonderful. If you'll follow me, I'll take you to your villa."

We follow her back through the open door and into the twilight where she hops nimbly onto a waiting golf-cart and gestures for us to follow.

"This is amazing," I say as we pull up to an exquisite little cottage five minutes later.

"It's even better than it looks online," Leo admits. "Better than a two and a half?" he adds smugly and I grin.

Ingrid whizzes through the small space, giving us a brief tour and then tells us that dinner is served between seven and nine before she finally leaves us alone.

The second she's gone, Leo opens the mini-bar and extracts a bottle of champagne. I can still hear the high whine of the golf-cart's engine as it heads back to reception.

"Should we sit outside?" I ask, peering through the doors at the gorgeous view.

"No," Leo's answer is immediate, "because I plan on pouring this champagne all over you and licking every drop of it off and I really don't fancy that golf-cart rumbling through right in the middle."

"Okay, we're definitely up to a high seven," I say, my voice low and husky.

"Let's see if we can't get you to ten, Miss Holt."

Later, sated and tender, I hobble to the SUV, grateful that I thought to pack at least one cocktail dress and a pair of heels. Leo looks very pleased with himself, but then again, he should be.

"We must have hit ten somewhere in there," he muses, as he holds the door open for me.

"I think we may have peaked at around a thirteen," I agree, flashing him a wicked grin.

He dips his head and kisses me deeply, taking his time, reminding me that there is no hurry and nothing else for me to do but enjoy myself. The kiss is slow and sensual, and, despite our recent love-making, I feel the heat flare between my legs. Leo's hand comes to rest on my bare knee travelling slowly upward and I catch my breath, arching my hips toward him. When he stops suddenly, I give a groan of frustration. To his credit, he looks pretty pained himself, his blue eyes liquid with desire.

"First we eat," he says, with as much resolve as he can muster. "If I don't stop now I'm going to ruin that dress." His gaze falls on the shadow of my cleavage and he shakes his head ruefully before shutting the door.

Ingrid approaches us shortly after our appetizers – polenta squares topped with mushroom *ragu* which literally dissolve in my mouth. I've been watching her move between tables, checking on every guest and I knew it was only a matter of time before she reached us. Unfortunately, I had just shoved a forkful of food into my mouth when she arrived.

"Mr and Mrs Russell!" she greets us warmly. "How are you enjoying yourselves so far?"

"Thoroughly," Leo responds with enthusiasm and a devilish glance in my direction.

"Marvellous!" Ingrid looks suitably impressed. "Please let me know if you need anything at all. Breakfast is served from seven-thirty and I'll collect you from here at nine for your first treatment. I hope that suits you?" she gives us an arch look, displaying all the confidence of someone who knows that her guests have little choice in the matter.

"Sounds perfect," I say. "What treatments do we have scheduled for tomorrow?"

She allows herself a little clap of elation and I wonder how on earth she manages to be so permanently upbeat.

"You start with a Swedish full body massage," she begins, "followed by tea and scones on the terrace. Then it's on to a deep cleansing facial and a manicure or pedicure, whichever you prefer," she glances critically at the hand holding my wine and I hide the ragged fingernail of my thumb, "after which you have a private lunch booked in the cellar."

"The cellar?"

"The wine cellar," she clarifies quickly. "It's our coveted fine-dining experience. Mr Russell booked it in advance."

"Oh, did he?" I waggle my eyebrows at Leo.

"After lunch you finish up with a body wrap and then spend an hour in the *Rasul.*"

"What's a *Rasul?*" I ask, as the waiter arrives with our main course.

"Oh, it's the perfect pampering experience for a couple to indulge in! A *Rasul* is a traditional Arabian cleansing ritual which takes place in our herbal steam room."

"It sounds… interesting."

"Basically they slather you in mud and then you wash it off in an oversized shower," Leo offers helpfully.

"After that, it's dinner and then the rest of the evening is yours to do as you will," Ingrid says, sounding remarkably less hospitable.

"Thank you." I'm distracted by the mouth-watering sole on my plate, and Leo has already picked up his knife and fork.

"Well, I'll see you both tomorrow," Ingrid says, knowing when to make herself scarce.

The food is superb, and I polish off the lot. In keeping with the health hydro theme, dessert is an ample serving of strawberries in a balsamic glaze and dipped in dark chocolate. I pop the last one into my mouth and heave a sigh, leaning back in my chair.

"That," I announce, "was heaven."

Leo pours the last of the wine into my glass, much to the

chagrin of the hovering waiter. I've lost track of how many bottles we've had between us.

"Dinner on the one-to-ten scale?" Leo asks.

"Eleven, at least."

This brings a smug smile to his face. "Well, it's nice to know I outperform the food."

"You outperform most things." I take a deep sip of the wine, draining my glass.

"Would you like me to order another bottle?"

"No," I gaze at him through lowered lashes. "I'm stuffed. I think we should burn off some of these calories."

CHAPTER 16

I wake to the incessant ringing of my phone. Throwing off the eiderdown covers I sit bolt upright in the bed, rousing Leo who leaps to his feet with a yell of surprise.

"What?" he gazes around, bleary-eyed and I take the opportunity to admire the view of his stark-naked body. I know from practically living with him for the past month that he visits the gym at least three times a week, but I suspect that's simply for fitness. Leo has that lithe, muscular build that is simply the product of winning the genetic lottery. "What is that?" Leo squints around, trying to locate the source of the ringing. I suspect we may both still be a little drunk on wine and sex. I seize my purse, upending its contents over the rumpled bedcovers and snatch up my phone. I stab at the call button.

"Hello?" The ringing continues and we both turn to glare at the telephone beside the bed. A blinking red light confirms that the call is coming from there.

Leo's eyes widen. "What's the time?" he hisses, clambering over the bed and scooping up the handset.

"We're not late yet!" I reply, glancing at the digital clock on my phone.

"Hello," Leo says, in the tone that people use when they're trying to pretend they've been up for hours. I stuff a pillow over my mouth to stifle a laugh. Leo winks at me and listens intently for a moment. "Thank you," he says simply, replacing the handset. "That was our wake-up call," he tells me, pulling the pillow from my mouth so that he can kiss me good morning, "courtesy of the ever-efficient Ingrid."

"Breakfast?" I suggest brightly.

"I love how excited you get at the thought of food."

"I burned a lot of calories last night, in case you've forgotten."

"Sarah, how could I ever forget?" he trails his hand down my leg. "The image of these thighs wrapped around my neck is one I will treasure forever. In fact, I'm thinking of getting it tattooed on my forehead."

"It wouldn't go well with that scar," I tease, swatting him with the pillow. I hop off the bed, exposing my naked bottom to his hungry gaze. I've never felt self-conscious about my body in front of Leo, not since the first night we were together when we made out in front of the mirror. He likes to watch me and is utterly uninhibited in the bedroom which makes it less awkward for me. In fact, it does just the opposite – it turns me on.

I take a lightning shower, reluctantly washing the scent and feel of him from my skin and then I change into a pair of black leggings and a vest. Mindful of Ingrid's instructions, I slap on just a touch of moisturiser, leaving my clean face bare.

My hair is still dripping so I rub at it vigorously with the fluffy white towel provided and comb it through while Leo takes his turn in the shower, then we head down to the manor house.

The morning goes by in a blur. I manage to wolf down my breakfast and two cups of coffee before the pampering begins in earnest and by the time we finish lunch, I feel as though all the stress of the past few weeks have been massaged out of me. Until our final treatment, that is. I don't know whether to laugh or die of mortification as a pair of therapists paint Leo and I in a thick mud-like substance which they purport will not only smooth my skin and detoxify my body, but will also cleanse my respiratory system. I refrain from asking how, unless they plan on pouring it down my throat to coat my lungs. Leo and I are dressed in disposable underwear bottoms, which cover very little, and are naked from the waist up, which is fine for him. Lying on the freshly plastic-draped therapy bed, I glance down to find my breasts slathered in mud, so that there is no differentiation between nipple and flesh, while the therapist checks intently for any spots she may have missed.

Leo, of course, takes the whole experience with a pinch of salt, and, on completion, looks like an Adonis. Painting done, the therapists, whose names I can't remember, wrap us up in clear plastic and discreetly leave the room, dimming the light as they go.

"Oh God," I groan, opening my eyes to look at Leo. My neck itches where the mud is drying, but when I try to lift my hand to scratch it I find it pinned to my side. "I feel like a mummy."

"That was pretty weird," Leo agrees, chuckling.

"I'm itchy."

"Don't think about it."

"How long do we have to lie here?"

"They said forty-five minutes."

"I'm going to die."

His chest shakes with silent laughter and I start to giggle until I can't stop.

"Never ever did I imagine I would be spending the weekend coated in mud and wrapped in plastic."

"What can I say, I aim to please."

I close my eyes and allow my mind to wander, trying not to think about the fact that now my ass is itching. The music playing through the room is haunting and soft, and slowly, I drift off, lost in that delicious place halfway between dream and reality. Before I know it, the therapists are back. They drape our gowns around us and carefully slip our feet into pairs of disposable rubber slops before we shuffle across the room and out into a small hall. The *Rasul* is basically a cosy steam-room and, at the touch of a button, a gentle mist of warm water sprays down from the domed ceiling. My therapist turns to us with a smile.

"Please feel free to come out whenever you are ready." We shuffle inside and she closes the door behind us.

I turn to Leo and burst out laughing. "Get me out of this, please?"

Leo, frees his hands easily, pulling the plastic down to his feet in one swift motion. He looks surreal, a bronze sculpture – naked and yet fully covered. Even the underwear is stained the same brown as the rest of him, but he tears it off in one swift motion, exposing a triangular portion of unpainted skin. He steps out of the plastic coiled at his feet and kicks it aside before coming to stand beside me under the centre of the dome. The mist-like spray has already settled on his hair, leaving crystal droplets of dew on his golden mane. Gently, he unravels the plastic wrap from my body, bunching it in his hands until finally I feel the blessed relief of the last stretch pull away from my skin. Leo has the mud-like substance on his hands as he lifts his thumb to my cheek, stroking my jawline. It smells nothing like mud – rather a delicious combination of rain and herbs. I shut my eyes and lift my head, letting the drizzle wash over my face. Leo's lips brush mine, once, twice, and then I open my mouth to allow him access. We kiss for what feels like forever, a gentle, heady sensation while the gentle hiss of the *Rasul* resonates around us. It is warm in this room, and even warmer when he takes me in his arms and pulls me against him. I rest my head in the hollow of his chest as his hands move gently over my shoulders, trailing heat down my back.

Infinitely slowly, his hands wash the mud from my body and I return the favour, massaging, teasing, touching. Leo gets onto his knees to lather down my legs and my knees tremble at his breath on my thighs. I wonder idly how many couples have made love in this room. My pulse quickens at the thought of making love to Leo right here, right now, but he makes no move other than the relentless touch of his hands and lips caressing every inch of my body until it is full to bursting with love and longing.

We emerge from the *Rasul* ensconced in our robes, eyes sparkling and holding hands. The therapists are nowhere to be seen, no doubt ordered to stay away and allow couples their privacy. Somehow, I feel even closer to Leo after this experience. It was almost better than sex - more intimate, somehow. The connection was less physical, but deeper, more meaningful, and I stroke the ball of his thumb as we walk, not wanting to break the connection.

We fall asleep almost instantly when we return to our cottage, my back pressed up against Leo's chest, his hand resting on my heart. The feel of his bare skin up against me lulls me to sleep with a light heart and a rested soul.

CHAPTER 17

"*I* still can't believe I let you talk me into this," I grumble, sticking my foot right through a brand new pair of black pantyhose.

"Who am I to stand in your way?" Leo teases, his blue eyes dancing with ill-concealed mirth.

"Sarah, you're doing us all a favour," Dylan chips in, clapping Leo on the back. "Mike is the only guy in the entire office who couldn't find a date. He'd be the laughing stock of the entire firm."

"You're rendering a great service, Sarah," Leo adds solemnly, and then he and Dylan fall about laughing.

"You both suck!" I snap, tearing the pantyhose off and hurling the offending item at them. "And I swear, Dylan, if Mike so much as lays a hand on my leg I'll…"

"Woah!" Leo raises his hands, "if Mike lays a hand on your leg, I'll be dealing with him myself."

"Don't worry, Leo, I'll keep my eye on her," Dylan vows.

"But I doubt she'll need me to. I'm pretty sure Mike bats for our team."

"Then why didn't you ask Tom to go with him?" I ask, slipping on a pair of black heels and smoothing down the front of my dress.

"Mike's in denial. Now shake your ass, we're picking him up in fifteen minutes."

"Who are you taking?" Leo asks.

"Lucy," Dylan rolls the name around his tongue, "but I'm meeting her there."

"You're not picking her up?" Leo's sense of propriety is obviously appalled.

"She's the secretary," I point out.

Leo processes this for about half a second and then he claps Dylan on the back.

"Good man!"

I roll my eyes at both of them.

"Right, I'm going to grab a jacket," Dylan announces, checking his watch. "I'll meet you in the hall?"

"Fine," I grumble.

The second Dylan is gone Leo pulls me to him, nuzzling my neck and breathing in the faint trace of Chanel behind my ear.

"You look beautiful," he murmurs, "and you're doing a really nice thing here."

"Don't try and butter me up," I say. "You are so not getting any later." My playful smile belies the threat and Leo runs a long finger down my bare arm.

"We'll see." His eyes hold a sensual promise and we both know that he will absolutely be getting some later.

"Sarah!" Dylan sticks his blond head around the front door.

"I'm coming!" I snatch up my purse and blow Leo a kiss as I follow Dylan outside.

To his credit, Mike has made a concerted effort with his appearance this evening. His suit is clean, at least; no ketchup stains in sight and he's attempted to comb his thatch-like hair.

"Thanks for doing this Sarah," he says as he gets into the car and his appreciation is so genuine that I immediately feel guilty for all my griping.

"It's my pleasure!" I say brightly, "I'm sure it's going to be fun!"

Dylan gives me an arch look in the rear-view mirror but I ignore him.

"I feel like a chauffeur," he grumbles.

"Lucy's meeting you there?" Mike asks and I detect a trace of disappointment in his voice.

"Yeah," Dylan grins wickedly at us over his shoulder, "that way if things don't work out I'm not obligated to take her home."

"You are so full of shit," I say, and Mike's cheeks flush with pleasure.

"You do know your friend Mike has a thumping crush on that twig you call a date, don't you?" I ask Dylan when I manage to corner him at the food table two hours later. Dylan raises his handsome head to peer at Mike who is offering to buy Lucy a drink at the free bar.

"No he doesn't."

"He does," I insist. "And it's breaking his poor heart to watch her fawning all over you like a cat on heat."

Dylan casts an appraising eye over Lucy who is bursting out of her hot pink dress.

"That's actually a good analogy," he laughs, "she looks like she'd be a tiger in the sack."

"Dylan!"

He does a double-take.

"God you sound like mom!"

"Mike is your friend."

"Yeah, but…" the sight of my raised eyebrow shuts him up. "Aw, come on, Sarah! It's not like Luce is going to look twice at Mike, even if I do turn her down."

"That's not the point."

"Fine," he grouches, tossing a half-eaten *vol-au-vent* back onto the table.

"That's a good boy," I tease, patting him on the head and flattening his deliberately mussed hair.

For the remainder of the evening Dylan studiously avoids Lucy, sulking all the while. I grin every time his wounded eyes find mine and give him an exaggerated thumbs-up. To my surprise, I'm enjoying myself far more than I thought I would. With Dylan out of the way, Mike is following Lucy around like a puppy dog, which leaves me free to wander about. Pulling out my phone I see a message from Leo, sent almost an hour ago. I open it and give a gasp of shocked surprise as I read the dirty text, outlining exactly what he intends to do to me when I get home.

"Where are you going?" Dylan asks as I pass him on my way to the stairs.

"Just getting some air," I reply, not having to fake my breathlessness.

I emerge on the roof, which is isolated save for a couple

with their backs to me, gazing out at the view. I retreat to the far side, out of their field of vision, and lean out over the railing.

I've never 'sexted' before, but reading the words on the screen my stomach curls itself into a delicious hot mess.

I quickly type my response, which is only a single word.

Wow!

Good wow or bad wow? The reply comes through instantly.

Definitely good wow.

How's your evening going?

It just got a whole lot better.

In that case, keep your phone on you.

For the rest of the evening Leo sends me sporadic texts, outlining in the most intimate detail every single thing he has planned for my return. By the time Dylan finally calls it quits, I am bubbling with desire, the entire lower half of my body turned to jelly. Heart hammering, I barely hear a word Dylan says the whole drive home.

He yawns as we reach his door.

"Sleep tight, sis, and thanks for doing that. For Mike, I mean."

"No problem," I grin stupidly at his closed door for a minute and then I rush frantically toward my own, fumbling through my purse for my key. The door opens as I reach it and I fly through it, hurling myself on Leo like a woman possessed. His response is just as enthusiastic, the hours of exquisite foreplay reducing us both to a frenzied primal desire. There will be no gentle lovemaking tonight. Instead, it is hard, fast and furious, and it still takes my breath away.

CHAPTER 18

J am thinking back to that wild night when I hear the front door slam. The icy chill of winter air breezes into the room, bravely taking on the heating.

"Please tell me you got the Christmas crackers?" I call.

"You sent me out for crackers," Leo drawls, coming around the corner laden with two huge boxes, "what else did you think I'd come back with?" He dumps both boxes unceremoniously on the kitchen counter.

"Oh, I don't know... cheese?"

"Smart ass." He grabs my backside and gives it a good squeeze, and the gesture reminds me so much of my parents that I can't help but smile.

"Your hands are freezing!" I exclaim as the cold permeates the denim of my jeans.

"Nothing like Christmas time in New York. What time are we leaving tomorrow?"

"Around ten. My parents like to do presents before lunch."

Leo and I have been dating for two-and-a-half months and

since he is practically living with me, I've decided it's high time that he met my parents.

"Is Dylan driving down with us?" Leo has flopped onto the sofa, his long legs disappearing beneath the coffee table. Dylan and Leo get on far better than I expected, which is a relief, but I had to re-institute the 'no visitation without prior warning' rule after I found the two of them drinking beer and playing PlayStation one afternoon. It wouldn't have been such a bad thing if I hadn't been wearing nothing but a new Victoria Secret twin set and an overcoat, which I'd bravely tugged open the second I walked through the door. Dylan insisted that he had to wash his eyes out with soap.

"No," I round on him, "he's taking his own car. Apparently he's bringing a girl!" Much to everyone's surprise, Mike had finally succeeded in getting Lucy to go out with him. Dylan, of course, was taking credit for master-minding the whole thing, but he hadn't been on a date since the dinner. For Dylan, sixteen days must be a new record.

"Marvellous." Leo grins wickedly, "It'll take the heat off me."

"My parents will adore you," I promise, dropping onto the sofa beside him and curling into his side. His clothes still carry the chill from outside. His arm comes around my shoulders and I heave a sigh of contentment.

"Did you finish your assignment yet?" I ask lazily. Leo had been given a mountain of work to do over the Christmas break and so far I hadn't seen him so much as pick up a pen.

"No," he groans.

"I'm going to start dinner, then," I say cheerfully, "while you get some work done."

"Do I have to?"

"Yes. Jess and Tom are popping in later so you can stop when they get here."

"But it's Christmas Eve?"

"Exactly," I say, "just think - tomorrow you get the whole day off." He gives a grunt as I shove his work bag at him.

Much to Leo's delight, Tom and Jess arrive early, bringing another gust of icy wind in with them. Jess's eyes are slitty beneath her beanie and her scarf is pulled up over her chin.

"God, it's cold," she announces, handing me an unwrapped bottle of wine. "Merry Christmas."

"Yes, Merry Christmas," Tom adds, handing me an identical bottle, with a broken strand of tinsel draped around it.

"So fancy, Tom!" I tease, picking it off and holding it up.

"I stole it off the cash register at the bottle store," he admits proudly. "Sorry we're early, but we're off to the pub in a bit, so we thought we'd stop by first."

"No problem at all," Leo assures him, packing away his books with a gleeful expression.

I make my way over to the tree that Leo and I decorated only last week and pull two bottles of red from its base.

"Merry Christmas!" I say, handing one each to Tom and Jess.

"I take it none of you believe in wrapping paper?" Leo drawls, watching us in amusement.

"No point," Jess informs him, "we're going to drink it now anyway."

The four bottles of wine are consumed in almost no time at all, and Jess and Tom make their exit, Jess considerably less affected by the cold.

"Tell your folks I say hi," she says, giving me a hug. "And Merry Christmas!"

"I will, and Merry Christmas to you too!"

Leo gives me a curious look when they're gone.

"You don't want to go with them?" he asks.

"I never do," I reply easily. "Christmas Eve is one night I like to stay in. They're used to it."

"Why do you like to stay in?"

"I don't know, I just do. There's something magical about Christmas Eve." I catch his eye and I can see he's trying not to smile. "I also don't particularly enjoy spending Christmas with a hangover," I insist, smacking his arm. "Now, I'm going to finish that dinner, and you, Mr Russell, are going to get back to your books."

I'm peeling potatoes when Leo's phone rings, the opening bars of Live's *Lightning Crashes* resounding through the room. Automatically he gets up and wanders down the hall. He can't stand still when he's talking on the phone, he has to pace, and I hear the deep thrum of his voice moving further away. I wonder idly what my parents will think of him. I'm sure they'll approve - there's nothing not to like about Leo - but I don't think it would be wise to let them in on our current living arrangements. As luck would have it, mom hasn't been to stay once since we started dating, so I haven't been caught yet, but I know she would frown upon her unmarried daughter living with a man. Of course, Dylan will probably take great delight in tipping her off, despite my plea for him to keep quiet.

I'm yanked from my musing by the change in Leo's tone. I don't think I've ever heard him raise his voice, other than the night Noah accosted me outside in the hall. Fearful of being caught eavesdropping, I tiptoe around the kitchen counter and stand just out of sight, behind the wall.

"Stop calling me," Leo is saying, his voice low once more. I frown, wondering who on earth he could be talking to. "That's none of your business," Leo continues. A pause, and then, "No really, it's not!"

There is a deathly silence and I picture him in my mind, standing in the hall, his eyes narrowed in anger. I wonder if he's hung up the phone and then I hear the soft footfalls of his return. I race back around the kitchen counter and pick up the potato-peeler as he rounds the corner.

"Who was that?" I try to keep my voice as normal as possible, but it sounds high-pitched, even to my own ears.

"Gordon," he replies easily. Gordon is a name I've heard often – one of the group of friends who was with him at the club the first night he bought me a drink – but we were never properly introduced and, in the months that we've been dating, I've never met any of Leo's friends.

"I still haven't met him," I say, keeping my eyes on the half-peeled potato in my hand. "You're not embarrassed to introduce your rich friends to your middle-class girlfriend, are you?" I expect him to deny it or to brush it off, but instead, he curses.

"What is that supposed to mean, exactly?"

I raise my eyes in surprise to find him glaring at me in genuine annoyance.

"Nothing," I retort, "I just find it odd that you've met all of my friends and I'm taking you to meet my parents tomorrow, but you haven't introduced me to a single person in your life."

"You wouldn't like my friends," he says. "I'm not even sure I do. And I've told you before, I'm trying to distance myself from them."

"Why?"

"Because!"

"That's not an answer, Leo and you know it." I slam down the potato-peeler and press my hands against the counter, my own anger roused. Leo pauses, takes a deep breath and seems to compose himself.

"They remind me of who I was before," he admits. "I have nothing in common with them anymore."

"So you just stopped seeing them, conveniently, at the same time we started dating?"

"Yes. Is it so hard for you to believe that you bring out the best in me? That I don't want to ruin what we have by bringing those types of people into it?" The fight goes out of me but there's still another issue to address.

"What about your family?" I ask. "You can't tell me you've cut them out of your life too? You see your sister often. Without me," I add pointedly. "And you're not even seeing them for Christmas!"

"My family don't celebrate the holidays, Sarah. It's not a big deal." He spreads his hands wide. "You want to meet my sister? I'll take you to meet her. We can go right now." He actually takes a physical step toward the door and I raise my hands.

"I don't need to meet her right now," I say, the thought alarming me more than I had expected. "I just want to know that you actually intend to tell her about us."

At this, Leo's jaw drops.

"You think she doesn't know?" he asks, and then his shoulders start to shake with silent laughter. "Sarah, she knows, trust me. In fact, I think she's sick of hearing about you... you're all I tend to talk about these days."

A warm glow suffuses me, obliterating all my anger and frustration. "Really?"

"Why do you sound so surprised?"

"I don't know, I thought maybe… I don't know what I thought." I shake my head, resuming my dinner preparations, but Leo marches up to me and takes the potato-peeler from my hand.

"I am not ashamed of you, Sarah," he says, his blue eyes holding my own without any hesitation. "You are the best thing that's ever happened to me."

"The *best* thing?" I smile shyly.

"Well, there was this Swedish model this one time…"

And just like that, our first official fight is over.

CHAPTER 19

"Mom! Dad! We're here!" I call, closing the front door behind me and peeling off my gloves.

"Sarah!" My mother bustles in from the kitchen, her blonde curls piled high on her head. Her hair is damp from the steam of cooking and she hasn't got a stitch of make-up on, but she still looks ridiculously youthful.

I accept a hug that is bone-crushing, particularly from someone so small and then turn to introduce Leo.

"Mom, this is Leo," I say proudly, "Leo, my mother, Eleanor."

Leo's hand dwarfs my mom's as he takes hold of it. "It's a pleasure to meet you, Mrs Holt."

"Eleanor, please," my mother insists, skittishly. I can tell she likes Leo – well, the look of Leo, at any rate. It's still too early for her to really know if he will live up to her expectations, but if this first impression is anything to go by, it's definitely a good sign.

"Your Dad's on the patio," Mom says, as I shrug out of my coat. "Go and sit, I'll be out shortly." Usually Mom enlists me to help with the food but Leo's presence gives me a welcome sabbatical.

Outside, Dad is reading the paper but, when he sees us, he folds it meticulously and sets it aside. Getting to his feet he shakes Leo's hand as I make introductions. Judging by the way Leo flexes his fingers afterward, I figure Dad gave him the old "flex test" and I smile inwardly.

'Where's your brother?" Dad asks when we're all seated.

"Late, as always," I say, and then, turning to Leo, "the Holt men are notoriously unpunctual."

"And the Holt women are always on time," my dad agrees cheerily.

Dylan arrives a few minutes later, with a slim, doe-eyed blonde on his arm who he introduces as Hannah. To my astonishment, she's not at all busty, and she has the poise and confidence that comes from absolute conviction of your worth. Beside me, Leo shifts in his seat and I notice he's avoiding her gaze.

"It's wonderful to meet you, Hannah," I say, giving Dylan some discreet wide-eyed approval. "This is my boyfriend, Leo." Leo finally looks up and Hannah shakes his hand politely. A tiny frown creases between her eyes as she meets his eyes.

"You look familiar," she says, "have we met before?"

"I don't think so," Leo replies, a little too quickly, "maybe I just have one of those common faces." Considering his face the comment is absurd, but I refrain from saying so.

"Maybe," Hannah agrees, but the frown doesn't subside.

"Right!" my mom announces, stepping outside. "Time for presents!"

My family have never been big on expensive gifts so when Dylan presents Hannah with a pair of diamond earrings we fall into an astonished silence. The fact that he is usually so tight with his money makes it all the more bizarre and I wonder just how long the two have actually been dating. Surely he wouldn't fork out for diamonds for a girl he's only just met? I rack my brain trying to remember if he's ever mentioned her before, but I can't recall a single name before Lucy the secretary. He turns them over so fast it's hard to keep track. Knowing Dylan, Hannah's probably been around a while, under the false pretence of exclusivity and I make a concerted effort not to mention Dylan's recent date. My dad gives an awkward little cough, indicating that we should stop gaping, and, as one, we all start talking at once to cover the stunned silence. I shove my badly-wrapped gift into Leo's hands.

"It's not that fancy," I admit, glaring at Dylan for good measure for setting such a high standard.

Leo, to my delight, isn't one of those men who shy away from present opening. He rips the packaging revealing the slim box within. Opening it, he quickly scans the embossed gift voucher – a weekend for two at *Serenity*.

"We're going back?" he grins, dazzling me.

"We're going back," I say.

"You shouldn't have done this," Leo grabs me in a bear hug, uninhibited by the fact that my family is looking on.

"Well, technically I bought it for myself, too, so I think it's worth it," I mumble into his shoulder, grateful for the navy sweater which is hiding my blushes.

"I think you're going to get a lot of use out of this one, sis," Dylan announces, handing me an oblong gift wrapped in newspaper. It's saving grace is a small gold bow, which is cello-taped so spectacularly to the paper that I don't even attempt to remove it. Inside I find a wooden sign with the word 'occupied' emblazoned in bold, block letters on the front.

"What does it say?" Mom asks fondly, trying to peer over my shoulder.

"It's for my bathroom," I say quickly, showing it to her, while Dylan shakes with laughter on the sofa opposite.

"How thoughtful!" Mom gives him an approving look, but the second she turns her attention back to me, Dad smacks him on the back of the head.

At last all the presents have been opened and we move to the table for lunch. My family are far too civil to say so, but the fact that Leo hasn't gotten me anything is an elephant in the room. My mom keeps casting disapproving glances his way over the condiments and my dad has fallen into a thoughtful silence.

"So, Hannah," I say, trying to redirect their attention, "what is it that you do?"

"I'm in sales," she replies, spooning peas onto her plate. "I sell medical laboratory equipment to hospitals and clinics." I clock the diamond bracelet on her arm and the impeccable cut of her tan trouser suit and figure she must be very good at her job.

"And how did you and Dylan meet?" Mom asks, finally tearing her eyes from Leo.

"Through a mutual friend." They share a secret smile.

"Oh?" I tease, "I wasn't aware that Dylan had any friends."

The tension eases slightly as everyone laughs at our typical sibling rivalry and I breathe a sigh of relief. I don't want my family to think badly of Leo. Of course I'm disappointed, not to mention the embarrassment of being the girl who didn't get a gift from her own boyfriend, but I figure maybe Leo's just not that into the whole holiday thing. He did mention they don't celebrate the holidays – maybe that includes gift-giving. I catch sight of the gorgeous knife-set on the counter that Leo presented to my parents. *Or maybe not*, I think wryly.

It's evening by the time we leave and, despite my best efforts, my disappointment has grown into an ugly, resentful sulk. My mom kisses me on the cheek and bundles me up in my coat, but the farewell she offers Leo is distinctly chilly. Leo seems oblivious, though, and he says nothing about it the entire way home.

I don't wait for him to open my door. Instead, by the time he comes around the SUV, I'm waiting on the sidewalk. He glances quizzically at me, but I ignore him, feeling tears of childish humiliation prick at my eyes.

"Sarah?" he asks, no doubt trying to discern the reason for my cool behaviour, but before he can go any further, a commotion breaks out to our left that drives all thought of presents, or lack thereof, from my mind.

In the four years that I have lived in Manhattan, I have never personally experienced any of the crime that runs rife in the city. Until now. A grubby, skin-headed youth lunges at us out of nowhere. Before I can even register that the glint of steel in his hand is a knife, Leo gives a bellow of rage and shoves me toward the SUV. I stumble on the uneven ground, landing painfully on my knees. Leo doesn't notice, stepping between me and the would-be assailant with single-minded purpose. His body is tightly coiled in a defensive pose, his hands balled into fists. The youth, not expecting such an aggressive reaction, hesitates. Leo doesn't. He lunges for the boy, grabbing hold of his knife hand and forcing it away. The youth gives a yell of pain as his wrist is twisted at an impossible angle and the knife clatters to the ground. Leo is taller and broader than the boy so I do not see exactly what happens next, but Leo's arm crashes into the youth's face with an audible crunch. When he draws his hand back again, his knuckles are bloody, but he strikes out again and again, landing blows wherever he can reach. With a shriek of fear and strength borne of terror, the boy manages to wriggle out of Leo's hold. I catch sight of his scarlet, mangled face and then he sprints off into the night, disappearing into the shadows as quickly as he'd come. Leo makes a move to follow him and I finally find my voice.

"Leo!" My fear and panic is tangible and brings him to his senses. He whirls around, his eyes searching for me.

"Sarah!" He is at my side in an instant, his hands gentle, his breathing laboured. The streets are quiet once more and no one comes to our aid. Through my adrenalin-fuelled daze, it dawns on me that the entire episode lasted only a few seconds and that my solitary scream was the only sound.

Leo helps me to my feet and somehow I manage not to give way to the panicked hysteria rising in my chest. My knees hurt and I'm trembling, but I keep a firm hold on my purse and let Leo lead me inside.

"Are you sure you're okay?" he asks as we ascend the elevator and I realise he must have already asked me this question. I nod, my heart-rate slowly returning to normal. "You sure?" His eyes are assessing every inch of me and he winces at the sight of my scraped knees through the tears in my jeans.

"He came out of nowhere," I gulp. Leo doesn't respond, but his shoulders are still taut with tension and a muscle is going in his jaw. "Should we go to the police?" I ask, leaning against him.

"There's no point. They won't do anything." There is such venom in his voice that I take a step away from him, but immediately he pulls me back. "Let's just get you inside," he murmurs into my hair. I can feel his heart hammering, but outwardly he maintains an eerie aura of calm. I lift his hand, seeing the scarlet streaks across his fingers. Two of his knuckles are split open.

"You're hurt."

"I'm fine," he insists. I think back to the sight of him thrashing the youth; the furious set of his body, the aggression that seems to emanate from him, so violent, so out of character. His reaction wasn't natural. *It doesn't matter*, I chide myself, *he probably just saved your life.*

"I have some Neosporin we can put on that," I say and, armed with a task, I feel better. I step out onto the landing with purpose.

"Sarah!" Leo calls as I slide my key into the latch, but it's too late. I open the door and am assaulted by the heady scent of freshly-cut flowers. I gaze around at him but he just shrugs, only half a crooked smile lifting his lips.

"This isn't exactly how I planned this, but..." he shrugs again, gesturing me inside.

"Seventy-eight," he tells me, as I take in the long-stemmed, white roses on every surface. "One for each day we've been together. Despite the fact that we were just accosted and the fear that has yet to wholly subside, I feel my heart lift.

"I thought you hadn't got me anything," I admit, a sob welling in my chest.

"I figured as much. You have a terrible poker-face." He

149

squeezes my hand. "But I thought it might be a bit over the top to have them delivered to your parents' place, and I didn't fancy bringing them all up from the car."

I move to pick up a rose nearest me and inhale the sweet scent. Leo picks up a festive-looking red envelope off the table in the hall. The sight of his bloody hands is painful to look at.

"Merry Christmas, Sarah," he murmurs, handing it to me.

I pull on the gold ribbon, which falls away and lift the flap. I gaze down at the tickets, incapable of speech.

"You always say how much you enjoyed that trip with your folks," Leo says, sounding unsure of himself, "and I've never been so...."

He doesn't finish, the wind knocked out of him as I throw myself against him, kissing him hard on the mouth. Inside the envelope are two open tickets to London.

CHAPTER 20

We didn't report the attempted mugging, although I became a lot more vigilant after that. Leo's hands healed and we put the incident behind us.

Time seems to have sped up during the winter semester. It's almost impossible to keep up with the workload and even Jess has cancelled Game Night three weeks in a row. Apparently all the mentors are trying to compete with Dianna and the library seems to be permanently packed with fifth-years. Thank God for Leo. He has taken to getting home early and doing the cooking, which tastes far better than anything I usually concoct. Most nights I get home late, fork up a few mouthfuls of dinner and then spend two or three hours at the small dining-room table, working on my thesis. Leo and I have both agreed that our London trip will have to be taken during the summer break – a celebration of my being awarded the advanced placement, he says. Or a commiseration if I'm not, I point out.

Despite my hectic schedule, I elect to bunk the day after

Valentine's Day. It turns out Tom Hardy really is featuring in the new *Mission Impossible* movie and his namesake, Tom, has it on good information that a scene is being filmed downtown on the 15th.

Feeling nostalgic, guilty and thrilled all at the same time, the three of us pile into a cab and make our way downtown. We can't get near the set so we walk the last few blocks.

"This could be it!" Tom is leading the way. "The beginning of the rest of my life!"

"You still think you're going to convert two hundred pounds of pure British testosterone?" Jess teases.

"You never know, Jess, my dear, you never know!"

We reach the edge of the crowd gathered around the set. There are barricades in place to keep the adoring fans out but somehow we manage to squeeze through the masses until we're pressed right up against them. There are strict 'NO ENTRY' signs posted at five-yard intervals.

"Oh my God, there he is!" Tom squeals, pointing at a short man with a baseball cap pulled down over his eyes. An excited ripple runs through the people nearest us at this proclamation. Jess squints at the man intently, ignoring the jostling.

"That's not him," she says. "He doesn't have a beard."

"Maybe he has one in this movie," Tom drawls, his eyes practically rolling up into his head at her ignorance.

"I don't know, I think Jess might be right," I say. The suspected Tom Hardy looks a little too rough around the edges and a little too old.

"You two are hopeless. You wouldn't know a megastar if he bit you in the ass."

Suddenly, Jess lets out a shriek of pure excitement.

"That's where you're wrong!" she gasps, waving her hands frantically to the left of a large trailer. "Holy shit!" I exclaim, as I see what she's spotted. Tom Cruise is standing only a few hundred yards away, dressed all in black and taking instruction from a man who I can only assume is the director. I whip out my phone, determined to get a picture.

The sight of him, however, proves too much for our own dear Tom. With a leap that would put even Omar McLeod to shame, he vaults over the waist-high barricade.

"Tom!" I yell, watching in shocked horror as he sprints across the space, dodging two beefy security guards. Spurred into action, the balance of the set's security team moves, forming a formidable line between Brooks and Cruise.

I look helplessly to Jess, but she's buckled over in hysterics.

"Go Tom!" she yells, fist-punching the air in encouragement.

Tom goes. He doesn't slow down, sprinting the last few yards before pummelling into the black-clad security guards nearest him. Meeting a wall of solid muscle, however, stops him in his tracks. I can hear him screaming, beckoning Tom Cruise over - as one does, Jess points out later, - but the actor's jaw is hanging open in a shocked expression and his stance has changed. He's getting ready to bolt.

His personal security usher him away as our friend continues to yell, waving his hands above his head, until they are forcibly shoved behind his back and a set of cuffs finally restrains him.

"Oh shit," Jess wheezes, unable to catch her breath. I glance down at her and my shoulders start to shake. Within seconds, we are both laughing hysterically, while the crowd around us tuts disapprovingly at such an outrageous display of lack of self-control.

Between us, Jess and I scrape together Tom's bail money. Leo offered to pay, but I refused. I had called him on the way to the police station.

"Don't you worry," I tell him, "Tom's going to pay every cent back."

"Damn right he is," Jess agrees as I hang up. "I can't believe the idiot actually did that."

"It was freaking funny, though. Should we take him out to dinner to lift his spirits? He can pay."

Jess shifts in her seat, looking uncomfortable.

"I can't," she says, "I have a whole bunch of work to do. Luke isn't happy with my lack of effort," she adds grumpily, but I have the weird feeling that she's not being entirely honest.

By the beginning of March my nerves are completely frayed; the stress and the late nights spent working finally catching up with me.

"That's it," Jess announces one afternoon, slapping her hands palm-down on the desk where we are working side-by-side. "Game Night is on this Friday, come hell or high water; I need a break."

"From what I hear you've hardly been slaving over your studies," Tom yawns from across the table. I frown in confusion as a red stain suffuses Jess's cheeks.

"What do you mean?" I ask Tom. He just shrugs, sticking his handsome head back into the textbook open before him. I know things must be bad if Tom is applying himself. The pressure of this year is getting to everyone. I glance between him and Jess. It's the first time I've spent time with them together in ages, but there seems to be an icy chill between them.

"Have you been partying?" I ask Jess dubiously.

"A bit," she admits.

An obvious snort comes from Tom's textbook.

"What?" Jess snaps.

"If you call going down to the pub almost every night 'a bit', then that's your business," he drawls, leaving the implication hanging.

"Jess?" I ask.

"Okay, a few times. It's hardly every night," she adds, glaring at Tom. He doesn't even lift his head.

"But you've cancelled Game Night so many times! I thought you were working!"

"Well I'm not cancelling this week! Besides, it's not like you've minded." I flinch at that. It's true, I've been nothing short of relieved for the extra time to work on my thesis and spend a few precious hours with Leo but Jess's sudden anger is so unexpected. She seems to realise this and adopts a friendlier tone. "So we're on for Friday?"

"Definitely." I nod.

"Tom?" she asks, glaring at the top of his head.

He peers at us over the book, looking more like his usual self.

"I wouldn't miss it."

Friday dawns and I drive into college with Leo. Due to my erratic hours lately I've been taking my own car or catching a cab home when I run expectedly late. Leo has been unbelievably understanding and just feeling the warmth of his hand on my thigh makes me wish this academic year was over.

"I cannot wait for London," I sigh, leaning over to rest my head on his shoulder. He drops a quick kiss on my forehead before turning his attention back to the road.

"I've been thinking," he says, and I raise my head to look up at him. "After London, when we get back... maybe I should put my apartment on the market."

I lean back slowly, sitting straight up in my seat. Leo risks a quick glance at me, trying to gauge my reaction

"I mean, I spend all of my time at your place and I just... it might be easier if we..." he trails off, his eyes flicking between me and the road. "Oh God," he groans, "you're not saying anything. Forget I mentioned it. Let's just rewind back to London and how excited you are about our trip."

"Are you asking me to move in with you?" I ask, and he hears the delighted teasing in my voice. "Well, technically, I'm asking if *I* can move in with *you*. Officially, that is."

It makes perfect sense. It's still a while away, but, after the summer, Leo and I will have been dating for a year, not that it matters. The heart doesn't beat to an appropriate clock. I love him. I want nothing more than to be with him and the more permanent, the better.

"I would love that," I say simply.

"It's my cooking that sealed the deal, isn't it?" he teases as we pull into the campus lot, but his crooked grin is impossible to miss.

I go about the day in a bubble of happiness. Not even my weekly meeting with Samantha in Dianna's office can dampen my mood.

"I'm impressed," Dianna says, once we've finished

presenting the week's work. "You've both accomplished a lot in a short space of time and you should be proud of yourselves." Coming from Dianna this is high praise indeed. "As you know, your final thesis will only be graded at the end of the academic year, to be counted toward your final mark, but the Burke & Duke selection committee will make their decision at the end of next quarter so the two of you need to be ready by then. They understand that they will only see the provisional draft, but I would like you to treat this as though it is your final. Don't let me down." Samantha and I both nod solemnly and Dianna smiles. "Now go and enjoy your weekend, I'll see you again next week."

I emerge from the campus building laden with files and textbooks and Leo rushes forward to help me.

"How did it go?" he asks as he relieves me of almost everything I'm carrying. He makes it look easy while I rub my aching back.

"Good. I just don't know how I'm going to finish by the end of next semester."

"You'll have to work through the break." He offers me an encouraging smile. "And I'm always here to help. It's only three more months of pushing and then you can relax."

"True," I sigh. I hate complaining, but I'm exhausted and the thought of spending the two-week break working isn't something I'm looking forward to, especially since Leo and I will be celebrating our six-month anniversary during that time.

"At least we have the weekend away," I say, the thought of two nights at Serenity brightening my mood considerably.

"Sarah, we can postpone that," Leo says gently. "If you have to work through…"

"No way," I state firmly, "I need to get out of here. Besides, it's three weeks away, I'll just pull a few all-nighters and get ahead of schedule."

"I'm glad to know that a dirty weekend away with me is worth your health for the next few weeks." Leo boasts as he loads my stuff onto the backseat of the SUV.

"You wish," I reply, laughing, "I'm going to spend that entire weekend sleeping."

"Even in the *Rasul?*" his blue eyes sparkle with ill-concealed mirth and my cheeks warm as I recall our last intimate experience in the steam room.

"I might be able to stay awake in the *Rasul*," I concede.

I lean back against the heated leather seat and close my eyes as Leo reverses out of the parking spot. I'd never admit it but I've grown to love his car and the luxury it offers. It certainly beats catching a cab and my Fiat, while reliable, is nowhere near as comfortable.

"Are we still on for Game Night?" Leo asks and I open one eye.

"Unless you want to call Jess and cancel?"

"Ah, hell no! I value my life."

"Then we're still on."

We stop for wine and grab a few bags of crisps to see us through and then head back to my place.

"I'm just warning you that Jess is probably going to drag us out tonight," I say as we take the short ride up in the elevator. "We haven't had a Game Night in a while and she's not going to let us off that easy. She's on a mission." In truth, even though I'm exhausted and I have a ton of work to do, I would go anyway. Jess hasn't been herself the past couple of weeks and I've had hardly any time to catch up with her. I don't know what's going on between her and Tom either, but hopefully tonight I'll get some answers. Guilt pricks at my conscience, but I push it away. I know that Tom and Jess are thrilled for me and they don't resent my relationship with Leo for a second, but I don't want to be that person who hooks up with a guy and abandons her friends.

"You know, party is my middle name." Leo gives a ridiculous disco impersonation and I laugh out loud as the elevator doors open.

I rush to take a shower and get changed while Leo prepares the snacks, which basically requires him to dump the crisps in a bowl and check that there are enough clean wine glasses. I leave the water running to heat up and pad naked down the hall to fetch a towel from the linen closet. Towels tumble to the floor in a heap when I open it. I really should repack it when I get a chance. I'm stuffing the towels back when I hear Leo's voice. Wondering if Jess or Tom have arrived early, I peek around the corner, wrapping a bath towel around my naked body just in case. Leo is standing alone in the living-room with his back to me, his phone pressed to his ear. So they haven't arrived yet. I turn to head back to the hot shower that awaits me, shivering with cold, when something in Leo's tone makes me freeze.

"Things have changed," he says flatly, "I can't let you drag this out any longer. I won't let you ruin this for me." There is a silence so deep that I fear he'll hear the frantic thudding of my heart. He turns slightly to the left and I slip back behind the wall, pressing my back against the cold surface. "You don't get to talk about her," Leo says, his voice low and threatening. Another pause and then, "Yeah, well I'm done being nice. Just stay away from me." I am so aware of him that, even with the space between us, I sense when he moves. I'm surprised he's stood still this long – he can never stay in one place when he's on the phone. Not wanting to be caught eavesdropping I bolt back down the hall. By the time he comes to check on me I'm in the shower, the warm water cascading over me doing nothing to melt the cold grasp of anxiety that has settled in my bones.

om and Jess arrive before I am out of the shower and I'm grateful for the distraction of their company, which at least keeps my mind off the strange, one-sided conversation I overheard. I keep replaying Leo's words over in my head but for the life of me I cannot figure them out. Was it an ex-lover on the phone or one of Leo's old friends – the ones he cut out of his life? And what could they possibly be threatening to ruin? I don't want to believe it could be our relationship, but if it is, surely I deserve to know what is going on?

On top of this concern I'm convinced that there is defi-nitely something going on between Tom and Jess. Usually, they're the life of any party and as thick as thieves – Tom and Jess against the world they always joke, which I usually kind of resented - but tonight they will barely even look at each other and all I want is for them to go back to the way they've always been. Things haven't felt the same between them since the day Tom was arrested for trespassing on the film set, which was the last time the three of us had been together, outside of campus. I've tried calling Jess a few times since then but she hasn't returned my calls, sending brief texts saying she's working.

"I'm on Sarah's team," Jess announces as she sets up the Charades board. Her eyes are glittering and she's even more energetic than usual, despite the fact that she refuses to even acknowledge Tom's presence.

"What's going on with you two?" I ask, keeping my voice down while the men are distracted.

"Nothing," she snaps. "I'm just sick of his constant judging. He should focus on his own life rather than getting all up in my business."

"I can hear you, you know," Tom drawls cattily. Leo, as usual, doesn't look in the least bit uncomfortable with their arguing as he opens a bottle of wine.

"Good!" Jess retorts, "then maybe you'll actually do something about it."

"I'm so sorry for trying to be a good friend, Jess. My bad! But have you even stopped to think that if you actually believed you weren't doing anything wrong you wouldn't be so secretive."

I try to wrap my head around his words. I must have missed something big, but for the life of me I can't figure out what it could be.

"Why don't *you* tell me what's going on, then?" I ask Tom, throwing discretion to the wind.

"Where do I start?" Tom says dramatically. "Well, first off, Jess is pissed because her divine crush is gay."

"He is not gay!" Jess yells, her tongue darting out to lick her lips.

"That's what this is about?" I would laugh if the situation

wasn't so absurd. "You're still arguing over that guy? It's been months!"

"His name is Jackson," Jess reminds me, "and he's not just some guy. And he's definitely not gay!" she adds, hurling the words in Tom's general direction. The cork pulls free of the bottle with an audible pop, as if adding emphasis to her words.

"Wine?" Leo asks the room at large, holding the bottle up in the air.

"I can't believe you two are fighting over a guy you don't even know," I snap, holding out my glass. Leo pours liberally, his eyes a gentle warning that my distress isn't going to help the situation.

"I do know him," Jess admits. "We've met up a few times."

"When?" I rack my brain trying to recall if she's mentioned meeting a man in the past month but nothing comes to mind. I can only assume that her recently mentioned visits to the pub had a hidden agenda.

"It doesn't matter," Jess seems to pull herself together and shakes out her arms. "I'm going to the bathroom and then we're playing. Leo, I would love a glass, thank you." She manages a small smile.

The second she's out of earshot I round on Tom.

"What the hell was that about?"

Tom looks pained. "Jackson's not a good guy, Sarah. I've heard bad things around town. Admittedly, I don't have any proof, but I've met him once or twice and I get that vibe, you know? Also, I'm telling you now, the man is gay. I've tried to talk to Jess about it but she keeps shooting me down and now she'll barely speak to me."

"Jess is too smart to fall for an idiot," I say, mostly to myself, but I know this isn't exactly true. Jess is no fool, but she's a magnet for trouble. If someone asked me to identify the serial killer in a room full of people, I'd send Jess in and pick the one she latched onto first. "Just because Jess likes bad boys doesn't mean this Jackson person is all bad," I add unconvincingly.

"Right," Tom rolls his eyes. "Look, all I know is that there are rumours doing the rounds that he's into drugs and all sorts of shady business."

"Drugs?" I shake my head, "Jess would never do drugs."

"Jess wouldn't do a lot of things - like ignoring our calls and going out without us, and yet that's exactly what she's been doing!"

I open my mouth to protest again but I can't bring myself to do it. Jess has been acting strange, to deny it would be pointless. Leo is watching me with a guarded expression.

"What do you think?" I whisper, hearing the sound of running water from the bathroom.

"I think we should keep an eye on her," Leo replies levelly. "If we don't look out for her, who will?"

"Let's just keep her calm for now, okay?" I ask Tom. "It's not worth fighting over. If she's heading for trouble the last thing we want to do is alienate her."

"It might be a bit late for that," Tom points out, but he reluctantly agrees and, by the time Jess returns, the atmosphere has lightened considerably. We manage to get through three rounds of Charades without incident, but I notice that Leo is watching Jess very closely, a small frown pulling between his eyes.

As the red wine warms my chest, I find myself relaxing. Tom is making a concerted effort to be nice to Jess and she is, if not entirely responsive, at least not casting him filthy looks.

Progress, I think. Everything will be fine - we'll work this out. We've argued before and it never lasts.

"Let's go out," Jess announces suddenly after the final game. Tom and Leo beat us three out of three games, but Jess's heart wasn't in it. She's distracted and fidgety, barely paying attention. She's also drinking far more than the rest of us, if her frequent trips to the bathroom are anything to go by.

"What exactly do you think she's doing in there?" Tom hisses after the fourth trip. His eyes are dark with worry, but there's also an angry set to his jaw.

"She wouldn't be doing drugs in my bathroom!" I reply, praying that the words are true.

"Well, unless she's suddenly developed a weak bladder, something's going on."

"I think Tom might be right," Leo says gently, mindful of my rising fear. "She's not herself."

"She's not going anywhere without us," I reply determinedly.

We've all been drinking so we catch a cab downtown. Jess practically falls onto the sidewalk, Tom's lightning reflexes the only thing keeping her steady. She shrugs off his helping hand and struts inside with barely a backward glance.

The music inside the club is loud and pounds painfully inside my skull. I haven't had enough to drink to really enjoy this and I'm worried about Jess. I wonder if being with Leo is changing me, feeling slightly guilty that I'm not having as much fun as I normally would, and that I didn't notice Jess's erratic behaviour earlier, but I quickly push the thought aside. I'm tired and antisocial because my thesis is sapping every waking hour of my day, and, if anything, Leo helping at home makes my life a whole lot easier. God knows what I'd do without him.

"Oh hell," Tom mutters behind me and I turn to him questioningly. "That's him." He points at the bar but I already know who he's talking about because Jess has rushed over to throw her arms around the stocky, raven-haired man lounging arrogantly against it.

"Jackson, I presume?" I ask and Tom nods. Even from here I can see the double, studded earrings in his ears and the ink trailing below the tight sleeve of his T-shirt. "Let's just keep an eye on her," I mutter, heading for the opposite end of the bar. We watch for a while, sipping our drinks slowly. Jess doesn't even acknowledge us and she's openly making out with Jackson now.

"This makes me really uncomfortable," Tom says after about half an hour of watching.

"Agreed," I say.

"It doesn't look like she's going anywhere in a hurry," Leo points out, and then, getting off the bar stool, he takes my hand. "Dance with me?"

Twenty minutes later, sweaty and breathless, we leave the dance floor. Tom joined us for a while but he's disappeared and Jess is still draped over Jackson at the bar. She's chugging back a Red Bull and her eyes are unfocused. I wave, finally getting her attention and beckon her over.

"Hey!" she shrieks, descending upon us maniacally. "Where have you guys been?"

"Dancing," I say, keeping my voice light, "I have a real knack for it. Where's Tom?"

"Don't know, don't care," she slurs, waving the tin around and sloshing Red Bull over her hand. She doesn't offer to introduce us to Jackson and I don't know if I'm relieved or infuriated.

"Hey," I grab her arm as she stumbles into a couple at the edge of the dancefloor. "Maybe we should get you home, Jess." I've never seen her like this – so drunk and out of control. I notice Jackson watching, a Cheshire cat's grin on his face and when he sees me looking, he winks. It makes me feel dirty. What on earth does Jess see in this guy?

"Home?" Jess laughs, the sound thick and unnatural. "I'm not going home!" To my horror, her eyes roll up in her head momentarily and she stumbles again. I don't understand how she deteriorated so quickly and I have the sickening feeling that maybe Tom is right about the drugs. I look around trying to find him, but he's nowhere to be seen.

"Yes, Jess," Leo interrupts, his brow furrowed, "you are." He seizes her by the wrist, none too gently, and starts making his way toward the exit. I almost expect Jackson to intervene, but he watches us go, unperturbed, and I feel the fury rise in my chest. He doesn't give a shit about Jess. Turning back I see that I've lost them in the crowd and I struggle to keep up, pushing through the crush of bodies.

I can't see Jess's face but, from the back, it looks as though she's going along with Leo willingly. Then the crowd parts briefly and I notice that her feet are dragging behind her. Leo must be supporting most of her body weight. I move faster, shoving people aside in my haste to catch up.

The fresh air assaults me the second I step outside and I gulp in a few deep breaths. It's colder than I remember and my breath billows in plumes of white smoke. I cast a frantic look around and spot Leo a few yards away engaged in a tussle with Jess, who is obviously protesting their sudden exit. Thankfully the icy air seems to have sobered her up, enough for her bolshiness to have returned in force, anyway. I swallow a sigh of relief and hasten over. As I reach them Leo is trying to draw her further away from the exit, away from the prying eyes of the crowds who have come outside for a smoke.

"I'm fine," Jess insists, yanking her arm back. So typically Jess. Even drunk she insists on her independence, although I can't help wondering whether, if Mr Vodka-Red-Bull were around she would refuse his help. I am about to ask when her eyes glaze over, and, with the faintest, most terrifying sigh, her legs collapse beneath her. She slumps for just a second in a kneeling position, before her eyes roll back and she hits the ground.

"Jess!" I rush forward. Her eyes are closed. I've never seen Jess pass out, from drinking or anything else. "How did she get like this so fast? We left her alone for like twenty minutes!"

Leo kneels at Jess's side, his eyes relaying a deeper emotion than my own concerned amusement.

"Would drugs make her pass out?" I ask. My limited knowledge doesn't include frequent known side-effects

"I don't think it's that simple," Leo murmurs. He feels gently for Jess's pulse and my heart-rate spikes.

"Why are you doing that?" I ask, a feeling of dread coming over me. Leo doesn't answer, completely focused and I snatch up Jess's other hand. It's cold and clammy. "What's going on?" I demand, but Leo holds up a hand, silencing me immediately. He lowers his head to Jess's chest and listens for a long drawn-out minute.

"What's wrong with her?" I repeat.

"Phone 911, Sarah," Leo announces suddenly, without a trace of humour. "We need an ambulance here, now."

CHAPTER 22

The ten minutes we spend waiting for the ambulance to arrive are the longest ten minutes of my life. Leo doesn't speak to me once, all of his attention on Jessica. Every few minutes he feels for her pulse, watching his wristwatch as he does so. I don't ask him what's wrong with her. She's pale and still unconscious, and, despite my craving for information, I am too frightened to ask again.

The sound of the sirens is the sweetest thing I've ever heard and I watch with relief as the flashing lights draw nearer.

"Sarah!" Leo's voice interrupts my daze. "Flag them down!" He is so calm under pressure and, grateful for something to do, I step onto the street, into the path of the ambulance, waving both hands in the air. It pulls up onto the curb drawing the attention of the nearby crowd of people. Curious, they shuffle forward, craning their necks to see what is going on, but I don't pay any attention as two paramedics leap onto the tarmac beside me and immediately move toward where Jess is lying. Both are dark-haired and of average height, but one is wearing glasses, making him distinguishable from the other. He meets Leo's eye and falters for a second, but recovers quickly.

"Leo." I hear his single-word greeting and watch in confusion as he inclines his head toward Leo before dropping to his knees beside Jess.

Leo doesn't respond. Instead, he says, in a voice I have never heard before, "She's been drinking all night, including a lot of Red Bull and she may have taken drugs." I cringe at his bluntness but I don't contradict the statement. The truth is he's probably right and now is not the time to worry about Jess's reputation. A titter runs through the gathered crowd and I fight the urge to scream at them. This tragedy isn't gossip and the fact that they find it entertaining makes me sick to the stomach.

"Her pulse is fast and I listened to her chest," Leo continues, throwing out facts with complete calm. "Her heart-rate is definitely out of rhythm. I can't be certain," his eyes flicker briefly toward me, "but I think it may be an atrial fibrillation."

The entire time he is speaking, the paramedic is assessing Jess, following the same pattern Leo did. At the words "atrial fibrillation" he lifts his head from her chest abruptly and gestures for his crewmate to assist. Between them they lift Jess off the ground and carry her over to the waiting ambulance. Leo follows behind.

"Drip," the first paramedic instructs and the second starts prepping without question.

"Matt," Leo breaks his silence. "While he's prepping the electrolytes, run an ECG, will you? Just to be sure."

I stand, frozen, as the man named Matt nods, reaching for

leads and stickers. The doors slam as they cut open Jess's tank top and, with a whirr of the sirens, the ambulance pulls away.

Leo doesn't hesitate. He grabs my hand and hauls me down the street, flagging down the first cab we see. He barks my address at the driver, tells him it's an emergency and hands over a twenty for good measure. Catching sight of my panic-stricken face he takes hold of my hand again and gives it a reassuring squeeze. "Don't panic," his voice is level and soothing, "she's going to be okay." The words are clichéd and contrived – something you say to make someone feel better, whether or not you believe them yourself.

"What is it? What's wrong with her?" I try to recall the exact words he used but my mind draws a blank.

"I can't be sure, Sarah. We'll know soon enough." He fixes his eyes on the road ahead, seemingly unable to look at me.

"You seem to know a lot more than you should." I can't help myself and the words are cold and accusing.

Leo shakes his head, opens his mouth as if to explain and then shuts it again. Choosing the lesser of two evils he returns to discussing Jessica's condition.

"It's hard to explain, but basically it's an electrolyte problem. The booze and drugs in Jess's system may have created a short circuit in the electrical pathway of her heart. It may not be pumping properly."

"Is she going to die?" I find that my mouth forms the words even though I cannot accept them.

"Her blood pressure is low and her heart-rate's skyrocketed, but she should pull through. We caught it quickly and she's getting the best treatment."

Even through my panic, the word 'we' jolts me. I don't think he intended to say it – to lump himself in with the emergency services – but he did and the words were natural, almost habitual.

"You knew," I mutter, roused from my stunned silence. "You knew what it was. You knew she needed to get to the hospital. How... how could you possibly have known that?" Had Leo been a paramedic before? And if so, why wouldn't he tell me?

"I think we should discuss this later, Sarah. Once we know how Jess is doing."

"No," I shake my head at him. "No! We discuss it right now. Atrial fibrillation," I pull the term triumphantly from my memory, "that's not exactly something you learn in your average high school biology syllabus. How *did* you know, Leo?"

"I..." he curses, the word filling the space of the moving cab and raising the tension even higher. The cabbie casts me a concerned look in his rear-view mirror. "Not now, Sarah," Leo repeats, as the driver swings the wheel and makes a tight left turn. I slide across the seat toward Leo, but the second we're on straight road again, I shift away from him.

"We're almost there," Leo speaks again and I recognise the familiar views of my neighbourhood. I sit in stunned silence, my brain trying to process this new information and what it could mean.

I leap from the cab as soon as it stops, reaching the Porsche seconds before Leo, who stops to pay the fare.

"Keep the change," I hear him say, and then he is there, unlocking the car and we both tumble inside. We don't speak a word as Leo navigates the roads at alarming speed.

It's a merciful relief when we finally pull into the hospital parking-lot. Leo screeches the Porsche to a halt in one of the parking spaces reserved for emergencies and medical professionals. At this moment I don't give a damn that another patient could be affected by our discourtesy, I only care about Jess. I scramble out of the car, leaving my purse on the seat, but Leo still reaches the automatic glass doors before me. He gestures me through first though, ever the gentleman, even in a crisis, and I fight the urge to laugh. Or punch him in the face.

The reception table is a broad half-moon manned by two identical, immaculate dolls with all the poise and grace under fire that one would expect of hospital staff; the same courteous detachment displayed by the paramedics earlier and by Leo when he spoke to them.

"Jessica Atkins," I manage, looking between the two interchangeable women. "She was brought in just a few minutes ago?" The brunette on my left gives me a patient smile and taps a clean fingernail to her screen. The brunette on the right, however, has spotted Leo and her words, when they come, fill my ears with a statement that brings my world crumbling around me.

"It's nice to see you again, Doctor Russell."

"Julie," Leo nods, his voice clipped. To my credit, I don't react. I don't take my eyes off the woman on the left who is now squinting at her screen with zero-urgency. "We don't have time for this," Leo insists. Brunette number two flushes under his scrutiny, her fingers taking flight across the screen as she tries to find information on Jess. "They'll have her in the ER," Leo says, finally dragging his eyes to mine. "You wait here, I'll go and see what's happening."

Somehow, my feet drag me to the uncomfortable sofas in the reception lounge. The inquisitive stares of the women follow my progress, but from here I can only see their eyes over the high counter of the reception table. I get the sense that below my line of vision their lips are moving – talking about me, talking about Leo. My gut churns with fear for Jess. If Leo's expression back at the club was anything to go by this is serious. If only I had been with her, if I hadn't left her alone. Usually, though, Tom was Jess's wingman. *Oh God! Tom*! I should let him know what's going on but I've left my purse back in the car with my phone tucked safely inside it and Leo has disappeared with the keys.

Doctor Russell. She called him Doctor Russell. There's no way I imagined that and no way she was mistaken. Leo knew her, he called her by name – Julie. He knew Matt, the paramedic, too. The memory of Hannah, Dylan's posh girlfriend, flashes through my mind. "Have we met before?" she had asked. Leo had denied it, but I remember his discomfort under her scrutiny. Hannah sells medical equipment – her clientele would include doctors.

I sit in the eye of a private storm, my concern for Jess and the secrets Leo has so obviously been keeping tumbling around my brain on an endless spin cycle. I need to do something, to speak to someone, but fear and solace holds me back. Fear for my friend and fear that the man I am falling for is not what he seems. So, instead, I simply sit – sit and watch and wait. Helpless.

After what feels like an eternity I hear the soft fall of footsteps on the polished, clinically white tiles.

"She's going to be okay," Leo says as soon as he reaches me.

"She's stable." His face is weary and guarded, but the news he brings is enough to buoy my spirits.

"Can I see her?"

"She's been taken to High Care but I've arranged for you to see her. Just for a few minutes," he adds apologetically. I don't ask the obvious question. I need to focus on one thing at a time and Leo's authority in this hospital is not something I can deal with before I see for myself that Jess is okay.

Leo leads me past the quizzical look of the receptionists to the elevators and presses the button for the second floor.

"Sarah," he says, the minute the doors close on us. He steps instinctively toward me but I hold up a hand to keep him at bay.

"Don't," I plead. "Not now."

He falls silent and I take a deep, steadying breath. The elevator emits a soft ping and I am out of the doors before they've even opened fully.

"This way." Leo gestures with a sweep of his arm and I head in that direction, reading the overhead signs as I go. We reach the High Care unit and I pause outside the automated doors. They don't open. A nurse glances up from the nurse's station just inside and, at a nod from Leo, she presses a button which opens the doors.

"Doctor." The nurse nods as we pass and a tide of nausea washes over me. I think I might be sick, but I swallow down the bile rising in my throat and keep my head held high. My legs are moving of their own accord, step by step through the silent ward, until finally we reach Jess's room. She's alone, a single empty bed opposite and when she sees me, she manages a tired, sheepish smile.

"How are you feeling?" I ask, approaching with caution,

intimidated by the machines monitoring her heart-rate, her blood pressure and other things I don't understand. Out of the corner of my eye I see Leo checking the monitors, running a practiced eye over the high-tech equipment. Doctor Russell – a man I don't recognise.

"I've been better," Jess admits. Her hair is escaping her traditional messy bunches and her eyeliner is streaked so far down her cheeks she could pass for a member of KISS.

"What happened?" I ask firmly. I don't want to be cruel in the face of her recent ordeal, but I demand the truth. Jess lowers her gaze, picking nervously at the crisp white sheets. "Jess?" I prompt.

"I took something," she finally admits, speaking so softly I have to strain to catch the words.

"Drugs?" My voice is a whip cracking in the quiet room and she winces. I look to Leo for confirmation and he gives a small nod of his head.

"Apparently they're not very good for you," Jess mumbles and I'm relieved to see how shame-faced she is.

"What happened?"

"Something called an amniotic vibration, I think."

"An atrial fibrillation," Leo corrects, almost automatically. We both glance across at him but he offers nothing more.

"What I meant," I continue coldly, addressing Jess, "is *how* did this happen?"

"Beats me if I know," Jess shrugs. "Apparently too many Red Bulls don't mix well with the odd recreational drug."

"Jess…"

"I got it from Jackson, okay. I wanted to impress him and, before you tell me he's no good for me, I've figured that out all by myself. Spare me the lecture will you, Sarah." Tears well in her eyes and her mouth contorts with the agony of keeping them in. I bite my lip to keep from saying something I might regret.

"Where's Tom?" Jess asks, in a voice that is too small to possibly belong to her. "I think I owe him an apology."

"He doesn't know you're here yet but I'm pretty sure an apology will be the last thing on his mind when he hears what's happened."

"Dude," Jess manages a wry grin, looking a little more like her usual self, "it's Tom!"

"True," I relent, "so it'll be the second thing on his mind. The first will obviously be getting the number of any cute male nurses."

Jess perks up. "Did you see any?"

"You're impossible."

"I know." To my absolute horror she loses the battle with her emotions and the tears spill over, tracking a sad, sorry path through the mascara-streaks on her cheeks. "I'm sorry, Sarah," she gulps.

To hell with the machines. I scoot up onto the bed beside her and hug the parts I can reach.

"I love you," I say, "and I swear to God if you ever do anything like this again I'll kill you myself."

CHAPTER 23

By the time I've retrieved my phone and updated Tom on Jess's condition, convinced him not to race over to the hospital and explained that none of this is his fault, we're almost at my apartment. The tension in the car is so thick I could cut it with a knife. Leo glances across at me as I slip the phone back into my purse, waiting for me to go first. I take a second to mentally prepare myself and then I meet his eyes briefly.

"Spill," I say.

"I'd far rather have this conversation when we get home, Sarah."

"Home?" I laugh, a dry, rasping sound. "You mean to my place – which you're no longer welcome in unless you tell me the truth right now."

"It's a very long story." A pause, and then, "I don't really know where to start."

"How about at the part where you're a doctor?"

"Surgeon."

"What?"

"I'm a surgeon. I *was* a surgeon," he corrects. "A trauma surgeon."

"Go on," I snap after a moment's silence. Leo scrubs at his face, the five o'clock shadow darkening his jaw visible even in the gloomy interior of the car.

"I did my residency at Jansens," he names the very hospital we've just come from, "and I was good enough at my job that they offered me a shareholding. Up until a few months ago I held a place on the board."

"What happened a few months ago?"

"I resigned."

"That's not an answer and you know it."

"Sarah, look, I know you're upset, but this isn't who I am anymore. I changed; I told you that part."

"Do you want a medal?"

"Don't be like that."

I curb my anger. "Why did you resign?"

"I didn't want to do be a doctor anymore."

"That doesn't make any sense."

"It does to me. You said it yourself – we only have one life. I'm trying to make every second count. And I am sorry I didn't tell you, but this has nothing to do with *us*." The word hits me like a punch to the gut.

"How can there even be an 'us' if you can't be honest with me?"

"I never lied to you."

"Don't! Don't you dare use that line. Keeping the truth from me is the same thing as lying to my face."

"It's nowhere near the same thing!"

"It is, it's exactly the same. Why the hell would you

register as a first year architectural student when you have a PhD anyway?"

"I told you, I changed. I wanted a new career."

"Changed *how*?" I am done tiptoeing around the subject and Leo seems to sense it.

"I used to be different," he hesitates, not sure how to continue. "I wasn't a very nice person. The money, the status…"

"This car?" I know I'm being petulant but I can't help myself.

"Yeah, this car," he nods angrily. "I just didn't want to live like that anymore."

"*Why?*"

"I just didn't!" We've arrived at my block and Leo pulls up to the curb. He leaves the engine running for the heat, but shifts the car into neutral and turns to face me. His eyes are bruised, haunted, but his words ring true.

"Okay," I say, rubbing my temples, "so you wanted a change. But to give up your career – one that would've taken you years to build? Why not just downscale - do some *pro bono* work; join Doctors without Borders or whatever it's called – why change your entire life? And, more importantly, why not just tell me?"

"I don't know," he admits. "Maybe I didn't want you to know what I was like before."

"Do you even *hear* yourself? You didn't want me to know that you were successful? That you saved lives? That just doesn't make sense."

"I know!" He is practically yelling and the shock must show in my face because he turns away, squeezing his eyes shut in frustration. "I'm sorry, Sarah, I'm just… this isn't how I wanted you to find out."

"Were you ever going to tell me?"

"What do you think?" His eyes are challenging now.

"I don't know what to think."

"Sarah," he takes my hands. "I don't know if I'm going to become an architect. I don't know if this is something I want to do for the rest of my life. This year was supposed to be a sabbatical – a chance for me to reassess and find out what I really want." He gives a hollow chuckle. "And do you know the only thing I know for sure?"

"What?" The word is a whisper of breath.

"That I want you. You are the one thing I am sure of. You're the last thing I planned for, but the only thing that matters. I'm in love with you, Sarah, God help me."

He falls silent and I feel the burning prick of tears fill my eyes.

"Please say something," Leo says eventually.

"You should've told me," I murmur, but I don't pull my hands away.

"I should have told you," he agrees. "But you can't tell me that this changes how you feel about me. Everything I am – everything we are – that's real! Me being a doctor before doesn't change that."

I digest this. He should've told me, but in truth he's committed no crime. I don't like secrets but does this change the way I feel about him? The answer is a resounding NO. He was a doctor, he's not anymore. He didn't like who he was so he made an effort to change, and that, in itself, is admirable. I have a sudden yearning for Jess and Tom and their zany, tactless logic, but the thought of my best friend in the hospital only makes my heart heavier.

"I'm so tired," I say, my voice small and unsure.

"I know." He sounds just as pained. "I'm sorry. I am so, so sorry."

"Would you have told me?" I ask again, needing to be sure.

"We wouldn't have had much of a future if I didn't," he replies levelly. "And I want a future with you, Sarah." There is no deception in that statement, it is pure truth, but I still want to hear him say it and he seems to sense this. "Yes," he says, emphatically, "I would have told you."

I watch the hope fade from his eyes as I slowly withdraw my hands.

Every movement is torture but I force myself to pick up my purse and meet his eyes. "I need time to think. I hope you understand."

"Of course," his voice catches slightly. He leans forward, automatically, to kiss me goodnight, but seems to remember himself and straightens up. The space between us burgeons, transcending physical distance until it feels as though we're miles apart.

"Thank you for all you did for Jess tonight," I say as I step from the car.

"I'm still a doctor," he smiles sadly. "I took an oath." As I close the door I hear his final words and my heart twists into a painful knot. "Don't give up on us, Sarah."

CHAPTER 24

*J*ess is full of beans the following afternoon when I pop in to visit her. It's Saturday, so the hospital is busy, but she's been moved to a private ward, courtesy of her father's perpetual generosity.

"He just left," she confides. "Thank God for the Hippocratic oath. I told him I ate a bunch of bad oysters. He wanted to sue the restaurant."

"How did you get around that one?"

"Easy," she grins wickedly, "I told him Tom made them."

"Did someone mention my name?" Tom sweeps into the room, his usual immaculate self. He also makes no effort to keep his voice down and a passing nurse throws him a filthy look as she passes the open doorway.

Oblivious, Tom makes his way over to stand on the other side of Jess. He takes in her bloodshot eyes, her pale skin and the fuzzy tangle of her hair. I notice the twitch in his jaw and a brief flash of anger at what Jackson's done to her, cross his face, before his usual bored expression falls back into place.

"God, you look awful," he exclaims.

Jess, however, doesn't laugh as she usually would. She looks embarrassed, not quite meeting his eyes.

"I'm sorry," she mutters, and in her defence she certainly sounds it. Her words are high and stilted as if she's trying not to cry.

"For what, exactly?" Tom asks gently. "Unless, of course, you're apologising for subjecting us to this bird's nest." He tugs at the knotty mass on top of her head.

"You were right about Jackson. You tried to warn me…" At her words I wonder how much I've actually missed about what's been going on between them. They must have discussed this Jackson character endlessly and in a lot more detail than I originally thought.

"You were right too," Tom says, brushing aside Jess's guilt. "It turns out Jackson is bisexual, so technically he's not gay, as I insisted. Looks like we were both right."

I can see how desperately he wants her to forgive herself, but Jess isn't letting herself off that lightly. "You told me he was trouble."

"Yes," Tom agrees, sitting down on the bed beside her without any regard for the tubes in her arm. One of the machines emits a frantic beeping sound but Tom doesn't even look up. "I did tell you that. And you should've listened. But when you told me to piss off and mind my own business I should've known better. I shouldn't have left you with him last night," his voice breaks and he takes Jess's hand and lifts it to his lips, giving it an emphatic kiss. "I guess we're both idiots. It's a good thing we have Sarah to balance us out."

"Me?" I scoff. "I'm the worst friend ever. I didn't even know what was going on."

"To be fair, the gloriousness that is Leo would distract even the purest of us," Tom says.

My face falls at the mention of his name, something my best friends don't miss, even through their mutual commiseration.

"What happened?" Jess asks, sitting up straighter in her bed.

"Trouble in paradise?" Tom is positively euphoric at the prospect of scandal – anything to distract him from feeling bad about himself for an extended period of time.

"Leo's a doctor," I blurt out. There's no easy way to put it. "A surgeon, actually. He's a shareholder in this hospital." Neither Tom nor Jess react to this save for their twin expressions of shock so I continue, the words tumbling out of my mouth in a confusing mess. "He says he didn't like who he was, that he wanted to make a change, so he left and enrolled in Holmes."

"A doctor?" Tom rolls the words out slowly.

"A surgeon!" Jess corrects, but she doesn't sound angry or indignant. If anything, she sounds kind of impressed.

"What kind of surgeon?" Tom asks.

"A trauma... wait, that's not the point, you guys! The point is that he lied to me."

"Well, not really," Jess points out. "I mean, did you ever actually ask him 'Hey Leo, are you a doctor?'"

"Jess!" I snap, not in the mood for games.

"Being a surgeon isn't the worst crime in the world," Tom adds. "I mean, maybe if he was married and didn't tell you, or if he didn't mention he was an alcoholic or that he used to be a woman – that would be unforgiveable, but really, there's nothing wrong with being a doctor."

"Surgeon," Jess corrects, but we ignore her.

"Exactly!" I tell Tom. "So why wouldn't he tell me?"

"Maybe he wanted you to love him for who he is, not what he is?" Tom is getting carried away, "like when Damon lied about meeting Elena first, because he wanted her to…"

"He didn't actually lie," Jess interjects heatedly, "he just made her forget. And she remembered eventually, when she became a vampire."

"Guys, this isn't about *The Vampire Diaries*! It's about my life!"

"Okay, fine!" Jess raises her hands in surrender. "It is kind of a big deal that he didn't tell you, but come on Sarah – he's a surgeon! And he's hot," she adds. Tom nods sagely at this, as if it concludes the matter. "How did you find out, anyway?" Jess asks. I give her a meaningful look. "Oh, God," she gasps, hand flying to her mouth. "Did he see me naked?"

"Wait," Tom is trying to keep up, "do you mean to tell me that Leo treated Jess last night?"

I nod. "Outside the club. She wasn't conscious, I would've thought she'd just passed out but he said it was serious… he told me to call 911."

"Wow." Tom has lost his habitual cool.

"Wow." Jess echoes.

Now that I'm saying it out loud I realise how big a deal it actually is. Leo probably saved Jessica's life last night. The reality of that fact hits me full force. No matter how angry I am at him, he saved my best friend's life.

"He told me he loves me." I say it almost without thinking. Probably because it's all I can think about. Leo and I have only been dating for a few months but I can't bring myself to discard his words as lip service. He meant it. I know that he meant it and I know that it's real, because deep down, even though I don't want to admit it, I feel the same way about him.

For once, Tom and Jess have no glib remarks.

"And you?" Jess asks eventually. "Do you feel the same way?"

"Insta love?" We have scoffed at the trope so many times together that I can barely believe she's even asking me. "Jess, it's not possible." She doesn't correct me but she doesn't agree either. Her caramel eyes are sparkling with knowledge – the clarity that comes from being on the outside and looking in. "I mean; we've only known each other a few months…" I trail off as it hits me just how pointless my denial would be.

"What's that got to do with it?" Jess smiles.

"Oh shit!" I put my head in my hands.

"She loves him," Jess announces triumphantly.

"You could do a lot worse," Tom consoles me, putting his arm around my shoulders and pulling me against him. "A hot doctor is hardly something to be embarrassed about."

"Surgeon," Jess corrects.

They are still pointing out the pros and prospects of dating a surgeon – the part about him resigning seems to have slipped their minds - when Jess's real doctor walks into the ward. He's older, with tufts of greying hair and the build of a once athletic man going to seed. His name badge identifies him as Doctor Fraser. He nods at Tom and I over his glasses but doesn't send us away.

"How are you feeling, Miss Atkins?" he asks, picking up her chart.

"Much better."

He scans the data print-out and then sets the file back on

LISSA DEL

the table apparently satisfied with what he sees. "Ready to go home?"

"Can I?" Jess's euphoria brings a small smile to his lips.

"You'll need a final ECG and a heart scan first, just to be sure there's nothing ominous going on, but, with any luck, I'll be signing your discharge papers before supper time."

"Hallelujah!" Jess flops back on the pillows contentedly.

"There are a few things we need to discuss before I let you go," Doctor Fraser's tone carries a warning. I start to retreat slowly from the room, but Jess waves me back.

"Stay," she sighs, and then to the doctor; "you can speak freely in front of my friends, Doc. They know I've been an idiot."

"You said it," Doctor Fraser agrees, but he looks comforted. "I believe you claim this was a once-off occasion and I hope for your sake that that's the truth." He peers at Jess over his glasses as though daring her to contradict him. Jess keeps her mouth firmly shut. "The most common cause of atrial fibrillation is stimulants," Doctor Fraser resumes, "so stay off the Red Bull, too much caffeine and any recreational drugs."

"And ordinary alcohol?" Jess asks in a small voice, sounding like a child in danger of having her favourite toy confiscated.

Doctor Fraser smiles at that. "Stick to a couple of glasses of red wine and you should be just fine. It's most likely an isolated incident, but I'd prefer it if you didn't test that theory."

"Deal!" Jess agrees happily.

"Okay, then that's it from me. They'll take you down for

188

testing shortly and, once I've seen the results, and if I'm happy with everything, you'll be free to go."

"Thank you, Doctor."

"Just doing my job. Take care of yourself, Miss Atkins."

I watch his departing white coat and make a lightning decision.

"I'll be right back," I tell Jess and Tom and then slip out of the door behind him. "Doctor Fraser," I call, getting his attention.

He turns immediately. "Yes?"

"I was just wondering about the man who was checking on Jessica last night – he used to be a Doctor here – Leo Russell. Do you know him?" Is it just my imagination or does he look more guarded at the mention of Leo's name?

"Yes, I know Dr Russell," he replies.

"Oh. Well, I was just wondering if you knew why he left?"

"The building?"

"No, the hospital. Apparently he resigned." I know I'm overstepping a boundary but I have to try.

"Do you know Doctor Russell?" Doctor Fraser fires back and I sense the protectiveness of establishment closing around us. If Leo was a member of the board at this hospital, the staff are hardly going to divulge confidential information.

"I… yes, I do."

"Then I suggest you ask him," Doctor Fraser says. His reply is short and clipped, but there is empathy shining in his intelligent eyes. I flush with embarrassment all the same.

"I will. Thank you for your time."

He nods. "Look after your friend in there."

CHAPTER 25

"*D*id I tell you they cut my favourite top?" Jess grumbles. She's been camped on my couch since last night, straight from the hospital, and thus far my Sunday has consisted of running around after her and listening to a long list of grievances she's building against the hospital and its staff.

"Yes, twice. And actually, that was my top," I point out, recalling the black tank top she had been wearing on Game Night. "You borrowed it a few weeks ago."

"You see! That's even worse."

"You were unconscious and you needed to be put on an ECG, Jess. What were they supposed to do?"

"Undress me slowly? I mean, if you're going to be seeing all of this," she gestures up and down her body, "you may as well take the time to enjoy it. Speaking of which, this body needs feeding."

"There is no depth to your depravity! And if you want a sandwich go and get one. There's nothing wrong with you."

"My knees hurt!"

"So you keep saying." I roll my eyes at her. "Those aren't even bruises." Jess's knees are a little scratched from falling on the sidewalk, but the way she's going on you'd swear both of her legs were broken.

"You're not usually this grumpy," Jess whinges. "I take it you haven't heard back from the delectable Doctor?"

"Don't call him that. And no, I haven't." I had left a message on Leo's phone last night once I had settled Jess in and she had called me an idiot for cutting him off without a word, but so far he hasn't returned my call.

"Maybe you should go over there?"

"What, and leave you defenceless? Who would change the channel for you?"

"I'll be okay for an hour or two, so long as you leave a bottle of wine within arm's reach."

"You shouldn't be drinking."

"You heard Doctor Fraser – red wine is good for me."

"I don't think those were the words he used, Jess."

"Close enough. Besides, Tom's coming over later."

"Of course he is."

I get up and head for the kitchen to make her a sandwich – partly to shut her up and partly to give myself something to do. I love having Jess here, despite our frequent disagreements, but this thing with Leo is really getting to me. I haven't spoken to him since Friday night after he dropped me home and I told him I needed time to think. Not that thinking has done much good. My heart doesn't want to listen to my brain. I don't know if I'm even angry anymore, I just want to talk to him and clear all of this up.

"I have arrived!" Tom's voice calls from the hall and a

second later he rounds the corner hefting two huge carrier bags. "And I come bearing gifts!"

Jess brightens perceptively at the sight of the bags.

"What is all of that?" I ask.

"It's dinner for her highness," he says, dumping the lot on the counter beside me. Then he lowers his voice. "Jess told me you have stuff to sort out with Leo. Go. I've got this."

"I don't even know where he is," I say, but already my heart is beating faster.

"No excuses, Sarah. Go sort your shit out. It's not every day that a handsome doctor saves your best friend's life and tells you that he loves you."

"Surgeon!" Jess calls from the living room.

Tom spreads his arms in a wide arc before turning to face Jess.

"She's al-i-i-i-ve!" he sings, in a perfect Victor Frankenstein imitation.

"He's right," Jess adds, giving me a stern look. "You need to sort your shit out, girlfriend."

I don't need any further prompting. Dumping the two slices of buttered bread in the trash I head for my bedroom. As desperate as I am to see Leo, I don't think my PJs are quite the right outfit for the occasion.

Ten minutes later I'm out of the door clutching Tom's car keys. My car is in the lot downstairs and I fear the battery might have run flat from gross underuse. Tom's zippy little hatchback is parked across the street and I pull off in a jerking plume of white smoke and the awful smell of burning clutch as I try to manage the stick shift.

I head straight for Leo's apartment.

RIVEN

"Good afternoon, Miss Sarah," the doorman greets me fondly.

"Hi James! Is Leo home?"

"He's not, I'm afraid. You're welcome to wait, though." It's not like I have any idea where else he could be, so I nod and take a seat in the lobby.

As it turns out I don't have to wait long. I'm flipping idly through a magazine when I spot Leo coming up the front stairs. I scramble to my feet tossing the magazine aside. My heart catches in my chest at the sight of him and then nose-dives into my stomach when I spot the attractive brunette beside him. A part of me hopes that perhaps they both happen to live in this building and have arrived at the same time, but her body is wedged into the space beneath his shoulder and she is smiling up at something he is saying.

There's nowhere for me to hide. I consider throwing myself behind James's station but it's too late. Leo lifts his sunglasses up onto his head as he comes through the glass door, pushing his hair back off his forehead. He looks happy and carefree, and it irks me that he's not suffering in my absence. While I fret over this, Leo is still talking, perfectly at ease with the woman beside him. She sees me first, offering the polite smile one assumes for strangers and passers-by. I don't smile back. My face is frozen, my jaw stiff.

"Sarah?" Leo has finally noticed me.

"Hi," I look up at him and then back at my feet.

"What are you doing here?"

"I came to see you. I left you a message but I didn't hear back." I risk a glance at the brunette who is assessing me silently.

"I'm sorry, I didn't get any message. We left early this

193

morning and I haven't really had time to check my phone." I cringe at the carelessness of his words – the implication that he has obviously been enjoying the pleasure of the brunette's company far too much to be burdened with his mobile.

"Leo," the woman speaks for the first time and her voice is deeper than I expected and oddly reassuring. "You might want to explain me."

"What?" he looks genuinely confused.

She smiles at me, shaking her head. "Men! I'm guessing you're feeling pretty uncomfortable right about now?"

Leo looks between the two of us and understanding dawns.

"Oh! No! Sarah, this," he gestures at the two of them, "this isn't what you think. Ellen's my sister."

The whoosh of relief that flows through me is so intense I actually feel faint. Leo has spoken about his sisters a lot over the past few months but I haven't met either of them yet, despite our conversation at Christmas.

"Ellen." She sticks out her hand and clasps my own in a firm handshake. "I've heard a lot about you Sarah." Her tone gives nothing away – whether she's heard good or bad I can't tell, but I smile anyway.

"It's very nice to meet you, Ellen."

There's a small, uncomfortable silence during which Leo stares down at me.

"You said you left me a message?" he asks, his eyes never leaving mine.

"Yes." I glance at Ellen. "I wanted to talk to you. But I can come back later…"

"No!" he lowers his voice. "I mean, you don't have to go. What is it you wanted to say?"

I look toward Ellen again and she gives a knowing smile.

"I'll leave you two to it," she says.

"You don't have to go," Leo insists, but he sounds far less emphatic and he's still looking at me.

"We'll chat tomorrow," Ellen says, rising up on her toes and kissing his cheek. "It was nice meeting you, Sarah."

"You too," I reply, but she's already heading for the door, casting a concerned look over her shoulder as she hits the steps.

"What did you want to talk to me about?" Leo asks again. His face is alive with excitement, his eyes sparkling with possibility. I don't really want to have this conversation in the lobby as James watches us with all the curiosity of a man whose only entertainment is the comings and goings of the buildings' tenants. He doesn't even have the good grace to turn away.

"Can I come up?" I ask, blushing.

"Of course." Leo draws me towards the elevator. The gesture is very controlled, his fingers applying only the slightest pressure as if he's nervous to touch me, but even that faint contact sends a warm tingle up my arm.

We don't speak until the apartment door has closed behind us. Leo fetches two beers out of the fridge without asking and hands one to me. The bottle is cold against my palm and oddly calming.

"Let's sit outside," Leo suggests. It's a beautiful afternoon, only the slightest of breezes taking the edge off the heat of the afternoon sun. I don't sit. Instead, I walk to the edge of the terrace. I lean against the railing and take a swig of my beer.

"It really is beautiful up here," I say to Leo, who has come to stand beside me.

"So you keep saying."

I turn to find him facing me, one arm slung across the balcony railing. His posture is relaxed and a semblance of my favourite crooked smile plays on his lips.

"Why are you smiling?"

He shrugs. "I'm just happy."

"I know you better than that. What is it?"

"You're here." He gives me a look that is both confident and sheepish.

"Yeah, I'm here. So?"

"So," he edges closer to me, his fingers trailing the railing close to my own, "you said you needed time to think, but I figure you wouldn't be here if you'd decided you never wanted to see me again."

"How do you know I'm not here to tell you I never want to see you again?" I tease.

"Because I know you better than that."

We lapse into a comfortable silence. Leo still hasn't touched me, but his hand is resting close to mine. I resist the urge to take it.

"You should have told me," I say.

"I know." In the quiet moment that follows this admission, I look up at him as if I'm seeing him for the first time. His unnerving self-assurance, his natural competitiveness and his keen mind – it makes perfect sense now. How could I ever have deluded myself that he was simply a student – a trust-fund baby with no ambition?

"It's not something you should be ashamed of," I murmur. He cocks his head in my direction, waiting for me to explain. "You obviously worked very hard to get to where you were and you had to have been good at it, considering your age and your success. I don't understand why you would want to keep it a secret."

"I get how you would think that," he concedes finally, "but I'm not ashamed of my career. I'd like to think I did a lot of good in my time at Jansens. I just…" he takes a swig of beer, trying to find the right words. "A lot of people don't understand my decision. They're trying to talk me out of it. I didn't want you to be one of them."

I open my mouth to insist that I wouldn't, but I close it again without uttering a word. I'm already wondering why Leo would walk away from his medical career – who's to say I wouldn't have encouraged him to go back to it. If I'd learned the truth without knowing how strongly he felt about it, would I have done exactly that?

"Do you have any idea how refreshing it was to have you not know? To tease me mercilessly about my car, about this apartment? You laughed at me, not judging my decision, just being you. And letting me be me. I didn't want that to change." His eyes meet mine and darken with a challenge. He wants to know if things have changed after all. I hold his gaze, losing myself in his eyes and then finally, I speak.

"I guess I shouldn't tell you, then, that I really like your car?" I say, the teasing in my tone impossible to miss.

"I don't care what you say, so long as you forgive me."

We lapse into a comfortable silence. I still have a million questions about exactly why and how he gave up his entire career but they can wait. Leo steps closer to me, offering his hand and this time I reach for it. His fingers close around mine instantly and he tugs me toward him, spinning me around so that we can both watch the glorious view. As his arms come around me I lean back against him, my head tucked neatly into the curve of his neck. The smell of his aftershave drifts down over me and I melt against him, breathing it in.

"You saved Jess's life, didn't you?" I ask, as the sun lowers on the horizon.

"It's possible."

"Probable," I correct.

Leo nuzzles my hair, his mouth close to my ear. "I'm glad I was there."

"Me too."

He brushes a kiss across my neck. "And I'm glad you're here."

"Me too."

CHAPTER 26

"You look like a woman who's been up all night getting her brains screwed out," Jess announces the second I come through the door. She's dressed and ready for the day, grinning crazily as she watches me do the walk of shame down the hall. I have borrowed one of Leo's sweatshirts but I'm still wearing yesterday's jeans.

"We're going to be late by the way!" she yells as I scuttle into my bedroom.

"I'll be ready in five minutes!" I shout back. I've barely pulled a clean sweater over my head when she appears in my bedroom doorway.

"I'm taking it you and McDreamy sorted out your issues?"

"You could say that," I tease, and then, sniffing the air, "what is that awful smell?"

"Tom burned the dinner last night. I'm surprised he didn't set off the fire alarm."

"I suppose I should be grateful he didn't burn the place down."

"You should be," she replies, deadly serious. "Are we still going to look at the warehouse this morning?"

"Yeah. You don't have to come with me, you know. You should work on your own thesis."

"I don't feel like it."

"You're running out of time, Jess."

"I'm hoping watching you work your magic will inspire me."

"Here's hoping." I yank my hair out of my sweater and tie it in a ponytail on top of my head. "Ready!" I say, flashing her a broad grin.

I spend most of the morning on site, measuring and making notes on my final design. My project proposes tearing down most of the warehouse, but I would like to keep some of the framework and incorporate it into my design. It makes the project more difficult, but I'm hoping it will earn me extra credit for effort.

"Done!" I announce with a flourish. Jess looks up from her phone for the first time in hours.

"I'm glad I could inspire you this morning," I add teasingly. "Who are you talking to anyway?"

"No one."

"Jess?" For an awful moment I wonder if she's still in contact with Jackson, despite her assurances that he's a pig-dog who should be drawn and quartered.

"No one!" she shows me her screen as proof.

"Seriously? Candy Crush?" I shake my head and then stick out my finger and finish the level.

"How do you do that?" Jess laments. "I've been stuck on that level for weeks!"

"It's a gift."

I'm at my desktop in the library when Leo tracks me down in the afternoon. The mere sight of him brightens my mood and he looks just as excited to see me. The few days we spent apart weren't easy for either of us. Leo has a pile of books in his hands and he dumps them unceremoniously on the table beside me before pulling me up from my seat and giving me a lingering kiss. The library is empty for a change and he doesn't bother keeping his voice down.

"I missed that."

"So did I," I say, feeling the familiar lazy swirl in the pit of my stomach that only he can incite. "What's with all the books?"

"I don't know how you managed to get through first year," he grumbles.

"It can't be harder than med school."

"Ah, but in my first year I studied the human anatomy." He leans forward and trails a finger over my shoulder and into the hollow of my throat. "It was far more interesting."

My breath quickens but he doesn't go any further. I look up at him to find he's no longer focused on me. I follow the line of his sight and, to my dismay, I spot Noah standing at the end of the long table. He turns away almost immediately, but not before I catch the furious look on his face.

Leo gives a small chuckle and takes a seat at the table.

"I had better get started," he says and opens his books. "Are you still okay with going to Ellen's for dinner?" He had texted me this morning saying his sister wanted to meet me properly and of course I had said yes. She had seemed nice enough when I met her yesterday and I wanted the chance to get to know her.

"Of course."

We work side by side for most of the afternoon. Every now and again I cast a discreet look at him. Despite his protests, he is utterly focused, his pen scrawling across the page. Every few minutes he consults another book, his golden hair flopping forward. From this angle his scar is more pronounced, the ridge in his hairline clearly visible.

"I should've known you were a doctor," I say, leaning forward and tapping his notebook. "You have awful hand-writing."

"They teach us that in second year," he grins. "How are you doing?"

"I'm done for the day, I think." I stretch my neck and rotate my shoulders, trying to ease the tension that has settled in after so many hours hunched over the keyboard. "You?"

"Almost. Give me twenty minutes?" he slides his car-keys across the table.

I log off and collect my bags, dropping a kiss on the top of his head as I pass.

I dump my stuff on the back seat of the SUV and then lean up against it. It's almost dark, but even so a few stars twinkle over-head, braving the twilight.

"I see you and the first year are still getting along famous-ly." The sound of Noah's voice ruins my moment of content-ment. He is standing a few feet away, heading away from the main campus building. "Nice car, by the way." He sneers at the Porsche with envious disgust.

"Hey Noah. You on your way home?" My attempt at civility.

"Actually, no," he hesitates and then admits, almost sheepishly, "I have a date."

"How nice!"

"No need to sound so relieved," he says, but there is a pleasant teasing in his words.

"I didn't mean it like that. I'm happy for you. I'm glad you're moving on."

"I am," he nods as though the thought has only now occurred to him. "I'll see you around, Sarah."

"See you." I watch him walk away, a weight lifting from my chest. Things are definitely looking up.

CHAPTER 27

"Are you sure this is okay?" I ask Leo as we head uptown. We didn't have time to go home and change and my jeans and sneakers combination is hardly smart. At least I have a pretty floral cardigan to pull over my vest.

"It's fine," Leo doesn't even look at me to see what I'm wearing. "Ellen's very relaxed."

"What does she do again?" I know that one of his sisters is a physiotherapist, the other a teacher.

"Physio."

"Ah. Trisha's the teacher?"

"Look at you, paying attention."

"I'm a quick study, Mr Russell."

"That you are, Ms Holt."

Ellen's apartment block isn't quite as upmarket as Leo's but it's close enough. There's no doorman, at least, but as we enter the elevator and Leo presses the button for the top floor, I groan. Of course, she stays in the penthouse.

"Is anyone in your family middle-income?"

"Trisha's a teacher," he points out, and then, with a wicked grin, "but she married an attorney."

"Of course she did."

"Can I help it that success runs in my genes?" he teases.

"Easy there, Steve Jobs – you haven't even passed your first year exams yet."

Leo laughs and I try to remember everything he's told me about Ellen. She's the eldest of the siblings, a couple of years older than Leo. She's not married, but she has a long-term partner named Bruce who has been trying to coerce her down the aisle for years. They don't have any children.

The elevator opens up onto a tiny landing with only one door. Leo raps hard on the polished wood. I barely have time to smooth my hair when the door is yanked open.

"If you salt that rice one more time I'm going to cut off your balls and feed them to you!" Ellen is yelling over her shoulder. Without missing a beat she turns to face us wearing the same crooked grin as her brother. "Welcome!" she kisses Leo's cheek and then gives me a polite smile, "Come in." She sweeps us inside. The apartment is high-ceilinged and beautifully decorated, but it's inviting and reassuringly untidy. Jackets draped over chairs, shoes discarded on the floor and unfinished cups of coffee create a colourful clutter that makes me feel instantly at home. Ellen is holding a glass half-filled with wine and, without asking, she leads us to the kitchen and pours me a glass of my own.

A man who I presume must be Bruce is standing at the stove stirring the contents of a bubbling pot. He is of average height with a slight pot-belly and his hair is shaved in a manner that suggests he is hiding a bald spot. His sleepy yellow eyes, however, twinkle with humour and lust for life. As we enter, he discreetly pushes a salt cellar behind the coffee machine.

"Leo!" he roars, seizing Leo in a bear hug and clapping his back enthusiastically. "Thank God you're here. Your sister's boring me to tears."

"I saw that," Ellen reproves, lifting one finger off her glass and wagging it in the direction of the salt cellar.

"Leave him alone," Leo says, "we both know you can't cook." He winks at her and then draws me forward proudly. "Bruce, this is Sarah."

"Welcome, Sarah!" Bruce hauls me into the same bear-hug he gave Leo but thankfully minus the back-clapping. It probably would have brought me to my knees.

"Thank you both so much for inviting us."

"Don't thank us yet. So far all we have is rice and lumpy gravy."

"And the rice is probably over-salted," Ellen adds.

"Ellen says you went to Monarch's for lunch yesterday?" Bruce asks Leo and then they're off, typical men discussing food, sports and politics.

"Let's leave these two to the cooking," Ellen whispers and I follow her into the living-room. To my surprise she stops only long enough to snatch up a packet of cigarettes and then continues out onto the balcony. "Sorry, it's my guilty pleasure," she says, promptly lighting up. "Would you like one?" she offers me the packet and I shake my head. "I keep threatening to quit but Bruce says he couldn't live with me if I did. I tried once before – it lasted a week and he told me if I ever do it again he's packing his bags."

I smile. "How long have you and Bruce been together?"

"Forever. We met in high school. I was actually dating his brother at the time."

"And how did his brother take it when you and Bruce hooked up?"

Ellen pauses to flick her cigarette ash into the silver ashtray on the table.

"I think he was relieved, to be honest. He was dreadfully unhappy, but a bit of a wimp. I don't think he had the balls to break it off. Bruce did him a favour."

By the time we head back inside to refill our glasses, Bruce has managed to fry up some pork chops and boil a pot full of peas. We take our seats at the dining-room table, Leo and I sitting opposite Ellen and Bruce sitting at the head.

"It's just for show," he tells me as he takes his place. "Ellen lets me look important when we have guests over."

"Enjoy it while it lasts," Ellen quips, loading her plate.

Watching them together it strikes me that I've never seen a couple so attuned to one another. I can't help but think that if Tom and Jess ever got married, this is how their relationship would be. Ellen and Bruce's constant sniping is delightful, a playful game for two people who are obviously very much in love. You can tell by the way they look at each other, the way they subconsciously lean toward one another, that they are as close as any two people could be. And yet, despite the relaxed atmosphere, I get the sense that there is something I am missing. As comfortable as Ellen and Bruce are with one another, and as hospitable as the couple may be, I get the sense that they are watching me, assessing me. It's not something I can put my finger on, but I can't shake the feeling that, beneath their friendly manner, Ellen and Bruce are not entirely comfortable with me being here.

By my third glass of wine, however, I've convinced myself that I'm imagining things. Ellen is now smoking openly at the table and Leo and Bruce are trying to convince her that she should stop being stubborn and just marry Bruce already.

"I don't believe in marriage," is her simple answer.

"How can you not believe in marriage?" Bruce laments. "It's the ultimate commitment."

"I'm utterly committed to you," Ellen persists, "I don't need a piece of paper to prove it. Besides, I don't want to change my name."

"What do you think, Sarah?" Bruce appeals to me.

"I think there's nothing wrong with a woman keeping her name," I reply, deliberately misunderstanding the question.

"Would you keep yours?" Leo asks lazily. He's had more than a few beers so I guess we'll be calling a cab to get us home.

"Um…" I hesitate, not sure how the conversation turned on me so quickly, "I haven't really thought about it."

"I'm old school," Leo muses, his blue eyes slightly unfocused. "If we got married I'd want you to take my name." Ellen and Bruce have fallen silent and I give a nervous laugh while Leo taps the neck of his beer thoughtfully. "Would you take my name?" he asks again. I can't tell if he's teasing or not.

"I'd have to give it some thought," I say, trying to brazen it out.

"You're not marrying her." Ellen's voice has lost all trace of frivolity.

Leo's eyes slice to hers. "I didn't say I was."

"You may as well have…"

"Ellen," Bruce issues a low warning.

"No," Ellen rounds on Bruce. "This is ridiculous!"

My head spins in confusion, trying to figure out how everything went bad so quickly. Another part of me is spitting mad and I feel a rush of anger toward Ellen, who has been so lovely to my face, but obviously thinks I'm not worthy of her brother. I get to my feet stacking the empty plates. The clatter of porcelain on porcelain is too loud and I force myself to calm down.

"I'll just take these through to the kitchen," I mumble, my eyes pricking with tears of embarrassment.

"No, Sarah, you relax!" Bruce says, pushing his chair back. "I'll take those through."

"Its fine, I've got it," I insist. I'm already walking toward the kitchen. I hear the clink of glasses behind me and a moment later Bruce joins me at the sink. I switch on the tap, running water over the plates for want of something to do.

"Do you wash by hand or are you loading the dishwasher?" I ask, trying to keep my voice natural.

He opens the door of the dishwasher under the counter and starts taking the plates from me one by one.

"She didn't mean it like that, you know," he murmurs. "Sarah," his voice is kind and gentle as he straightens up and his fingers close over mine, switching the water off. I set aside the plate I'm holding and lift my eyes to his. "She didn't," he repeats. "Ellen likes you. You may not think so but..." he trails off, looking pained, as though the right words to express himself are just beyond his reach.

"It was a stupid conversation," I say. "I think Leo's had a bit too much to drink. Maybe I should just get him home."

Bruce looks at me for a long moment and then he nods and steps aside, allowing me to pass.

I leave him behind in the kitchen and head back to the

dining-room. Leo's in no state to drive and I stop in the hall to fetch my phone from my purse. I can hear the water running again in the kitchen – no doubt Bruce gets lumped with the washing-up as well as the cooking, I think spitefully. I dial the cab company, walking unenthusiastically back to the dining-room when I hear Leo's voice. I freeze, hidden behind a single brick wall, my hand dropping to my side.

"It's none of your business," Leo snaps.

"Of course it's my business," Ellen replies, "it's all of our business!"

"It's *my* life, *my* decision."

"Yes and I respect that, in case you've forgotten. I've supported you even when everyone else refused to. How long has it been since you spoke to Trisha, hmm? How many months since you cut her off? I've respected your wishes, Leo, but you can't possibly think that this relationship…"

"I love her, Ellen!" It is a desperate proclamation, one that both fills my heart with joy and terrifies me at the same time.

"I have no doubt of that." Ellen's voice is laden with disap-pointment.

"Then why are you being like this?"

"You know why, Leo."

"Well, you're just going to have to accept it. I love Sarah. And she loves me," he adds proudly, as though that fact in itself is an accomplishment.

"Does she?" Ellen asks wearily. "Does she really? Does she even know the truth?"

I wait for his confirmation, secretly hoping he'll put her in her place - that he'll tell her I know all about his past – about him being a doctor and his decision to change. Let her stew over that. Instead, Leo repeats himself.

"I love her."

A long moment and then I hear Ellen's small sigh. "The worst part is that I believe you. She's a wonderful girl, brother, but she has no idea what she's getting herself into. Either you tell her, Leo, or I will."

I wait in the hall while Leo says his goodbyes. Ellen and Bruce try to act normal, as though nothing has happened, but I can't help stiffening as they hug me goodbye. Ellen's eyes are shrewd and she gives me an almost sympathetic look but she doesn't apologise for her outburst. *Stuck up cow*, I think.

"I hope we see you again soon, Sarah," Bruce says as I pull away from him. *Over my dead body*, I think to myself, but I manage to nod in response.

I get Leo home and into bed, my heart heavy. I almost wish I'd never asked to meet his sister, because I'm pretty sure that nothing I could come up with on my own would be as awful as what happened in real life. Almost asleep, Leo pulls me up against him and I allow myself to be comforted by the warmth of his arms and the smell of him, the familiar smell of his aftershave and the faint apple of my shampoo. I wonder if he had been sober whether he would have called Ellen out on her threat to tell me the truth when he'd already done so. It hurts me that she would talk about me like that, but even worse is the fact that he tolerated it. My mind is a tumultuous sea of doubt and I stay up long after Leo's soft snores rend the air.

CHAPTER 28

*W*e drive down to Serenity on the last weekend in March. The spring quarter starts on Monday and, with the advanced placement selection only weeks away, my anxiety levels are through the roof. I worked through the break, as promised, so that I can enjoy our anniversary weekend, guilt-free, and as the warm breeze lifts my hair through the open passenger window, I feel myself relaxing for the first time in weeks.

"I can't believe we've been dating for six months," I muse, watching the City give way to budding green.

"Time flies when you're having fun." Leo squeezes my leg and I turn to peek at him, my head resting on my arm. I hadn't mentioned the conversation I'd overheard at Ellen's and, as much as it pains me, I've resigned myself to the fact that perhaps she and I just weren't destined to get along.

Ingrid, the Spa Manager, is delighted to see us, toting Leo's Platinum card, and she greets us warmly.

"Of course I don't need to explain anything to you," she

winks, as though our one-time previous visit makes us regulars, "so, I'll just show you to your villa."

We don't have the same cottage as before, but the one we are assigned is identical to the first, down to the tiny silver sugar-bowl on the left of the kettle.

"Your treatments tomorrow will be as before," Ingrid advises before she leaves. "And breakfast is served from seven-thirty."

"Thank you, Ingrid."

The second she is gone, I flop onto the king-sized bed, rubbing my cheek against the smooth cotton pillow.

"Tired?" Leo asks from the foot of the bed.

"You have no idea." I sigh. Leo chuckles and then I hear him move away. I open one eye but I don't follow him and a few minutes later the bed dips under his bulk. I snuggle into his chest.

"Where did you go?"

"I ordered our dinner in."

"You are a legend."

He kisses my forehead. "Sleep, Sarah. You need it."

I wake up to the feel of his fingers stroking my hair and I smile contentedly before I even open my eyes.

"Hey." My voice is husky from sleep. "Is it time to get up already?"

"It's time to eat. Our dinner's arrived."

The two-seater dining table beckons, but I pass it by, heading for the patio instead. Leo follows me but we have barely sat down when the sound of his phone ringing breaks the peaceful silence. Leo groans.

"Start without me," he says, loping back inside.

I pick at my food, half an ear on his conversation. I hear

the words 'hospital' and 'operation' and my curiosity is piqued. Casually I lean toward the open section of the sliding-door and Leo's voice grows louder.

"I don't know how many times I have to tell you; I won't do it. I don't care what he says." There's a pause and then, "Yeah, well I'm a surgeon too, and even if I was interested in doing it, the risks are too high."

I risk a quick glance around. Leo has his back to me and he's walking back toward the bedroom. His voice fades and I feel an overwhelming frustration. Determined, I get to my feet, but, in my haste my knee catches the edge of the table and sends my fork clattering to the floor.

"Dammit!" I curse, retrieving it and hurrying inside. I'm too late. Leo is walking toward me, his phone nowhere in sight.

"Who was that?" I ask. My contentment has evaporated, replaced by a nagging suspicion that is becoming all too familiar.

"My sister," he replies smoothly. I turn my back on him so he won't see the look on my face. He's lying.

My suspicion stands between me and a weekend of bliss. Not even the strong hands of my masseuse can relieve the tension in my body as I silently battle the feelings of mistrust building inside me. Leo doesn't seem to notice and my traitorous body responds to his every touch. Leo toys with me throughout the day – a sensual touch here, a gentle stroke there, between every treatment and over a lingering lunch in the cellar where his eyes make promises that have me squirming. By the time we enter the *Rasul* my body is screaming for release and my mind is all too happy to go along for the ride, letting Leo make love to me so passionately that it obliterates every misgiving I have, even if only temporarily.

"I love you." He breathes the words into my mouth through the heat and mist, his lips warm and wet as the water drips from his mouth into mine. He buries himself so deep within me that I cry out, my nails digging reflexively into his back and I let myself become lost in him. I let myself drown in him.

"It's a surgery only he can perform," Jess whispers confidently. "It has to be." We are sitting in Noah's lecture hall, the dull monotone of his voice washing over us. I take comfort in the fact that this is the last semester I will ever be subjected to Noah's teaching.

"I thought of that, but surely when you stop practicing you can't just flit in and out of theatre?" I reply. "Don't surgeons have all sorts of insurances and things? Those would have lapsed!"

"Maybe he kept them paid-up? Or the hospital did – maybe he's just that good." Typical Jess, always looking for the attractive option.

"That's a lot of maybes." I tap my pen on the blank page before me. "But even if that's the case, why not just tell me? Now that I know all about his past, why keep it a secret?"

Jess has no answer for this one and I drop the pen with a sigh, rubbing my temples. I look up to find Noah regarding me curiously and I paste a smile on my face.

"We'll figure this out," Jess reassures me. "Leo's one of the good guys, Sarah. I bet there's a perfectly reasonable explanation for all of this. But if you need answers we'll get them."

"How?"

"You sure you don't want to just ask him?" she repeats the same question she asked me ten minutes ago and I nod. Between the conversation I overheard at Ellen's and the telephone call on Friday night, the secrets are piling up. I'm going mental thinking about it all but I can't bring myself to bring it up with Leo. Partly because I'd have to admit to eavesdropping, and partly because I don't know if he would tell me the truth. "Okay, then we go to plan B," Jess says.

"Which is?"

She grins conspiratorially, a gleam of mischief in her eyes. "Tom."

Jess's plan consists of snooping around the hospital. The details are vague but Tom is required to wear black.

"Why don't I just walk in with a mask on my face?" he snorts, when she outlines her idea.

"Too obvious," Jess replies, completely seriously.

"They won't tell us anything," I insist, thinking back to my conversation with Doctor Fraser.

"Tom can charm the pants off any woman who lays eyes on him," Jess reminds me. Tom, who has his *Mission Impossible* face on, nods in sage agreement.

"You think this is a good idea?" I ask him.

"I think you need answers, Sarah. And if Leo's not going to give them to you, then we'll have to find another way."

CHAPTER 29

"If they ask why you want to know tell them you're a friend of his sister, Trisha, and you want to get in touch with the family," I hiss, as Tom and I walk up to the automatic doors at the Jansens Hospital. "You and Trisha are about the same age so it's not too much of stretch to believe you went to school together."

"Just leave it to me!" he snaps back. "I know what I'm doing!"

"Don't let them know you're gay!" He flaps his hands at me in a very non-straight way and I shut up. As we reach the familiar half-moon counter I veer left, pretending to be on the phone. I risk a peek at the two receptionists on duty and breathe a sigh of relief. They're not the same night-shift brunettes who were on duty when Jess was admitted.

"Hello," Tom greets them both. The woman on the left merely glances up and then continues sorting through the stack of patient files before her, but the one on the right's face splits into a beam and Tom subtly shifts his body towards her.

"Nicky?" he asks, having clocked her name badge. "I wonder if you could help me."

"Of course, Sir, what do you need?"

"Well, for starters, my name is Tom, not Sir," he is unabashedly flirting, "but I've been known to answer to both." I think he might be overdoing it a bit, but Nicky seems delighted.

"What can I do for you, Tom?" For a name with only a single syllable she manages to drag it out into a purr.

"It's about Doctor Russell," he begins, but before he can go any further, she speaks, eager to impress.

"Sure, third floor, Suite 3C."

I blink in confusion and even Tom falters. "I thought Doctor Russell was no longer practicing?" he stammers, and I turn away in dismay at his complete meltdown under pressure.

"Oh, *that* Doctor Russell," she giggles, and I relax, "sorry, but you're right. He's taken an extended leave of absence."

Tom feigns genuine disappointment, "Any idea when he'll be back?"

Nicky's eyes narrow slightly, but I can see her fighting an internal battle between wanting to please him and doing the right thing. Her companion shows no such compunction. Sliding a hand over the mouthpiece of the telephone she's now speaking into, she leans across the counter until she's under Tom's nose.

"May I ask what this is in connection with, Sir?" She deliberately refrains from calling him by his Christian name.

"I'm a friend of the family," Tom replies smoothly, "I was at school with his kid sister, Tasha."

I stifle the urge to scream. *Trisha, Tom, it's Trisha!* Fortunately, it doesn't appear these women know the difference.

"I'm in town for a visit and wanted to get in touch with her," Tom continues, "but she's unlisted. I remembered her brother worked here, so…" he lets the obvious conclusion hang in the air. It's a lame argument given that he's just admitted he knows Leo no longer practices. The bolshie receptionist seems to come to the same conclusion.

"I'm sorry, Sir, we aren't permitted to disclose any personal information about members of staff," she states bluntly. Nicky gives Tom an apologetic look.

"That's okay," Tom says, drumming his fingers twice on the polished wood surface. "Thank you for your time, ladies." He saunters away and I rush to meet him at the main doors.

"Well that didn't go as planned," Tom admits.

"You think?" I sigh. "What do I do now?"

"You ask him straight up. This is ridiculous Sarah – just ask Leo."

Over the next few weeks I try on numerous occasions to bring it up but my courage fails me. Leo is more attentive than ever, and with the deadline for my thesis submission looming, I find myself leaning more and more heavily on him for emotional support. Dianna will be submitting our final projects to the Selection committee mid-May and in the three weeks leading up to D-day I am operating on an average of three hours' sleep a night.

"You look terrible," Leo sympathises on the morning of the fifteenth, handing me a cup of coffee in bed. I accept it gratefully, wondering if the caffeine in my system will get me through the day. "How are you feeling?" he asks, climbing onto the bed beside me. The mattress groans in protest under the additional weight.

"I'm just glad it's finally here. The only good thing about having to prepare earlier than everyone else is that I can basically coast through the rest of the year."

"There's that silver lining. Why don't we go out for dinner tonight to celebrate?" It's a sweet gesture but he takes one look at my face and bursts out laughing. "Or we could just stay in," he offers. "Pizza and a movie?"

"That sounds amazing."

"Good. There's something I want to talk to you about."

"What?"

"Not now," he says, getting to his feet, "we'll talk later." He looks almost uncomfortable.

"Now you've got me worried."

"Don't worry," he gives me the benefit of his crooked grin, "it's a big day. I just wanted to mention it so I don't chicken out later."

"It's going to bother me all day."

"Well then I suggest you hurry home." He kisses me again and leaves to me to get ready.

My stomach is in knots as I enter the campus building. This thesis is the culmination of years of hard work. I've had my heart set on the Burke & Duke internship since the first day I set foot on the Holmes campus, since before I even enrolled, and it all comes down to this. If I lose, I could probably still land an entry-level position in a smaller firm, but I want to work at Burke & Duke. It's the Mecca to my pilgrimage.

"Sarah," Dianna greets me as I walk through her office door. I set down my 3D model on her desk, along with my perfectly-bound thesis document. It hits the desk with a thud and she nods in approval, but her lips are tight. She gets right to the point.

"I had a chat with one of my ex-colleagues at Burke & Duke last night. I called in to confirm the submission requirements. She had some interesting information to share."

"Oh? What is it?"

"She mentioned that one of their staff is dating someone here at Holmes." She gives me an arch look and my heart sinks.

"Noah?"

"It looks that way."

I cast my mind back to that afternoon when Noah threatened me with his friendship with one of the Burke & Duke panellists.

"Is this woman's name Amanda, by any chance?" I ask Dianna wearily.

"Indeed," she confirms. "I'm sure it's nothing to worry about, but, given your history with him, I hope you heeded my advice. Of course, our personal lives should have no bearing on our professional lives but as you know it doesn't always work that way."

"Noah wouldn't sabotage my career," I say. I cast my mind back to the last time I saw him – in the parking-lot outside this very building. He had been amicable enough toward the end, but I couldn't forget the look of anger on his face when he saw Leo and I together, or the viciousness he'd displayed the night he learned we were dating.

"Are you sure about that?"

No, not really.

"If anything were to go wrong couldn't you speak to your colleagues?" I ask nervously.

"The apprenticeship selection falls wholly under the appointed panel. My colleagues are not likely to get involved with a junior position placement and to ask them to do so would be, quite frankly, insulting. It would also reflect badly on me."

"Of course, I'm sorry. I shouldn't have asked."

"I'm sure everything will be fine, I just wanted to let you know what I'd heard."

"Thank you. I appreciate it."

The second I'm outside I call Noah's number on my phone.

"Sarah!" he doesn't sound half as shocked as I thought he'd be, hearing from me.

"Hi," I keep my voice calm, "how are you?"

"Good. What's up?"

"I… there's no easy way to say this, but I heard that you were dating someone from Burke & Duke."

"Amanda? Yeah, she works at Burke." He says it lightly but I can hear the satisfaction in his voice, knowing that he's rattled me.

"Noah, you know this internship means everything to me."

There's a long silence. "Sarah, are you asking me to influence Amanda to vote in your favour?" His indignance is so fake I feel sick.

"Of course not! I'm asking exactly the opposite."

"So you think I'd plot against you?"

"I didn't say that. I'm just asking that you don't do anything, either way. Please."

Noah laughs. "So now that you want something from me you're prepared to be nice – is that how this works?"

"I don't want anything from you, Noah. Please, just... just leave it alone. You know how hard I've worked for this."

"As has Samantha," he points out.

"Yes," I grit my teeth. "As has Samantha. I want it to be a fair fight."

"I really don't know what you expect me to say, Sarah."

"Forget it, I'm sorry I called."

"Hold on a second." When he speaks again his voice is further away. "It's my ex-," he says. I hear a woman speaking in the background and then he's back.

"I'm sorry, I have to go. Amanda isn't pleased." He hangs up and I feel the bile rise in my throat. I've just blown it.

CHAPTER 30

By the time I get home I'm fuming. Noah set me up, the bastard! I replay the conversation in my head, cringing at how it must have sounded to Amanda, who was, no doubt, sitting beside Noah throughout.

"Son-of-a-bitch!" I yell, hurling my purse at the table in the hall. It slides across the smooth surface and drops innocently to the floor with a dull thud.

"Hey!" Leo pokes his head around the corner, "what's up with you?"

"I think I just lost the internship."

"But aren't they only announcing the winner next week?"

"Noah's dating one of the selection committee."

"Only one of them?" Leo raises his brow. "He must be losing his edge."

"It's not funny."

"It's kind of funny. Hey," he pulls me toward him, his strong arms coming around my waist, "Why are you so upset?" For the briefest moment he looks horrified, as if, perhaps, I'm jealous.

"I called him," I admit, and the jealousy festers. Leo arms begin to withdraw, "to ask him not to get involved, not to influence the panel." I explain quickly and he relaxes. "She was with him." I finish.

"Oh shit!"

"Yeah."

"Surely she wouldn't be petty enough to hold it against you. I mean, you guys are over."

"It's not that. Noah made it sound like…"

"Made it sound like what?"

"Like I was trying to cheat. He twisted my words around and she was listening."

"Oh, Sarah," he sounds oddly disappointed. "Why did you call him?"

"I don't know! I just wanted to make sure he wasn't going to screw this up for me! He's been so angry, and I… I need this, Leo. I've worked for it. I could out-design Samantha with my eyes closed!"

"I know that; you don't need to prove anything to me, but bringing her down isn't the right way to go about it."

"I'm not bringing her down I'm just saying it how it is."

"Could you calm down, please, I'm not the one who got you into this mess, neither is Samantha, for that matter. Your phone call to your ex- did that."

"Seriously? You're saying this is my fault?" I pull away from him, storming through to the kitchen.

"Sarah…" he watches as I open a bottle of wine, pulling the cork out with such a vengeance that I hit my hand on the overhead cupboards. "Maybe you shouldn't drink that. I know you've had a bad day but drinking isn't going to fix anything."

"A bad day?" I laugh, sloshing wine into my glass. "It's a bit more than just a bad day."

"I know, and I'm sorry. I don't want to make it worse, but I do need to talk to you, remember?" In all the drama with Noah I'd forgotten about his words this morning. It had seemed like a big deal at the time, but now all I can think about is how I've screwed up my career. "There's something I've been wanting to tell you but I didn't want to do it until your thesis was finished," Leo continues hesitantly.

"So talk," I splay my hands in front of me. "I'm listening. My thesis is finished, as is my career, probably, so I have all the time in the world."

"Not until you've calmed down."

"I'm calm. What is it you want to tell me, Doctor Russell?" Usually I use the term as an endearment, but this time I throw it in his face and he flinches visibly.

"Sarah, this is serious. Could you please calm down? I can't talk to you when you're like this."

"Oh, I'm sorry, Leo. I didn't mean to make everything about me. We should focus on you and your issues." It comes out acid on my tongue, but the weeks of suspicion and doubt are clawing to the surface, riding the wave of my anger to freedom.

"What is that supposed to mean?"

"You're so smart why don't you figure it out."

Leo stares at me for a long moment as if he's looking at a complete stranger and then he snaps.

"I'm not doing this," he growls. Before I can formulate an

answer he's snatched up his keys and stormed out of the apartment.

"Shit!" I hurl the contents of my glass down the sink, the magenta stain pooling around the plug-hole bringing me to my senses. I catch Leo waiting for the elevator.

"Where are you going?"

"Home," he snaps. "I'm not staying here with you acting like this."

"Like what?"

"Like a royal bitch."

I don't even flinch, too worked up to care what he thinks.

"So you're just going to walk away?"

"That's exactly what I'm going to do."

The elevator doors open with a cheerful ping and he steps inside. Even from here I can see the muscle working in his cheek and the furious glint of his eyes.

"Call me when you've calmed down," he says as the doors close.

"Asshole!" I kick at the metal door and then let out a shriek of pain as my big toe connects with the unyielding surface. I hop back to my apartment in a foul temper and refresh my glass of wine – seeing as Leo's made himself scarce I have no reason to stay sober – before calling Jess.

"What are you up to?"

"Not much," she sounds bored and half-asleep. "Why, what's up?"

"Do you want to go out?"

Jess is immediately suspicious.

"Where's Leo?"

"We had a fight. I don't want to talk about it."

"I'll be ready in ten," she announces breezily.

Neither of us feel much like clubbing, so we settle for supper at one of Jess's favourite restaurants. *Jimmy's* is a prawn shack only a few minutes from her apartment, the best place in town for seafood, and, best of all, it offers a complimentary bottle of wine with any platter ordered.

"So," Jess asks, armed with her first glass of red. "What happened?"

I start by telling her about Noah and the phone call. Her caramel eyes open wider and her choice of curse words goes a long way to appeasing my sense of injured indignance.

"He's a real piece of work," she huffs when I'm done.

"Yeah," I agree wholeheartedly, spearing a piece of calamari.

"I don't get what this has to do with Leo, though?"

"He thinks I brought it upon myself."

"No!" Jess is outraged. "What an asshole."

"Yeah," I agree again, but this time I can't put quite as much enthusiasm behind it.

"So he's left?"

I nod.

"For how long?"

"I have no idea."

"Well good riddance! I can't believe he'd think this is somehow your fault."

I hesitate, peeling a garlic prawn slowly and thoughtfully.

"Sarah?" Jess's brows are raised and a knowing look is dawning on her lively face.

"What?" I ask innocently.

"Why do I get the feeling you're not telling me the whole story?"

"I am!" I insist. "Leo said I have no one else to blame but myself."

"Um-hmm," she drops her fork and fixes me in a challenging stare.

"He did!"

"So you are absolutely blameless in so far as his departure is concerned?"

"Well, not exactly," I mumble, and she preys on my moment of weakness.

"What did you do?"

"Nothing."

"Liar!"

"I didn't do anything."

She goes ominously quiet and I start to feel a bit like a criminal in an interrogation room. Jess's tactics are militant and it doesn't take long for me to cave in.

"Okay, I'm not admitting any guilt, but I may have been a bit of a bitch."

"Explain."

"What do you want me to say, Jess? I was in a bad mood, okay! I just learned my entire career could be jeopardised. Can you honestly blame me?"

"No," she relents, chugging back a spectacular sip of wine. "I don't blame you. Tonight, we commiserate. But I have a feeling tomorrow you're going to need to do some serious sucking up."

"I'll think about it tomorrow," I grin, and I raise my glass to hers.

I wake up with the mother of all hangovers. I barely remember catching a cab home, and after a lengthy search I finally locate my cell phone in the laundry basket under a tangle of clothing. The battery's dead so I plug it in to charge while the coffee brews. After a cool shower I feel marginally more human and I check my messages. There's nothing from Leo. Ignoring the tug at my gut, I get dressed and resolve to find something productive to do today, but when I yank open my front door I walk right into him, his key in his outstretched hand. He takes in my pallor and the scruffy bun on top of my head and his frown deepens. In comparison, he looks fantastic. He's wearing his gym clothes, still damp with sweat, and his hair is slicked back over his forehead, making his scar more prominent.

"Hi," I say, feeling shy and awkward.

"Hi," he takes in my bruised eyes and makes the obvious deduction. "Heavy night?"

"Jess and I went to *Johnny's.*"

"I'm glad you enjoyed your evening." There's a hard edge to his voice.

"I didn't know if you'd be coming back this morning, after what happened last night." I say.

"Why wouldn't I come back?"

"I don't know," I shrug, "things got pretty heated."

"We had a fight," he corrects. "I'm not in the habit of ending a relationship just because of an argument." He regards me levelly. "May I come in?"

"Of course!" I swing the door open and pad back into the living room. Leo flops onto the sofa beside me.

"I'm sorry," I say, "I was an absolute bitch."

"Yeah," he runs his hand through his hair. "You were. But, to be fair, I didn't help matters much. I was stressed out to begin with and I overreacted. Have you heard anything else – about the internship?"

I shake my head.

"No."

"Nothing from Noah?"

The mere thought of Noah's name makes me sick to my stomach.

"No. And I doubt I will. He got what he wanted."

"I can't believe he would be so petty."

"That's Noah," I sigh.

Leo takes my hand hesitantly and I lean into him, letting my head rest on his shoulder. It's awkward for both of us, but as his thumb strokes the palm of my hand I slowly relax against him. My eyes are half-closing when I feel him shift beside me.

"I'm going to make some coffee. You want some?"

Something isn't right. He's acting strangely, as if he's nervous, and I recall with a start that he has something he wants to tell me.

"No, I just had," I say, and then, taking the bull by the horns, "you wanted to speak to me about something?"

He stands abruptly and heads toward the kitchen.

"I'm going to have a cup," he calls over his shoulder. Intrigued, I follow and watch as he switches on the machine.

"Leo?"

His back is to me, but his shoulders slump and his hands clench into fists at his sides. Without saying a word, he switches the machine off.

"There's no easy way to say this," he announces. He puffs out a long breath of air and then finally turns to face me.

"I want your word you'll hear me out before you say anything. No," he insists, as I automatically nod in agreement, "your word. Once I'm done you can throw things around, kick me out, do whatever it is you need to do, but you hear me out first. Give me a chance to explain myself."

"What's going on?" For the first time I almost don't want to know. The way he's acting is scaring me. "Does this have anything to do with your sister or the hospital?"

"Why would you say that?"

"Um," I cast my eyes downward in embarrassment, "I overheard you and Ellen talking that night we were there for dinner. And I've overheard a few of your telephone conversations."

Leo looks visibly shaken. "Why haven't you brought it up before?"

"I don't know," I admit, "I was scared, I guess. Is that what this is about?"

"First, I want you to promise," he reminds me.

"I promise I'll hear you out." Then, after a quiet minute, "Should we go sit down?"

"No," he shakes his head and I wait for him to explain why not, but instead, he drops the bombshell. "Sarah, I'm married."

Words form in my mouth but they don't trespass past my lips. I bite down hard on my tongue, trying to control the urge to react, to yell at him, to demand answers. I promised I would hear him out and despite the dizzying nausea and the silent screaming inside of me, I wait.

"My wife and I separated almost a year ago," Leo is hesitant at first, but his voice grows stronger as he speaks. "I'm not in love with her anymore but she won't give me a divorce. I haven't had anything to do with her," he is pleading with me to believe him, "not since months before I met you. In my heart it's over, but she won't accept it."

In the pause that follows there are a million things I want to say, but I can sense he's not done yet, so I ask the most obvious question first. "Why won't she accept it?"

"It's complicated," he tugs at his hair again. "I told you about how I changed – how I want different things?" I nod my confirmation. "That's when I left. Clare is part of the me I don't want to be anymore."

The casual mention of her name is my undoing and my knees buckle beneath me.

"I need to sit down," I say, practically sprinting from the kitchen. Leo is beside me in an instant, his strong hands holding me up, but I shove him away.

"No," I say, my voice cracking with the strain. I perch on the edge of the sofa and he retreats to a respectful distance, but his blue eyes watch over me in concern. "Your wife... Clare," the name is bitter on my tongue, "is she by any chance a doctor too?"

His eyes widen. "Yes. How do you..."

I give a harsh bark of hysterical laughter. "Lucky guess."

"Sarah?"

"I went to the hospital after our last trip to Serenity to try to do some digging. There's a Doctor Russell on the third floor."

A pained expression pulls at his face. "That's her. She's in radiology."

I close my eyes. "Of course she is." Because why wouldn't she be? A successful, beautiful, talented woman who is the perfect match for a brilliant surgeon.

"Sarah, please. Don't..."

"So that's why your sister threw such a fit when you

mentioned marriage! Of course you can't marry me – you already have a wife!"

"Sarah," he tries again, but I'm on a rollercoaster and can't stop myself.

"You know what I don't understand?" I sob. "Why someone who has the perfect life – a brilliant career, more money than he can possibly hope to spend, a flashy car and a beautiful, successful wife on his arm, would give it all up to slum it in college with a mediocre girl who hasn't even got a job!"

This time his arms close around me in a vice-grip and he ignores my attempts to push him away.

"I'm not letting you go," he growls, impassioned, as I lash out at him. "Stop it, Sarah! You are beautiful and perfect, and everything I want and need in this world. You inspire me every single day to be better and you are so much more than you give yourself credit for." The words fall over me leaving a searing heat in their wake, but still, I fight. "Don't fight me, please," Leo's voice is broken, too – desperate, lost and beautiful. "Don't fight me," he repeats, holding me even tighter and his scent assaults me, the hard contours of his chest smothering my face. And now the tidal wave of emotion crests, swelling and rising until it breaks across the fragile threads of my heart and streams down my cheeks in an unending flow.

Leo lifts me in his arms and lays me across his chest on the sofa, holding me so tightly that I couldn't lift my head even if I had the strength to try. I sob until my body is heaving - dry, retching gasps. Leo's shirt is soaked, my face a blubbering mess, but I don't care. I wouldn't care if the world around us imploded - in fact, it would be a blessed relief.

When I finally struggle to a gulping stop, I am too

exhausted to even raise my head. I curl into his chest, my arms clutched tightly around myself. The silence between us grows but Leo doesn't let me go.

"I'm not in love with her, Sarah." He sounds almost like he's talking to himself, as if he doesn't believe I would listen. "You are the only thing I care about." Galvanised by my lack of response, he continues, "I should have told you. I know I should have told you, but I didn't expect any of this. In the beginning I figured you had no right to know and by the time I realised how serious I was about you, I was afraid you'd leave me. I have no right to expect you to understand, but I've never betrayed you. In my heart, I'm divorced."

"But you're not divorced." I draw on all of my strength to push myself up, shuffling backward until I'm sitting cross-legged, facing him. I pull one of the sofa cushions against my chest, cradling it against me like a shield.

"Not for lack of trying," he replies. He sounds as exhausted as I feel.

"Why are you telling me this now?"

"I've wanted to tell you for a long time – since you found out about me working at the hospital - but I didn't know how. Then you got so busy and I convinced myself it wasn't the right time. In truth, I was just shit scared, so I vowed I'd tell you the second your thesis was done and not a moment later."

"I don't even know how I'm supposed to react," I admit. "You're married. Oh God, you're married!" The revelation hits me anew and I smother my face in my hands, taking deep gasping breaths, trying not to break down again.

Leo waits for me to compose myself, his hands stroking my back as if he is comforting a child.

Eventually I force myself to continue.

"When did you last speak to her?"

"Yesterday." I do a double-take and he hastens to explain. "She calls me every couple of days. Often I don't even take her calls, but I can only ignore her for so long before she becomes persistent."

"She must think there's a chance that you'll get back together or she wouldn't bother, surely?"

"She thinks I'm going to go back to the way I was before. To the person I was before."

"Have you ever considered that she might be right?"

"No," he shakes his head vehemently, "she's not."

"How can you be so sure, Leo? You woke up one day and threw your life away on a whim. Who's to say in a few more weeks or months that you won't decide to go back to it?"

"I won't. I know it's hard for you to believe but I didn't just decide to live a different life, I changed, Sarah, deep down in my core. I'm not the same person I was." He sounds so certain, so assured, it's hard not to believe him. "What's more important," he adds, doubt creeping back into his voice, "is whether you believe that or not. Whether you'll stay."

"I don't know," I rub my face. My eyes are burning and my cheeks are hot. "You're asking me to take one hell of a risk. If you… if you decided differently, I don't know if I'd recover."

"I'm asking you to trust me, to trust how I feel about you," he corrects when I give him an arch look.

I gaze up at him. The truth is, I do trust how he feels about me. I know that Leo is in love with me, just as I know that I feel the same. If he's telling the truth – if it really is over between him and his wife, isn't it the same thing as if he was legally divorced. *No*, a tiny voice whispers inside of me, *it's not.*

"I can't be with you if you're married," I say. "Whether you're separated or not doesn't matter. I won't be the other woman."

"You don't have to be. I hired an attorney this morning. Clare can't keep me in this marriage against my will." He gazes down at me, a fierce look in his eyes. "Can I stay?" he asks gently, unsure what my response will be.

"I don't know what to do."

"You should speak to Ellen." The suggestion is so unexpected that I sit straight up, baulking at the very thought.

"There are things she can tell you that I can't," he offers gently. "If it's the truth you want Ellen will give it to you. Just don't judge me too harshly when you hear it."

The thought of speaking to Ellen is daunting, but he's right. It's the only way I'll know for sure whether Leo's marriage is over. Ellen will tell me the truth.

"I'll go and see her in the morning," I say, my heart heavy. Leo's arms come around me and squeeze, crushing me against him as if I might be swept away at any minute.

"I love you," he says, breathing the words into my hair. "Whatever happens, remember that. Please don't give up on me." I lift my face to his and he brushes his lips across mine, kissing away the tears that he caused.

"It hurts," I sob against his lips.

"I never meant to cause you any pain. I tried to stay away from you when we first met, but I just couldn't."

I remember how he had declined my offer of tutoring, how he hadn't kissed me after Game Night.

"You may not have meant to cause me pain but you did," I say.

"Then let me take it away, please," his voice is heartbroken and despairing. "Let me love you, Sarah. It's what I was meant to do."

CHAPTER 31

"Sarah," Ellen waves me inside. If she notices my puffy eyes and blotchy skin she's polite enough not to comment. I called her first thing this morning and she told me to come over immediately.

We walk toward the kitchen where Bruce is brewing a pot of coffee. He gives me a sympathetic smile and I try to return it as we pass, heading for the patio. Ellen looks resigned, but she lights up a cigarette the second we step outside.

"Sit," she waves me toward a chair and I sink onto it, trying to keep my knees from trembling.

"Thank you for agreeing to see me," I croak, my voice still husky from last night's sobbing.

"Of course." Ellen hesitates a moment and then takes a seat beside me. She examines my face in an almost clinical manner. "You look terrible," she admits.

"Leo told me about Clare."

"I figured as much. I'm relieved, actually, given what I said at our disastrous dinner and how it must have made you feel."

"I thought you just didn't think I was good enough for your brother," I say, and then I drop my head in my hands as the emotion overwhelms me once more, "God, if only that was the case." I take a deep breath. "A bitchy sister I could deal with. A determined wife… I'm not so sure."

We're interrupted by Bruce who steps out onto the patio with a tray laden with coffee pot, cups, sugar, milk and a bottle of brandy.

"I thought you might need it, sweetheart," he tells me, setting the tray on the table. He leaves us, but not before placing a comforting hand on my shoulder. "I hope you're okay, Sarah." His kindness is almost my undoing but I manage to hold it together. Ellen waits until Bruce is gone and then pours us each a cup of coffee, adding a liberal splash of brandy.

"What exactly did Leo tell you?" she asks, handing mine to me.

"That he's married. That he's changed and he wants a divorce, but she doesn't. Why?" I ask, catching sight of her expression, "is there more?"

"Did you tell him you were coming to see me?"

"Yes. He said it would help."

"Then yes, there's more." At these words the air leaves my body in a high-speed sprint, as though someone has punched me in the gut. I don't speak, waiting for the hammer to drop, but Ellen doesn't elaborate.

"Do they have children?" The thought had occurred to me but I didn't think it was probable, given how much time Leo spends with me.

"No," Ellen actually smiles and the weight on my chest

eases, "it's nothing like that. Leo told you the truth – he does want a divorce and Clare is refusing to give it to him."

"You don't sound disapproving." It strikes me as odd, given her brother's wishes, that Ellen wouldn't hold it against Clare. Unless…

"Are you and Clare very close?"

"I have the utmost respect for my sister-in-law but I wouldn't call us close," she says, almost apologetically. "She's a good wife and she adores my brother – in her own way."

"So you think it's right that she refuses to divorce him?" It sounds absurd. Regardless of Clare's spousal acumen there is no situation I can possibly consider where it would be right to trap someone in a marriage they don't want to be in.

"Yes and no," Ellen answers cryptically. "I'm not saying that she's right, but I don't blame her for what she's doing. It's an unprecedented situation. Who knows what's right and what's wrong." She senses my agitation and shifts her body so that she is facing me directly. "Do you love my brother, Sarah?"

I don't hesitate. "Yes."

She nods. "And I know that he loves you too, not least because he's told me repeatedly." A pause. "Are you sure you're ready for this?"

"Yes." This time the word is softer, less certain and I cringe at the sound of my own fear. It seems good enough for Ellen though, because she continues.

"A little over a year ago Clare was working late. She does that a lot," Ellen adds, and I gather from her tone that she doesn't approve. "When she pulled into the drive two men accosted her."

"*Accosted* her?"

"Yes," Ellen nods grimly, "although whether they were after her or the car we still don't know. Leo heard her screaming and, well it's hard for you to understand, but the way Leo felt about Clare back then… let's just say he went a little crazy." My mind flashes back to the night at my apartment when we were attacked by the knife-wielding youth and Leo's violent reaction. I actually do understand, but I say nothing, needing to know what happened next. "Leo tried to stop them," Ellen continues, "he got between them and Clare. There was a struggle and one of the assailants panicked. He…" she stops for a second, incapable of going on.

"What happened, Ellen?" My heart is racing in my chest.

"They had a gun. Leo was… Leo was shot."

I clap my hand to my mouth, the thought of Leo being hurt almost too painful to comprehend.

Ellen visibly pulls herself together.

"He survived, obviously, but the bullet penetrated his skull. It lodged in his skull cavity and caused significant pressure to the left frontal lobe of his brain. The doctors managed to save him but they couldn't remove the bullet at the time."

"His scar," I breathe. "Wait - you said 'at the time' – so they removed it after?"

"No."

I think of the raised lump beneath Leo's scar that I've touched a hundred times.

"You're saying that there's a bullet in Leo's head?"

"I wouldn't believe it myself if it hadn't happened to my family," Ellen says softly, "but yes, there's a bullet in Leo's head. With his life out of immediate danger the doctors were happy to leave it there until a surgical plan could be put in place to remove it, but none of us were prepared for what it did to Leo."

"What? What did it do to Leo?"

"The bullet is putting a significant amount of pressure on the frontal lobe of Leo's brain. It's the area of the brain responsible for personality."

"I'm sorry," I interrupt, trying to gather my scattered wits about me, "but I have no idea what you're talking about."

"I was getting to that. After the initial surgery Leo started behaving differently. We thought it was post-traumatic stress, but, after the swelling went down, the doctors discovered that Leo's personality was being affected by the pressure the bullet was exerting on his frontal lobe. They were confident that once it was removed he would come to his senses, but Leo refused to go through with the surgery."

My coffee has gone cold so I toss it out into a potted plant beside me and fill the mug with neat brandy. I take a huge swig, the fiery liquid burning down my throat and into my chest. Ellen watches me thoughtfully and then does the same.

"Apparently," she sounds like a person who wouldn't believe it herself under ordinary circumstances, "there have been recorded cases where an individual has suffered blunt trauma to the left frontal lobe and gone through an entire personality shift. Hold on…" She stands, making her way back inside. I take another swig and refill my mug. "Here," she announces, appearing once more with a slim green folder in her hands. She hands it to me and I open it in a daze.

"Phineas Gage?" I ask, glancing up. "Who's Phineas Gage?"

"The most famous case," she explains. "Phineas was a construction worker whose head had been impaled on a metal rod. Miraculously he survived, but friends and family reported that the effects of his injury included profound changes in his character and behaviour – to the point that they claimed he was no longer Phineas."

"Is this a joke?" I snap, shoving the papers back at her and getting to my feet. The brandy churns violently in my stomach and I put out a hand to steady myself. "Some sick, twisted plot that you and Clare came up with to scare me off?"

"Seriously?" she laughs, a desperate, hollow sound. "Do you think I could come up with this shit on my own? Do you think I haven't read this file and wondered if this is God playing a sick joke on my brother – on Clare – on all of us?"

Her words hit home and in the instant that I bear the full brevity of what this family has gone through, the guilt surges up, pushing everything else aside.

"Oh God." Suddenly Clare is no longer my competition. She's not the evil, clingy wife I've created in my mind. Instead, she's a woman who has lost everything through no fault of her own. "No wonder she won't divorce him."

"The reason she won't divorce him," Ellen states slowly, as if weighing up how painful this will be for me to hear, "is because the damage is reversible."

I listen while she tells me that Leo's doctors are confident that they can remove the bullet and that the subsequent reduction in pressure will probably result in Leo reverting to how he was before – to who he was before the injury.

"He'll return to being in love with her, won't he?" I whimper.

"That's what Clare is hoping for." An honest answer, no matter how painful.

"But he refuses to go through with the surgery. Why? Why would he do that?"

For the first time Ellen gives me a smile.

"Have you *met* my brother?" she asks wryly. "He's a stubborn ass. Leo doesn't want the surgery because he doesn't want to go back to how he was before. I think he likes this new version of himself and he has no intention of changing it. Also," she adds, "there's you to consider."

"Me?" For the life of me I cannot understand what I could possibly have to do with this.

"Yes, Sarah, you. Leo is in love with you. I can certainly see why – I know you probably don't believe me but I don't want to see you hurt either. This surgery could turn your whole world upside down."

"I'm nobody," I say, "he has a wife, Ellen. She's the only one whose opinion matters."

Ellen takes my hand and it's so uncharacteristic of her that I'm stunned into silence.

"No, Sarah. You are just as invested in this as she is. You both love him and, to be honest, I'm not so sure that this new Leo isn't the person he was supposed to be all along. As a little boy he was the same – headstrong, determined, full of potential and larger than life. I watched him grow into someone I almost didn't recognise – the money, the trappings – it changed him. Do you know they never wanted children either?" I shake my head, but the question is rhetorical. "They were so focused on their careers, so ambitious, they forgot to enjoy themselves – to enjoy their lives. After the accident, I noticed the change in him before Clare did. Not because she didn't love him, but because they had already become so distanced from one another. Their work was the one thing that brought them together and the thing that pushed them apart. I don't even remember the last time I saw them eat a meal together..." she trails off and I let go of her hand.

"It doesn't matter," I insist. "Whether he's a better man now or not, it's still not right. He has to do this."

"Do you really believe that or is it because you believe it's the right thing to do?"

"It is the right thing to do! If you're asking me if I want this, then no, of course I don't!" my voice breaks and I take a steadying breath. "I don't want any of this. I want Leo to stay with me. I want us to have a chance, I want to be able to think about marriage and babies and growing old together. But I don't have any of that - Leo doesn't belong to me."

"He doesn't belong to her either," Ellen points out gently. I press my lips together and fight the tears that threaten to overwhelm me.

"That's where you're wrong."

"Sarah..."

"No," I shake my head, "thank you for telling me, Ellen, I appreciate it, I really do, but there's no hope for me in all of this." I get to my feet and stumble for the door.

"What are you going to do?" she asks as I yank it open.

"What I have to."

"Can I just say one thing?"

I nod, not trusting myself to speak.

"Try to remember that my brother didn't do anything wrong. Life dealt him a shitty card but he's picked himself up and he's never shown even the slightest hint of self-pity. Maybe he didn't tell you the whole truth, but he does love you."

"I know he does. It's the one thing I am sure of."

"He's a good man, Sarah – he's always been a good man, but he's an even better one with you in his life. Try to remember that."

CHAPTER 32

"I need Clare's number," I tell Ellen before I leave. Fuelled by self-pity and a healthy dose of brandy, I know I need to meet Leo's wife, to see her for myself before I make any decisions.

"Sarah, that's not a good idea."

"I have to speak to her. Please, Ellen, just give me her number."

Bruce has come to see me out and he gives her an imperceptible nod.

"Okay," Ellen relents, and she calls it out as I punch the digits into my phone.

Clare gives nothing away over the phone. I explain who I am and she doesn't sound altogether surprised to hear from me. She gives me her address immediately and I cut the call, my stomach still churning. Driving down the street she has specified I can only marvel at the houses. When I spot number 29 I pull up to the curb, killing the engine, but I don't get out straight away. There's a sleek silver Mercedes parked in the drive. I check my phone – Leo has called four times but I've ignored him. No doubt Ellen has told him where I'm going or she's told him I've left her place and he is frantic to get hold of me. The phone rings again in my hand, Leo's name flashing painfully in my face. I put it on silent and stuff it in my purse.

We sit in the living room. Clare straightens the magazines on the coffee table and, for a minute, only the gentle ticking of the clock above the fireplace fills the space between us. Then I hear her draw in a deep steadying breath and she begins.

"I want you to know I don't blame you, Sarah," she says, which is pretty big of her, considering that I'm sleeping with her husband.

"I didn't know," I reply, feeling the need to justify my actions. "I didn't know Leo was married, I didn't know about the shooting, I didn't know any of it."

"I'm not surprised," she smiles sadly. "Leo doesn't like to talk about it." I feel a stab of spite and anger when she mentions Leo so casually, a subtle reminder that she knows him far better than I do.

"It was awful," Clare continues, oblivious to my thoughts. "When the gun went off… well, I immediately thought the worst, naturally. My attackers fled I didn't even know which way they went and Leo was on the ground. He was unconscious but there wasn't any blood to start. I couldn't find the wound at first, can you believe it? My husband had been shot in the head and I didn't even know it…" She stops suddenly, turning her head away so that I can't see her face.

"Ellen told me," I say. I don't want her to relive it. I don't want to hear it from her point of view.

"Ellen doesn't really like me, did she tell you that?" the

abrupt change of topic catches me unaware and I shake my head.

"No, she didn't. She speaks very highly of you."

"We've come to a mutual understanding over the years," Clare explains, and I feel as though she's not even talking to me, but rather stating facts, "and she's been very supportive of me since the accident but she never approved of our marriage."

I say nothing and she slowly seems to become aware of me again.

"You love Leo, don't you?"

"Yes," it's the smallest admission, but it makes my cheeks burn.

"He loves you too. I knew there was someone else but it's only recently that I realised how serious it was. He's never pushed so hard for the divorce and he's never been so cold toward me. Despite his feelings changing, he's always been sympathetic to mine, until a few months ago. That's how I knew. It's not easy hearing your husband say he's in love with someone else."

"I'm sorry. I don't know what else to say."

"Please don't apologise. This isn't anybody's fault. It just is."

She gets to her feet, seems to realise that she has nowhere to go and sits back down. My heart aches for her, for the discomfort and the pain she is so obviously feeling.

"I'm going to break it off with Leo," I say. The words cut into me like a knife through butter, slicing through every fibre of my being, but I speak the truth. As much as I love Leo, I cannot be the person who holds him back.

"That's very noble of you," she smiles. I almost wish she'd tell me not to, that she'd be like Ellen, but, who am I fooling?

She's his wife. "I know this must be very painful for you," Clare continues, "and I'm sorry you got mixed up in all of this. Leaving Leo alone will go a long way toward getting him to see reason." She pauses and I have the awful sensation she's not quite done with me yet. True enough, her next words confirm it, "I take no shame in fighting for my marriage, Sarah. There's nothing I wouldn't do to get Leo back. I know that sounds insensitive, but I've lived for over a year without the man I love and if there's even the slightest chance of getting him back, I have to take it. So, with that in mind, I'd like to ask one more thing of you."

"What could I possibly do?"

She sits up straighter and looks me dead in the eye. "Leo needs to have that surgery."

The question is implied and I consider it for a long moment. Deep down, I know that she's asking because he won't listen to her, but he might listen to me, because right now, I'm the one he loves – the one he cares for. And if I convince him to go ahead with this surgery, I won't be anymore.

"I know the sacrifice I'm asking of you. I know how badly this will hurt you and I'm truly sorry. You seem like a nice person, but he's my husband. I've loved him since med-school. You've had seven or eight months with him, but I've had over a decade."

I watch in mortified horror as her eyes pool suddenly, glittering for only a moment before a solitary tear spills over, gliding quickly down her cheek as if it has somewhere important to be. In the brief time it takes that tear to reach the curve of her chin, my heart breaks.

CHAPTER 33

$\mathcal{I}$ walk to my car in a daze. I look back at the house one last time, the white columns bordering the mahogany door, the perfectly trimmed verge, even the rose bushes which seem to stand to attention and I am struck anew at how different it is from my own home – cluttered, messy, imperfect. Why would Leo ever want me when he has this, I think, and then, laughing almost hysterically, it occurs to me that he has *bona fide* brain damage and it makes perfect sense.

I get into my car and dig in my purse for my phone. There's another missed call from Leo. I ignore it and find Jess's number in my call log. She answers on the second ring.

"Jess," I manage to croak before my voice fails me.

"Sarah?" she asks frantically. "Sarah, what's wrong."

"Leo's married," I gulp.

There's a long pause and I try to catch my breath. Here, in the claustrophobic confines of my car, the reality of what's just happened crashes over me in a stifling wave.

"Where are you?" Jess asks.

"In my car." I can't bring myself to tell her I'm outside his house. Not yet.

"Get over here now. You come straight here, Sarah, no stopping. I'm timing you."

Somehow I manage the drive to Jess's apartment, although the tears blurring my vision impede my progress. By the time I knock on her door she has worked herself up into a frenzy. She yanks open the door and pulls me inside.

"Thank God," she says, flinging her arms around me. "I thought something had happened. What took you so long?"

"She's a doctor," I sob into her shoulder. "And she's nice. I wanted to hate her, but I can't."

"You met her?" Jess pushes me gently away, holding me at arm's length so she can see my face. "Oh Sarah, why would you do that to yourself?"

She lets me cry it out. We sit on the sofa and I tell her everything. Halfway through Tom arrives, but I don't stop, the words pouring out of me in a river of sadness and heartbreak. When I finally finish, they sit, stunned, digesting.

"I can't actually believe it," Jess says eventually. "What a mind-fuck."

"What are you going to do?" Tom asks, not unkindly.

"What else can I do? He has to go through with the surgery, obviously."

"Why?" Jess demands, looking angry. "He's happy, you're happy. This Clare woman has no right to ask this of you."

"She does, Jess! Of course she does. She's his wife."

"From what you've heard from Ellen she wasn't exactly a good wife."

"It doesn't matter. He married her – he took a vow long before he met me. She has to come first."

"That son-of-a-bitch!" Jess's anger changes direction so quickly I struggle to keep up. "I'm going to kill him."

"It's not really his fault," Tom points out, playing devil's advocate, but he falls silent at Jess's fierce look.

As if on cue my phone rings. I retrieve it from the depth of my purse and fresh tears well in my eyes.

"Give me that," Jess demands, snatching the phone. She scowls at Leo's name and then gets abruptly to her feet. I slump on the sofa beyond the point of caring whether she yells at him or not. I feel numb, like a hollowed-out version of myself, but I know it won't last. My body is holding my emotion at bay to protect itself but I'll have to face it eventually.

"Listen here, you son-of-a-bitch," Jess snaps into the phone, "you stay away from Sarah. Don't you dare come looking for her. If I see you within a hundred yards of my place I'm calling the cops. And get out of her place," she adds menacingly, "Tom's coming to pick up her clothes and he's got my pepper spray." She disconnects the call and switches my phone off.

"I have to talk to him, Jess," I say in a small voice.

"Yes," she agrees, "but not today you don't. Let him wait. You don't owe him anything." She strides across the room and digs in her own purse. "Here," she says, tossing it to Tom.

"What the hell are you giving me this for?" Tom asks.

"Didn't you hear me?" Jess's eyes widen with irritation. "You're going to get Sarah's stuff."

"I am not taking your pepper spray over there," he retorts.

"What if Leo's there, huh? What are you going to do?" she challenges.

Tom looks at her as if she's sprouted a second head.

"Um… I'm going to say 'Hi, Leo, I'm here to pick up Sarah's stuff'. Jeez, Jess, this isn't Def Con One."

"Whatever," Jess snaps in annoyance at his departing back. "And bring that bag of Jalapeno poppers in the cupboard above the sink!"

I spend the weekend fluctuating between bouts of deep depression and righteous anger. I cry buckets, fuelled by a never-ending supply of red wine. At night I sleep fitfully between my two best friends, their support and solidarity protecting me from the horrors outside of my weekend cocoon. So touching is their concern that Tom doesn't even complain about having to share a bed with Jess's feet.

"You do not have to go to college today," Jess announces when she wakes up on Monday morning to find me getting dressed. I hoist up my pants, Tom giving a cry of alarm as my butt veers dangerously in his direction.

"I do," I insist, heading for the bathroom. "They're announcing the advanced placement winner today." One look at my face in the mirror and I realise that no amount of makeup can conceal my puffy eyes or the pastiness of my skin. Still, I slap on some bronzing concealer and a defiant coat of red lipstick. I pull a face at my own reflection. I look like Dracula's bride.

By the time I emerge Jess is already dressed.

"I'm driving you in," she instructs. "Give me five minutes."

I make my way to the living-room while I wait and switch my phone on for the first time since Saturday night when Jess turned it off. I have thirteen missed calls from Leo and a bunch of messages. I don't read any of them.

"We're going to be late," I tell Jess when she finally comes down the hall. Her hair is gathered in the familiar messy bunches on top of her head and her eyeliner is so thick it looks like she's been punched in the face. Twice.

"Who cares?" she asks. "Are you sure you want to do this? You know he'll probably be there." Keeping Leo away from her apartment is one thing, but banning him from campus is beyond even Jess's control.

"I know, but I have to face him eventually, I may as well get it over with." On impulse I step forward and hug her. "Thank you for this weekend. I don't know what I would've done without you guys."

"We're a squad," Jess replies easily, "that's what squads do."

We are almost at the campus when my phone rings.

"Don't answer it," Jess warns.

"It's the college," I say, looking at the number on the screen.

"Hello?"

"Sarah," Dianna's gravelly voice doesn't sound pleased and my hand convulses over the phone.

"Dianna? What... what's wrong?"

She doesn't hold any punches. "Look, there's no easy way to tell you this, Sarah, but Burke & Duke have just announced the recipient of the internship. I wanted to tell you in person, but I stopped by your class and it appears you're not coming in today."

"I am, I'm just running a little late," I answer automatically, my mind still trying to process what she's just said. "I didn't get it," I whisper. Jess's head whips toward me but I can't look at her. I keep my eyes on the road ahead.

"No," Dianna heaves a weary sigh, "I'm afraid you didn't. They gave it to Samantha."

I try to swallow down the hard lump which has formed in my throat but it won't budge.

"Well," I say, trying to feign camaraderie, "she obviously deserved it."

"Actually," Dianna's voice drops an octave, "Samantha didn't beat you. She won by default."

"Default?"

"Yes. She won because you were disqualified."

"Disqualified?" My cheeks flame, even though I know I have done nothing wrong.

"Burke & Duke claim you tried to influence the panel's decision."

We pull into the campus lot in a screech of rubber and white smoke, Jess's own anger weighing her foot down heavily on the accelerator. I am vaguely aware that Leo's SUV is parked a few spaces down, but I ignore it, focusing instead on the sporty Audi at the far end of the lot. I sprint into the main campus, the sound of my footsteps echoing through the halls. Jess falls behind but she doesn't call me back.

Noah's lecture hall is empty, the lights switched off, but I know he's here somewhere. I try the library and the administrator's office, but it is in the cafeteria that I finally track him down. Noah is sitting with Luke, Jess's mentor, and when he sees me, the look on my face wipes the smug smile from his.

"You son-of-a-bitch!" I yell, each word punctuated by a step. Noah scrambles to his feet just in time to meet my right hook, my closed fist slamming into his cheekbone. He stumbles back a few steps, much to my dismay. I'd hoped to at least land him on his ass.

A few cat-calls rise from the tables around us, but I ignore them.

"Sarah!" Luke grabs me from behind as Noah rubs his jaw. "What the hell do you think you're doing?"

"Ask him," I hiss, pointing at Noah. "You got me disqualified!" I yell, writhing in Luke's grasp.

"I don't know what you're talking about, Sarah," Noah says, but his words ring false. I'm obviously not the only one who thinks so, because Luke rounds on Noah, his grip on my arms loosening.

"Did you?" he asks incredulously. "Tell me you wouldn't stoop that low, Noah?"

"There's shark-shit that floats higher than him!" I cry, tears stinging my eyelids. "There's nothing he wouldn't stoop to."

"Prove it!" Noah retorts maliciously, his eyes gleaming. Of course I have no proof – that's the whole point. Noah has won and there's not a damn thing I can do about it.

"How could you do this to me?" I ask. The anger is draining from my body giving way to despair and hopelessness. Luke has released me and is regarding Noah with a disgusted expression. "I worked so God-damned hard, Noah. This is all I had left," I add, and then, like a cable being cut, I collapse. Or I would have, if strong arms hadn't reached for me, holding me up.

"I've got you." I hear Leo's voice, but my eyes feel too heavy to open. "And as for you, you conniving shit," he adds, and I feel his shoulder moving as he points at Noah, "I'll be dealing with you later. Don't get too comfortable."

"Are you threatening me?" Noah's outrage is evident, but his voice fades as Leo carries me from the room. I'm aware of a small figure hurtling past us in the opposite direction and then

I hear the sounds of a scuffle and Jess's high-pitched voice calling Noah out, permeated by the thuds of her handbag hitting his flesh and Luke Hanson half-heartedly telling her to cut it out.

"Sarah," Leo lowers me gently to my feet when we get outside. My legs are trembling but I hold onto his arm for support.

"I lost the internship."

"I figured as much." His eyes are searching my face, my own pain reflected in the blue orbs.

"And I met your wife," I add, tears splashing from my cheeks. He pulls me to his chest, his fingers tangled in my hair and an inhuman growl of anguish rumbles through him.

"I figured that too, love."

CHAPTER 34

I don't remember the drive home although at some point Leo called Jess and told her in no uncertain terms that she was to stay out of this until he and I had talked.

I stand as far from him as I can on the ride up to my apartment and he doesn't try to touch me. He steps out of the elevator before me, arm outstretched and, wordlessly, I hand him the keys.

"We're going to talk," he says, opening the door and gesturing me inside. "No arguments there." I square my shoulders and walk inside. The apartment feels cold and unfamiliar, as if all the happy memories of the past few months with Leo have left, along with the possibility of a future with him.

We stand in the living room facing one another. I want to keep him at a distance, but just the sight of him, his eyes as bruised as mine, the dark circles below them and his hair standing all on end, breaks my heart. He hasn't slept much either and I wonder who he turned to for support this weekend.

"Where have you been staying?" I ask.

"At my place." Alone, the words seem to imply.

"And you spoke to Ellen?"

"Yes. She told me about your conversation and that you were planning to meet Clare." There is an underlying question in his statement and I'm stunned to learn he hasn't confirmed this with Clare herself.

"I did. She's lovely."

"I wasn't looking for your approval."

"Well you've got it. Your house is amazing, by the way."

"Stop it."

I consent, the fight going out of me.

"What happened, Sarah?"

"I called her. I wanted to hear her side of the story after Ellen told me what happened." My eyes light on his scar and I lift my hand, tracing the raised ridge beneath my fingers. "You forgot to mention this part."

"I didn't forget. I just thought it would be better coming from Ellen."

"Why?"

"Because she's objective. Because you don't trust me as much as you did before. Because…"

"Because you don't like to talk about it?" I prompt, and he raises his eyes to the ceiling in frustration.

"You've definitely been talking to Clare."

"She loves you."

"I love you."

"You don't know that."

"Excuse me?"

"Think about it, Leo. If this injury is truly affecting you as Ellen explained, everything you think you know or believe to be true could turn out to be false when you're healed."

"No," he shakes his head so hard that his copper hair flies around his head. "Nothing is going to change how I feel about you."

"Prove it." He starts at this challenge. "Prove it," I repeat. "If you're so sure that nothing will change how you feel then have the surgery. Prove that you really love me. Prove Clare wrong."

"Sarah, that's ridiculous…"

"It's the only way I can be with you, Leo. I won't live a lie."

"I'm not having that surgery."

"Why? What are you afraid of? Deep down you must have some doubts or you wouldn't think twice about it."

"Wouldn't think twice about a potentially fatal surgical option that could leave me dead on the table or brain dead?"

"You're a doctor Leo, you deal with risk every day. I don't buy it."

"Why can't you all just let me be?" he yells, "I like who I am now, I don't want to change any single part of my life. Why isn't that enough?"

"Because it's not you! This isn't even your life! Your life was taken from you over a year ago and you can't just forget about it!"

"I didn't forget about it!" he roars, with the impassioned emotion of a man who hasn't been heard. "I remember everything! I just don't want it anymore!"

I bite my lip. It's killing me to do this but I can't turn back now. It would be so easy to just leave well enough alone and stay with Leo – with my Leo – the man he is today, the man who swept me off my feet and made me fall in love with him. But that would be the coward's way out of this.

"I'm sorry, Leo but I won't be with you like this."

"But you'll be with me if I go ahead with the surgery?" His voice is hardened by the fact that I've backed him into a corner, but beneath his anger I can hear the hope. Leo is actually considering it and this alone shatters my heart into a million pieces because if I had harboured any doubt before, this proves how much he loves me; enough to do something he is violently opposed to doing if it means we'll be together.

"Yes," I smile, a bittersweet, rueful smile that doesn't reach my eyes because I know, deep down, that Leo will not love me when this is over. He will love Clare – the woman he is supposed to be with. The woman he almost died to protect. The woman he took a bullet for. If he goes through with this surgery my Leo will be lost to me and the grief that fills me at the thought is almost too much to bear. His eyes are glittering with fear and regret and I know, without a doubt, that he knows it too.

He holds my gaze as the seconds count down and then, almost weeping, he nods and utters the words that cut through the tattered remnants of my heart.

"I'll do it. If it'll make you stay, then I'll do it. I can't live without you." I barely have time to register the enormity of what this means when he has me in his arms, crushing me against him until I am struggling to breathe. His lips are on my hair, my cheeks, my mouth and through the blind misery overwhelming me, I hear him whisper, "Please, Sarah, love me."

The words are desperate and frantic and I meet his need with a deep desire of my own. Passion, fury and regret meld into one, blazing hot through my body. This could be the last time I feel his lips on mine, feel his body, lean and hard, pressed against me, feel his fingers trailing liquid lava across my skin. I seize his hair, crushing my chest against his, pulling his mouth to mine. I sob into his lips, my breath becoming his breath and my heart beating fast enough for both of us.

Leo grabs my shirt and jerks it over my head, but even that infinitesimal separation is agony. My skin is burning, my breath coming fast and hard, and, as our lips collide once more, my tooth draws blood from his lip. Neither of us is prepared for the fire that sparks between us fanned by the fuel of an impending loss.

It's still dark when I wake to find the bed empty. I know a moment of blind panic thinking he's left without saying good-bye, but as I stretch my hand toward his side of the bed, I feel the warmth lingering there and I feel weak with relief.

I find him sitting alone on the sofa, his head in his hands.

"Leo?"

He turns to look at me, his eyes black orbs in a shadowed face and I tiptoe closer in the dark. When I get close enough he reaches for me, pulling me onto his lap and, like a blind man, he traces my face with his hands.

"Why are you doing this to me?" he gasps against my neck and I pull his head to my chest, feeling the shudder of his body beneath my hands.

"Because I love you. Because I need to know."

"I'm scared, Sarah," he admits. "I'm scared of losing myself and I'm terrified I'm going to lose you."

"You could never lose me, Leo," I whisper, pressing my lips

against his forehead, kissing the raised ridge of his scar. "I'll always be here. And if you decide that's not what you want, then I guess you haven't lost anything." I don't mention that I'll lose everything. I don't want him to be any more afraid than he is and I fear that if I tell him, I might never summon the courage to do what needs to be done.

I gently release him and get to my feet, my legs shaking with every step as I fetch his keys from the kitchen counter.

Leo takes them from me with an inhuman sound that comes from deep within him.

"I think it's time for you to go," I say. My lips are pressed so tightly together to keep from crying that it hurts. He gets to his feet, gazing down at me.

"I can't imagine my life without you in it."

"Yes you can," I remind him, "it's the life you had before."

"I don't want it. I want you, I want this."

"Shhh," I press my finger to his lips, steeling myself to stick to my course of action. "Tell me after."

CHAPTER 35

"So he's really going through with it?" Jess asks. We're sandwiched on my sofa, a giant-sized bag of crisps between us. It's been three torturous days since Leo left my apartment, three days since I said goodbye, and so far all I've managed to do in that time is watch two seasons of *Grey's Anatomy* reruns.

"Yes. The surgery is scheduled for Tuesday."

"And you haven't spoken to him at all?"

"No. I asked him not to contact me until after."

"He's going to come back," Jess insists.

"I don't think he is, Jess." I want her to argue but she doesn't. Instead, she offers me the bag.

"Well, I guess there's nothing you can do but wait and let the chips fall where they may."

"Yeah." I set my glass down, not much in the mood for drinking. I haven't set foot on campus for the past three days and I know I shouldn't let my personal life, or the fact that I've lost the Burke & Duke internship affect my career, but

I'm wallowing in a pit of self-pity that feels like home. I also haven't had the guts to face the consequences of my attack on Noah. I'm not sure whether he reported it or not, but since I haven't been called in for a disciplinary hearing, I suspect the fear of his own involvement in the Burke & Duke selection process being made public might be my saving grace.

"Tom's coming over later," Jess says, "let's make him dress up like a girl and do some cabaret."

"Sounds good," I smile, grateful for her effort to cheer me up.

"What should we do this weekend?" Jess is desperate to keep my mind off things but her words remind me that I have somewhere to be this weekend.

"I'm going to my parents on Saturday," I groan, "I'm spending the night."

"Don't sound so glum," Jess teases, "your mom's cooking will do you the world of good."

"Yeah," I agree half-heartedly. My phone rings from the kitchen counter but I ignore it.

"Aren't you going to get that?"

I shrug, non-committal, but Jess jumps to her feet and fetches the phone. It stops the second she hands it to me, but starts ringing again almost immediately.

I don't recognise the number and my greeting is hardly enthusiastic.

"Hello."

"Is this Sarah Holt?" A man's voice - abrupt, professional.

"This is she."

"Miss Holt, my name is Jeremy Langford. I'm an associate director at Burke & Duke Developments."

My heart gives an out-of-synch lurch. "Yes, Mr Langford, how can I help you?"

Jess raises her brow but I shake my head at her to wait.

"Jeremy, please," he insists. "It's come to my attention that you applied for our advanced placement program this year through the Holmes Institute. Your application was unsuccessful, is that correct?"

"Yes," I refrain from making excuses or screaming that Noah Allen sabotaged me.

"That's a pity. I'm sorry to hear it." I wonder if he's phoning simply to offer his condolences which, of course, makes absolutely no sense.

"Not as sorry as I was," I say, trying to sound nonchalant.

"Well, be that as it may, Miss Holt..."

"Please, call me Sarah," I interrupt.

"Sarah," he concedes. "I don't have much time, but I'd like you to come in for an interview next week. Would that be possible?"

"Um... of course, I can be there whenever you need me."

"Wonderful. Shall we say Tuesday at ten?" The mere mention of Tuesday sends a pang of heartache through me. Tuesday is the scheduled date of Leo's surgery.

"Absolutely, I'll be there," I reply after a small pause, and then, "has something happened to Samantha Simpson?"

"Samantha Simpson?" There is not a trace of recognition in his voice.

"She was awarded the advanced placement position."

"Ah, yes, I thought her name sounded familiar," he says, "but no, that position is still hers."

"Then, why do you need to see me? If the internship is hers then...?"

Jeremy Langford's chuckle is infectious.

"You misunderstand me, Miss Holt. I'm not offering you an internship, I'm offering you a job."

My mouth drops open and, for a moment, I am incapable of speech. Jess jabs me in the stomach.

"I'm sorry, I don't understand?" I wrack my brain and only one person springs to mind. After all Dianna had said about not calling in a favour would she really get involved after all?

"Did Dianna Marchant contact you?"

"No, although I know Dianna well. An amazing woman," he adds fondly. "We have another mutual friend, Miss Holt, and he put in a very good word for you."

My hearts stutters. Leo. It could only be Leo. No one else I know would have these types of connections, nor would they go to the trouble.

"The interview is merely a formality," Jeremy continues, oblivious of the emotional chaos he has wreaked upon me, "and the position is a junior one, although slightly more exciting than the advanced placement. Of course, it will only come into effect in the new year."

"I… I don't know what to say."

He allows himself a small chuckle. "You don't have to say anything. From what I hear you have exceptional talent and I know that nepotism isn't something Leo would stoop to. I've checked your submitted portfolio and, quite frankly, I'm not sure why the internship wasn't awarded to you in the first place."

"Thank you," I reply humbly, "that's incredibly kind of you. And thank you so much for the opportunity."

"No need to thank me, Miss Holt – Sarah," he corrects.

"It's the least I could do. Two years ago Leo Russell saved my son's life."

The emotional upheaval of Jeremy Langford's call is no way good enough to excuse myself from lunch with my parents, much to my dismay, and so, on Saturday morning, I wash my hair, get dressed and put on make-up for the first time in days.

My parents are naturally concerned about me and for the first time in my life they are treating me with kid gloves. I arrive early on Saturday morning and spend the better part of the day being waited on by my mom, while my dad attempts to draw me into conversations that are far better suited to Dylan.

My brother's arrival just before lunch is a welcome relief, but the sight of Hannah hanging on his arm sends me straight back to purgatory. Even her slight connection to Leo brings it all back.

"How are you holding up sis?" Dylan asks, with none of his usual sibling rivalry banter. Uncharacteristically he pulls me into a hug and I can sense his concern. Unlike my parents who have been studiously avoiding the topic of Leo, Dylan gets straight to the point. "Have you heard from him at all?"

"No," I shake my head. "And I don't expect to, for a while, at least." I steel myself and face Hannah, who now knows exactly who Leo is and why she recognised him. "How are you?" I ask.

"Good," she smiles. "I'm so sorry for what you're going through."

"Thank you."

I can barely finish my lunch with all the tea and biscuits

Mom has plied me with this morning, but I eat as much as I can, conscious of her scrutiny. I know I've lost weight over the past few days, existing on a diet of wine, caffeine and the occasional packet of crisps, but I'm confident that, at the rate Mom's going, I'll have picked it all back up by the time I leave tomorrow. In comparison to my pale lethargy, Hannah is practically glowing. Her cheeks are flushed and she can't tear her eyes from my brother. Her adoration is plain to see and I'm happy for Dylan, but it only serves to highlight my own misery.

Dylan waits for Mom to serve dessert – her legendary peach cobbler – before he drops the bombshell.

"I have something I'd like to tell you all," he announces. I don't imagine the nervous glance he gives me and I think I know what's coming. "Hannah and I are engaged," Dylan finishes. Dad gives a grunt of surprise. Mom covers her mouth with her hand, tears springing instantly to her eyes. I'm about to offer my congratulations when Dylan continues, looking straight at me. "I'm sorry sis, I didn't want to do this while you're going through such a tough time, but I also didn't want to leave you all in the dark." His eyes are genuinely apologetic and my face flames.

"Are you mad?" I squeak, leaping to my feet and rounding the table. "This is amazing news!" I pull his head into a headlock and plant a kiss on his blond head. "I'm so happy for you! My sympathies," I add, winking at Hannah with a hint of my old flippancy, "are you sure you know what you're getting into?"

My delighted response serves as a catalyst and everyone relaxes, ooh-ing and aah-ing as Hannah shyly produces the ring from her purse. It glitters on her finger, to be examined by all and sundry and Dylan looks absurdly proud of himself.

"We need champagne!" Mom announces, clapping her hands together. She scuttles into the kitchen and returns a few minutes later with a bottle of sparkling wine. "Close enough," she laughs, the sound tinkling around the room.

I manage to keep up appearances until Dylan and Hannah leave. I am thrilled for my brother but the announcement has also sent me into a spin, a poignant reminder of what could have been. I help Mom clean up and then I head upstairs to my childhood bedroom, collapsing on the bed in a flood of silent tears.

It's not long before a gentle knocking sounds at the door.

"Yes?" I call, frantically wiping my eyes on the sheet and leaving a black streak of mascara as evidence.

Mom takes one look at my face and gives a small sigh.

"Did you really think I didn't know, sweetheart?" she asks, coming to sit beside me. She pulls me against her chest as easily as if I am a child and I give an audible sniff.

"I'm really happy for them," I say, desperate for her to believe me.

"Of course you are; there was never any question of that! But you can be happy for them and sad for yourself at the same time." She rubs my back, her small hands strong and reassuring.

"I don't know what to do, Mom," I gulp, choking back sobs even while the tears run freely down my face. "How will I live without him?"

"I can't answer that, honey. I wish I could and I wish I could take away your pain. More than that, I wish I could force him to choose you, but he has to make the decision on his own."

"Jess says I should fight – that I should be there, at the hospital, reminding him what he's giving up." I feel her chest rise and fall with a small giggle.

"Why am I not surprised?" she says. "Jess has always been a fighter."

"Do you think I should?" I ask. "Fight, I mean?"

"It's hard for me to answer that, Sarah. I believe in the vows of marriage and I believe that they're not something to be taken lightly. This Clare girl – she's done nothing wrong either and Leo made her a promise. At the same time, you're my baby girl and I don't want to see you hurt. It's an impossible situation."

"Why is this happening?" My voice breaks and she holds me even tighter, sweeping my curls off my face.

"Sometimes bad things happen to good people," she replies simply.

We stay that way for long while, not saying anything, not needing to. I am almost asleep when she speaks again.

"Whatever happens, sweetheart you'll get through it, that I can promise you."

I nod against her chest, praying that she's right.

$\mathcal{I}$ should have known mom would call in the big brother police. When I let myself into my apartment on Sunday evening, it wasn't even a minute before Dylan arrived.

"I don't have any food," I grumble as I let him in.

"I'm not here for food, sis." His uncharacteristically serious tone stops me in my tracks and I swivel on the spot. His blue eyes are filled with concern, and that in itself brings fresh tears to my eyes.

"Oh God, I'm so sorry Sarah." He crosses the space between us in two enormous strides and pulls me against him. Dylan and I have never been the hugging type, but I collapse against him, clinging to his shirt and wishing I could absorb even the smallest bit of his solid, quiet strength.

"I miss him," I sniff.

"I know you do." He rubs my back in the same way that mom used to when we were kids and our hearts had been broken by simple things like the loss of a favourite toy, or a bully on the playground. "But you are going to get through this. You're a Holt, and we Holt's don't go to pieces in a crisis."

I give a half-laugh, half-sob.

"Did you come up with that yourself?"

"I may have had a little help from Dad."

We sit on the bar stools at the kitchen counter eating buttered toast, which is the only meal Dylan is qualified to cook. Still, it's a welcome change having him feed me for once. When he sets a steaming cup of coffee on the counter before me I manage a smile.

"You must be really worried about me, Dyl."

"I am," he replies, in all seriousness. Clearing his throat, he pulls his wallet from his pocket. My curiosity is piqued when he starts rummaging through it and withdraws a white business card. "Don't shoot me down, okay," he warns, holding it against his chest, "but I want you to go and see someone." He slides the card across the counter and I stare at the embossed print.

"A psychiatrist? You want me to go and see a psychiatrist?"

"Yes." He is unapologetic. "What you're going through isn't normal, Sarah, and I don't think you realise how traumatic this whole situation is."

"Of course I realise how traumatic it is, Dyl, I'm living it!"

"Just do this for me, okay? Hannah says he's one of the best." Hannah calls on enough doctors to have a lot of insight into the medical profession.

Gingerly, I pick up the card and squint at the name printed on it.

"You really think this Doctor Sheldon is going to wave his magic wand and make me feel better?"

"No," he shakes his head as if he wishes it was that simple, "but I do think he can help you deal with it a bit better." Sensing that I'm resigned to go and see this doctor, he relaxes. "I think they call them coping mechanisms," he teases.

"Maybe Hannah should go and see him, then. She's going to have to learn how to cope with your Godawful cooking."

Two days later I find myself perched on the edge of a sofa that reminds me of Clare Russell's. A petite young girl with a mass of dark hair pulled over her tear-streaked face emerges from the door behind me and I avert my eyes automatically so as not to embarrass her.

"Miss Holt?" The receptionist smiles politely at me, indicating the still open door. "Doctor Sheldon will see you now."

Cark Sheldon looks like the grandfather every child wishes they had. A middle-aged, bespectacled man with a receding hairline, a kind face and a gentle demeanour, he greets me warmly as he shakes my hand.

"Miss Holt, please, have a seat." I'm relieved to discover that, instead of the stereotypical sofa, he has two simple occasional chairs facing each other and separated by an oak coffee table. The box of tissues on top of the table, however, makes me baulk.

"I'm sure you won't be needing them," Doctor Sheldon smiles encouragingly, settling himself in the chair opposite me. "Now, why don't you tell me why you're here?" Of course, I promptly burst into tears.

The story emerges in stops and starts, punctuated by the sound of my nose-blowing as I drench one tissue after another, pulling them from the box as if it is a vending-machine.

"It's crazy, right?" I ask when I'm finally done.

"It's certainly not a typical situation," he replies. "And not an easy one for anyone involved."

"How is it even possible?"

"The brain is an amazing thing, Sarah. There are no limits to what it's capable of. We have guidelines, of course, but every now and then a case such as this one challenges everything we have been taught. My job is not to help you understand *why* this has happened, but to enable you to work through your own experience of it."

"I bet when I walked through that door you never expected anything like this. I must be the appointment you've dreaded your whole career. The freakish case nobody prepared you for."

He smiles at that.

"I counselled at a psychiatric treatment centre for many years. There is very little that surprises me. I can tell you with absolute certainty that this is not the most unique case I've ever heard of. It's not even the strangest I've personally been involved with."

"I find that very hard to believe."

He chuckles.

"You remind me so much of a girl I know. She too, had her share of heartbreak. And she too rose above the adversity she faced and went on to live a very full and happy life."

"Did you help her?"

A glimmer of sadness flits across his lined face, gone so quickly I wonder if I imagined it.

"I tried to. I hope that I did. Just as I hope I can help you."

"I don't know how I'll get over this. How I'll get over him."

"You may not. It is possible to love someone very deeply

without letting it consume you. Eventually, in time, things become easier and you move forward. You mentioned your passion for architecture? Can you tell me a bit more about that?"

The change of topic lightens the atmosphere and I manage to voice all of my concerns and fears for my career without breaking down again. When our hour is up, I feel as though I'm coming out of a daze, and I'm a little embarrassed by how much I've confided in this absolute stranger. It strikes me that he said very little throughout the session.

"Shall I come back again?" I'm unsure of where we go from here.

"That's up to you, but I would like to see you again, if you're open to it? It's difficult to resolve anything in one session."

"Okay," I nod, "yeah, sure. I'll just book at the front desk?"

"That would be perfect."

He opens the door for me and I notice his next appointment sitting on the sofa, averting her eyes. I turn back just before she gets expectantly to her feet.

"Doctor Sheldon?"

"Yes?"

"What was her name – the girl you mentioned before?" I don't know what makes me ask, perhaps its idle curiosity, or that the way he spoke of her gave me hope. He pauses, considering me for a moment and I wonder if this would be a breach of doctor-patient confidentiality, but then his face creases into a smile.

"Is," he corrects fondly. "Her name is Paige."

~

It's been a week since my interview with Jeremy Langford, which coincided with Leo's surgery and I'm four episodes into a *Masterchef* catch-up marathon when my phone rings. I glance at the screen and freeze. It's Ellen. I don't want to speak to her, to dredge up the pain that mentioning Leo's name will bring, but I can't ignore her. It could be important. I haven't heard any news since Leo's surgery, save for one text from Ellen telling me the surgery was a success. It was a nice way of saying Leo hadn't died on the operating table, but I had wept with relief. I haven't heard a word from him since the surgery.

I switch off the TV and hit the answer button on my phone.

"Hi Ellen."

"Sarah, how are you doing?"

"As well as can be expected. How's Leo doing?"

"That's actually why I'm calling. There's been a complication – I, I need you to come to the hospital."

"What? What happened?" I'm already on my feet, the bile rising in my throat. If something has happened to Leo…

"Something the doctors didn't anticipate," Ellen replies tersely. "Can you get here? Please?"

"I'm on my way," I say, already heading for the elevator.

I barrel through the revolving doors before they've even opened properly, knocking my arm painfully against the aluminium frame in my haste.

"Where I can find Leo Russell?" I ask, noticing with mild recognition that these two receptionists are the same ones Tom had tried to question so many months ago.

"He's in Gen 3," the one on the left tells me without consulting her computer.

"Are you Sarah Holt?" the second asks and I nod. "They're waiting for you," she says kindly.

I follow the overhead signs, my anxiety soaring out of control. They knew I was coming. In my experience the only time guests are allowed open visitation is to say goodbye.

I hurtle around a corner and almost collide with a man coming in the opposite direction. His arm shoots out to steady me.

"Sarah?" His voice is deep and familiar and I look up to see Ellen's partner, Bruce, towering over me. His hand around my arm relaxes instantly.

"Bruce," I gasp, clutching at his arm. "Bruce, where's Leo?"

"He's this way," he leads me toward the ward. "You got here quickly. We didn't expect you for at least another twenty minutes."

"I came as soon as Ellen called," I reply automatically, my eyes scanning each room as we pass.

"He's in here," Bruce gestures me forward and I step quietly into the room.

Ellen is standing beside the bed blocking my view, but, at the sound of my footsteps, she turns and I catch my first glimpse of Leo lying in the bed. He looks paler than usual and has lost weight since I last saw him, but the thing that strikes me the most is his shaven head - the glorious copper mane is gone - and the thin bandage wrapped around his temples.

"You're awake," I breathe, not daring to hope. Ellen gives Bruce a secret smile and steps aside.

"Hello Sarah," Leo's lips curl into the crooked smile that makes my knees go weak.

"Are you… Is everything all right?" I ask. "When I got the call I thought…" I trail off, not able to say the words.

"I'm fine," he insists.

"But…" I look to Ellen for answers but she doesn't look half as concerned as I thought she would.

"Well, my work here is done," she announces, lifting her purse off the table beside Leo's bed. "Thank you for coming, Sarah," she adds, squeezing my arm as she moves past me. I don't see Bruce leave, but a second later they are gone and I'm alone with Leo. I step forward slowly, gathering my wits.

"How have you been?" Leo asks, watching my every move.

"I think I should be asking you that question," I point out. I reach the edge of the bed and gingerly reach out to touch his head just above the bandage. "Does it hurt?"

"No."

"And you're not… you're not in any danger?"

"No more so than any other brain surgery patient post-op." He sounds so like himself and my heart gives a twinge of protest at being split open again. Yet another thing I will have to recover from.

"I don't understand why Ellen called me. I thought something terrible had happened."

"She called you because I asked her to."

"But she said there was a complication? Something the doctors hadn't foreseen."

"There was," he agrees. The dark shadows beneath his eyes do nothing to diminish their intense colouring. "The results of the surgery weren't quite what they expected." He is teasing me now and a rose of hope blooms in my chest as a few things suddenly become clear. Leo looks almost smug and Ellen was here with him - Ellen, not Clare. I bite my lip to keep from smiling as I realise exactly why I'm here.

"How so?" I ask, resting my hand on the sheet beside him. My fingers itch to touch him, but I hold myself back.

"Well," Leo is actually enjoying himself, "the doctors expected me to go back to how I was before. I believe you yourself were of the same opinion?" he asks innocently, and this time I can't stop the grin that spreads across my face.

"I may have expressed that opinion, it's hard to recall exactly."

"Right, well, it turns out that while you are an undeniably talented architect, you really are no brain surgeon."

"So," I stretch out the word, "what you're saying is…"

"What I'm saying, Sarah Holt, is that I love you. I may have changed after the accident, but being with you changed me on a much deeper level. This," he takes my hand, and his is warm and dry, "this is exactly what I want. I want you. I choose you. Always."

I close my eyes and feel the tears well up and push through my lashes, streaming down my cheeks and leaving the taste of salt on my tongue.

"Also," he adds, his tone playful, "I wanted to tell you I told you so."

I give a choked sob of near-hysterical laughter.

"Really Leo?" I ask, still not believing what's happening. "Is this really what you want?"

"This is what I want." He holds my gaze, his eyes sincere and filled with adoration and I kiss him full on the lips.

"Sorry!" I gasp as the lone monitor emits a high-pitched beep.

"Don't be," he grins against my lips. "It's just my heart-rate."

I step back, wiping tears from my eyes.

"What about Clare?" I don't want to mention her name, knowing it will break the spell, but I have to know. Leo's expression turns sombre.

"I told her this morning," he says. "She's hurting, but she finally understands. She can accept it now. She won't stand in our way." I feel a crushing heaviness weighing on my heart. Clare didn't ask for any of this and she certainly doesn't deserve it.

"Hey," Leo pulls me against him and I rest my head on his shoulder. It's the most natural thing in the world. "Don't feel bad; do you understand me?" he squeezes my shoulder in emphasis. "You did nothing wrong. And you stepped aside, you stayed away. No one could've asked any more of you than that. This was my decision, Sarah, and I made it long before I met you. My marriage was over - she just didn't want to believe it."

"But if you hadn't met me," I prompt, "do you think you would've given your marriage another chance?"

He doesn't answer immediately and I'm grateful that he's giving the question serious consideration and not just telling me what I want to hear.

"No," he answers eventually. "the Porsche is proof."

"The Porsche?"

"I love that car," he admits, "I loved it before and I love it now. And I guess somewhere deep down I loved it even when I was damaged, because, as much as I wanted to change, I never could bring myself to get rid of it. Clare and I were over... probably even before the accident, I was just too busy to see it."

I nod, the metaphor oddly reassuring.

"So," I muse, casting him an arch look, "you're keeping the car?"

"I'm keeping the car," he confirms happily.

"I guess I'm just going to have to get used to it, then," I tease.

"Don't act like you don't love it," he smirks as I snuggle up against him.

I lie that way for the longest time feeling the rise and fall of his chest under my fingers, his heart beating a steady rhythm that matches my own.

"I've got a job at Burke & Duke starting in the fall," I murmur. "I believe I have you to thank for that."

"Well I'll need someone to pay the bills while I work my way through college," he teases.

"You're not going back to medicine, then?"

"I don't know. I've been giving it a lot of thought and, for now, I think I'm where I need to be. The new me likes Holmes, although," he adds, and I hear the playfulness creep into his voice, "it may just be Samantha Simpson's cleavage that holds the attraction."

I start to laugh and find that I can't stop. I laugh until I'm crying, gasping for breath, and eventually, I stick my nose under his arm to stifle the sound. His arm tightens around me naturally and then he is laughing too, the two of us like a couple of kids without a care in the world.

"I can't believe I'm here," I say when we finally fall silent. My fingers trace the hard contours of his chest beneath the hospital gown, the lines of his abdomen, coming to rest on his hand. He squeezes my palm, his thumb stroking the ball of my thumb.

"Thank you," he whispers, so softly that I have to strain to hear him.

"For what?"

"For making me go through with this. For allowing me to know for sure. For making me whole again."

"I didn't think I'd ever see you again," I admit truthfully, and he pulls me tightly against him, squeezing out all my fear and doubt.

"You know what we're going to do the second I get out of here?"

"What?"

"Book that trip to London."

"Before we do that," I say, catching his eye, "we need to put your apartment on the market."

His eyes light up, his lips ensnaring mine and he kisses me deeply, a kiss filled with the promise of forever.

CHAPTER 37

*I*t's after midnight by the time I get home. Apparently, being on the Board, even if on a sabbatical, grants Leo privileges that don't apply to regular patients. I get into bed and hug myself tightly wishing he was here with me and delighting in the knowledge that soon he will be. With any luck his surgeon will be discharging him before the weekend.

In the morning I call Jess who insists on a minute-by-minute account of exactly what happened last night.

"God that's romantic," she declares when I'm done. "I feel like I should be smoking a cigarette."

"It was," I boast.

"What about the wife? Has she tried to contact you?"

"No," the twinge of guilt flickers to life but I force it down.

"What will you do if she does?"

"I honestly have no idea."

"Tom and I are meeting up for breakfast burritos at Tex-

Mex, why don't you join us? He's going to want to hear all the gory details, too."

"Why don't you guys pop over tonight? I'm stopping by the hospital on my way in to campus."

"Why are you even bothering? You've already got a fancy job lined up, unlike the rest of us, and now that your thesis is done you'll coast through the rest of the year."

"I want to talk to Dianna," I say, "and you know you have a fancy job lined up too." I remind her of her father's standing offer.

"Don't remind me. My dad's already earmarked a corner office with a shiny gold name-plate."

"Things could be worse. You could've been born into poverty and had to sell your ovaries for cash."

"God, you are a twisted cow! Give McDreamy a kiss from me."

"I will," I promise, "I'll catch up with you later."

I drive much more slowly this morning, shuddering at how reckless I'd been on the road last night. My frantic panic for Leo's safety had overcome my common sense and I'd jumped a few lights. I pull up in the hospital lot with my Leo-insulated bubble around me and head for the doors.

"I'm here to see Mr Russell," I tell the nurse behind the station in Leo's ward. Is it my imagination or does the blood drain from her face at the mention of his name?

"Sarah?" I freeze at the sound of my own name. I've only heard that voice once but I'd recognise it anywhere. I rotate slowly, my eyes finding Clare. Her hair is pulled back into a messy ponytail and the buttons of her shirt are done up wrong, causing it to pull to one side. My heart skips a beat as I notice her face is tear-stained and her eyes are red from crying.

"Clare," I begin, trying to find the right words to console her. "I'm sorry. I did what you asked, I really did, but…"

I'm not finished speaking when she gives a wail, rushing at me. I steel myself for a physical attack, but to my astonishment she throws her arms around me. The sound of renewed sobbing in my ear sends an icy dread crawling up my spine.

"Oh God!" Ellen's voice. I meet her gaze over Clare's heaving shoulders and my worst fears are confirmed. Ellen's face is a blubbering mess, her nose and lips swollen and, at the sight of me, fresh tears slip unbidden from her bruised eyes.

I disentangle myself from Clare's grasp and walk toward Ellen, my ears thundering as the blood rushes through my body.

"I was about to call you," Ellen sounds contrite through her despair and she glances at Clare as she adds, "the hospital still has Clare listed as the primary emergency contact."

Emergency contact.

"No!" I utter the word with conviction as though saying it will make it true. "No," I say again but this time my courage fails me. Because I know what she's going to say even before her mouth opens.

Ellen's face crumples. "It was a blood-clot. They didn't pick it up in the scans," she breaks off, unable to continue.

"No, please, no…" I mewl, shaking my head. "He's not. He can't be? Ellen, please tell me he's not…?"

Bruce appears at Ellen's side and she leans heavily against him. I suspect that without his solid bulk she would have toppled over.

"Leo's in a coma, Sarah," Bruce says. His eyes are red, his voice hoarse, but he has picked up where Ellen left off. Ellen's eyes are closed, shutting out the world.

"A coma?" Hope. Beautiful glorious hope raises her head. "So he can wake up. He's going to wake up, right?"

Clare is still sobbing, clutching a soaked tissue. She looks frail and isolated and I step closer to her, putting my arm around her shoulders.

"He won't wake up," Bruce says, speaking frankly and holding it together for Ellen's sake. For all of our sakes. "His organs are shutting down and there's zero brain activity. The only thing keeping him alive is the machines."

Without warning, my chest heaves. I turn away from Clare, trying to stop it, but my stomach purges itself of what little contents remain inside it. A nurse is beside me in an instant, holding a wad of tissues. I take them from her, wiping my mouth and trying not to be sick again. This isn't happening.

"I want to see him," I whimper, averting my eyes from the pool of vomit on the floor.

"Of course," Bruce gently pulls away from Ellen and she gives him a nod. Clare has fallen silent, her eyes watching me with a haunted expression as I follow Bruce to Leo's room.

Leo could be sleeping. The shadows under his eyes are darker and his lips are dry, parted around the breathing tube, but he looks like he could open his eyes at any moment. The bandage has been replaced and I wonder if they tried to save him - if they operated again - or if they simply didn't have time.

"We'll give you a few minutes alone with him," Bruce says. I don't respond and a second later I hear the door close. All is silent, save for the faint hum of the machinery surrounding Leo's bed.

~

I don't even realise I've moved until I'm standing beside him. His hand is warm, just like I remember, and in my imagination I can feel a pulse. Or it might just be the machines. I lift the blanket and squeeze up onto the bed next to him, the place where I lay last night when we laughed and kissed and made plans for our future. Leo can't shuffle aside now so there's not much room, but I manage it, draping my leg over his and curling myself into the nook below his shoulder, with my head resting on his chest. I'm not afraid of disrupting the tubes and sensors affixed to his body. I ignore them, choosing to see only Leo. In this moment we are alone, somewhere far from here.

"Leo," I say, willing the sound of my voice to bring him back to me. "I'm here. I'm right here."

I squeeze his hand, his lifeless, unresponsive hand. Less than twelve hours ago he was squeezing mine back, his crooked smile teasing me, his eyes reflecting endless possibilities.

"Please don't leave me," I whisper, tracing the line of his jaw. "Open your eyes, Leo, please. Open your eyes." His eyes – the incredible blue that defies genetics – stay shut, and it dawns on me that I will never see those eyes again. I'll never see the crooked grin or feel the power of his arms around me, keeping me safe. My chest constricts with pain, a shooting, heart-wrenching agony that sucks the breath from my lungs and sends my body into spasm. The tears that I cry are infinite, a never-ending stream that soaks us both, but which only I can feel.

I lie that way for a long time, a montage of images playing

in my mind: Leo's eyes in the mirror, his hands on my bare skin, Leo playing Charades, the sight of his broad shoulders as he walked away. Hunched over Jess's lifeless body, standing between me and a youth holding a knife. The crystals in his hair in the *Rasul*, his lips warm and wet on my skin. Leo in the library, Leo in the shower, Leo in my bed, naked and glorious and mine. Leo holding up a piece of paper: Only six more minutes.

"It's not fair," I murmur, kissing his shoulder, tasting the salt of my own tears. "This was the beginning, Leo, not the end."

CHAPTER 38

*A*s a doctor Leo had been vehemently against artificially sustaining life. His paperwork was all in order and the hospital had every right to terminate his life-support without consent. Out of respect, however, they called Clare into a private meeting to discuss it. I sit slumped in a chair in the compassionate room, Ellen, Bruce and Leo's sister, Trisha, opposite me. Trisha had arrived a few minutes after I had said my goodbyes to Leo, clinging to the arm of her husband. She hadn't spoken a word to me but I took no offence. Save for a short conversation with Ellen when she arrived, she hadn't spoken since.

I am surrounded by Leo's family but I can't bring myself to leave. I have nowhere to go – no place on earth will shelter me from the storm that is coming. I can feel the madness, the depression lingering just beyond my comprehension and I know that, when I leave this place, it will engulf me; so, terrified and heart-broken, I wait.

Ellen emerges from the private meeting within ten minutes her hand pressed against her mouth, her skin so alabaster white she looks like a walking corpse. To my utter astonishment she heads straight for me and I stumble to my feet.

"They want to turn off the machines." Her voice quavers, "I didn't want to agree until I heard what you think."

"Me?"

"You love him just as much I do." The use of present tense jars us both and we cling to each other, drawing comfort from the one person in the world who understands how we feel. "Besides," Clare draws in a shaky breath, "he loved you. He chose you. He would've wanted you to decide."

I agree, of course. It was Leo's wish, after all, and as the Doctor explained, there was no chance of recovery. Not even one percent. Clare and I stand side by side, shoulder to shoulder, as they slowly switch off the machines keeping Leo alive, and then we wait, hand in hand, as he leaves this world – as he leaves us both.

Leo Russell left a gaping hole in my life – an empty space where there should have been love and laughter, marriage and babies and sunsets and art. Light. Space. Beauty. I allowed myself to mourn him. The anguish that I had feared won me over for a time, but I surrounded myself with friends and family, letting them help me heal, help me get up and face a world without him. I cried every night for a month and then I cried every time I thought of him, and whenever I caught a glimpse of the Porsche parked outside.

And then, one day, I found myself smiling. Tom cracked what would later be referred to by Jess as the stupidest joke in the history of mankind, and, without realising it, my lips curved upward for the first time in forever. The smell of him faded from the pillow on my bed and the world kept turning, despite the fact that my own universe had imploded.

I didn't keep in contact with Clare. Our grief had brought us together, briefly, in the hospital that day, but ultimately we were two very different women who had fallen in love with two very different men. Unbeknown to me, Leo had done more than secure me a job with Burke & Duke. He had also changed his will before his surgery, leaving Clare the home they had shared and all of their mutual possessions. To me he had left his apartment, his savings and the Porsche.

It is remarkable how one tragedy can impact on the lives of so many and set on course a sequence of events beyond the control of the unwilling participants, but that is exactly what happened, for Leo and for me... and for everyone else caught up in the journey that changed the course of our lives forever.

In the summer, two weeks before I was scheduled to start working at Burke & Duke, I made the trip to London on my own. Jess had offered to come with me, but it was something I had to do alone. That journey was the start of my healing. I absorbed everything, lifting my face to the sun and letting the beauty of life wash over me. At night I wrote it all down, every experience, every moment that mattered. It was my ode to him. I know it sounds crazy, but I wasn't alone. He was there with me the whole way, right up until the moment I returned home and realised I would survive this.

Losing Leo was like losing light, losing space, losing beauty, but I couldn't let that be his legacy. And so, instead, I poured those things into my work. His legacy became the modern lines of a strong building made softly rosy in the dawn light, the clean, arching curve of a bridge. I sensed his spirit and his lust for life in the shapes and forms of strong, unique structures which stood apart in a sea of similarity, and through these, Leo lived. Through them, I lived.

AUTHOR'S NOTES

This book is based on the remarkable real-life tragedy of Phineas P. Gage; an American construction worker who was impaled through the head with a metal rod. The rod destroyed much of the left frontal lobe of Phineas's brain, the part of the brain responsible for personality. Miraculously Phineas survived, but the reported effects of his injury were such that his character and behaviour changed so profoundly that people who knew him no longer saw him as "Gage".

I read about Gage's case in my first year Psychology studies and it stayed with me throughout the duration of my degree, prompting me to continue with my studies in psychopathology. Both *Rainfall* and *Riven* were borne of this fascination. It is important to note, however, that I have dramatised and romanticised the injury and its effects for the sake of contemporary fiction, and that the possibility of this happening in a real-life scenario is improbable, if not impossible. The effects of left frontal-lobe damage, however, are real.

ABOUT THE AUTHOR

Lissa Del is the author of a range of contemporary women's fiction titles and the pseudonym for award-winning author, Melissa Delport. She graduated from the University of South Africa with a degree in English Literature and now lives with her husband and three children in Hillcrest, KZN.

SIGN UP FOR THE LISSA DEL MAILING LIST HERE!
www.subscribepage.com/g7q7u9

Like Melissa on Facebook at
facebook.com/TheMelissaDelportBookClub

Visit Melissa's website, and read her blogs, on
melissadelport.com

Follow Melissa on Twitter
twitter.com/melissadelport

CPSIA information can be obtained
at www.ICGtesting.com
Printed in the USA
LVOW07s1517051217
558726LV00004B/916/P